n did his ass start to look so damn good in
s?

Being around him made her skin feel hot and
tight and she was suddenly awkward about
thing. Did Mark notice the way her ass
ed when she walked? Did he sneak a quick
at her tits when she wore that red sundress that
ed off more cleavage than usual? The urge to
in her gut when he walked into the room was
t overwhelming in its intensity.

he thought of being in a bathing suit in front of
and his perfect, hard body made her feel
dly uncomfortable, so she settled for making
of iced tea instead. She was just pouring
a glass when she made the mistake of
g out the kitchen window. It faced the pool
backyard and Mark was hoisting his wet body
the pool. She sucked in her breath, the glass
tea forgotten as she stared wide-eyed at him.
dripped down his tanned, lean body and he
is hand through his dark hair before reaching
towel. As he dried his upper body, her gaze
to his crotch. His wet swimming trunks
his sizeable dick. Her mouth went bone
a spasm of pleasure rippled through her
elly. Her pussy started to throb in a way
ver felt before and when she swallowed she
e dry click of her throat.

tore her gaze from his crotch and stared at
of iced tea before she set it down on the
and left the kitchen. Her cheeks felt like
e on fire and she kept seeing the way the
dripped down Mark's chest and arms.

Undeniably Hers

RAMONA GRAY

Published by
EK Publishing Inc.

Adult Reading Material

Edited by
L. Nunn Editing

Cover design by
The Final Wrap

ISBN-13: 978-1-988826-18-9

Prologue

It happened a decade ag remember every little detail fr wearing jean shorts and a herself. It was the middle parents were at work and he some cooking class with his considering going for a swir had shown up half an hour to the pool. Lately, sh conscious around her brothe

Up until a month ago, s as anything more than Stanford may not have be he'd practically grown up teased and tormented her j

But for the last few herself staring at parts o noticed before, like his other night at dinner, she mouth. Had his lower would be delightful to s

whe
jean

too
ever
jiggl
look
show
suck
almo
T
Mark
decide
a jug
hersel
glanci
in the
out of
of iced
Water
raked h
for his
droppe
outlinec
dry as
lower b
she'd ne
heard th
She
the glass
counter
they wer
water ha

"Oh God," she'd muttered to herself, "it's like I'm in a damn porno. I'm the horny housewife and Mark is the pool boy."

She wanted to laugh at the absurdity of her thoughts, but they suddenly didn't seem so absurd. Lying naked on one of the deck chairs while Mark settled his body between her thighs seemed like a fine idea. He would kiss her and touch her, and suck on her aching nipples. She would gladly give him the gift of her virginity if it meant that this sudden throb of need in her pussy would be eased.

Another spasm of pleasure pulsed in her lower belly. She was actually heading toward the patio doors that led to the backyard before she got a hold of herself. What the hell was she doing? She wasn't interested in Mark that way. He was practically her brother for God's sake. Thinking about having sex with him was sick and twisted and wrong and – oh God – why couldn't she get the image of his mouth sucking on her nipples out of her head?

Snap out of it, Ames! Her inner voice said fiercely. *Mark is not attracted to you, and besides, do you really think he wants to see your naked chubby ass? He doesn't. All the girls he dates are thin and dark-haired and they have perfectly tanned skin. He is not interested in your blonde, pale chubby self.*

She took a deep breath and leaned against the wall. She was standing in the hallway next to the door. Through the narrow side window, she could see the mailman as he walked up the front steps. He waved at her and she waved back as he pushed the

3

mail through the slot in the door. The envelopes tumbled to the floor and she took a second, deep breath. She was not attracted to Mark. She absolutely was not. She was just having a weird little fantasy that was perfectly normal. It didn't mean a damn thing.

She walked to the pile of mail and bent to scoop it up. She rifled through the envelopes and her breath caught in her throat as she stared at the one addressed to her. The return address said Academy of Art University and her heart started a hammering beat that she could feel in her toes. She walked slowly into the kitchen and set the other mail on the table. Her hands shaking, she ripped open the envelope and pulled out the single folded sheet of paper. She closed her eyes and leaned against the wall for a moment.

She'd applied to three schools and she'd already received rejection letters from two. She was disappointed but not surprised. The Fashion Institute of Technology and Parsons were both in New York and both notoriously difficult to get into it. She would have been thrilled to be accepted to either, but it was this University, the Academy of Art in San Francisco, that she really wanted.

Still leaning against the wall, she unfolded the paper and opened her eyes. She scanned it quickly and as nausea rolled in her stomach, she blinked back the hot tears.

"No," she whispered. "No, this can't be right."

"What can't be right?"

She jerked and shoved the paper behind her back before staring up at Mark. He was still wearing just his swimming suit, but the death of her dream blotted out any of her newly discovered desire for him.

"Ames? What's wrong?" He asked.

"Nothing," she said.

"You're crying." He stepped closer and rubbed the moisture from her cheek with his thumb before showing it to her. "What happened?"

"Nothing happened," she said. "I just – nothing happened."

Oh God, why did he have to come into the house right now? She wanted to be alone. She wanted to go to her room and scream and cry and pound her feet like a little kid having a tantrum.

"You're lying," Mark said. "What were you reading? Let me see."

He reached for the paper still tucked behind her back and her fragile control broke. She burst into tears before pushing him in the chest. "Leave me alone, Mark! Get out of my way!"

"Amy?" He gave her a look of confusion as she pushed past him and ran out of the kitchen and up the stairs. She raced into her bedroom and slammed the door, wishing for the first time that she had a lock on her door.

She collapsed on the bed, buried her face in her hands and sobbed bitterly. The door opened and she screamed, "Go away, Mark!"

"Ames, tell me what's wrong," Mark said.

"Please leave me alone," she sobbed.

"I can't, sweetheart." He sat on the bed next to her and sat her up before pulling her into his lap like she was a child. She tried to squirm off his lap, but he held her tightly. She gave up immediately and wrapped her arms around his neck before burying her face in his neck and sobbing. His swimming shorts were wet, and she could feel her jean shorts soaking up the moisture, but she didn't care. Mark was pulling the piece of paper from her fist and she let it go.

A few minutes later, both of his arms were around her waist and he rubbed her back with his warm hands as he murmured, "I'm so sorry, Ames."

She cried even harder and he rocked her back and forth as he continued to rub her back. "I'm sorry, baby."

"They all rejected me," she sobbed against his throat. "All of them."

"They're idiots. It's their loss, Ames."

"They're the best fashion design schools in the country, and I was rejected by every one of them."

"It doesn't mean anything," he said. "You're still an amazing designer."

He leaned sideways and snagged the box of tissues from her nightstand. She grabbed a handful and dried her face before blowing her nose. She was still sitting on his lap and she rested her head on his shoulder as he kissed her forehead. "Better?"

"I don't know what to do now," she said. "I don't have a Plan B or - "

"Ames," he cupped her face and made her sit up, "you don't need a Plan B."

"I do," she insisted as a tear slid down her cheek. "I'm not good enough to design my own clothing line."

"Yes, you are." He rubbed his thumb across her

cheekbone. "You're smart, talented, beautiful and an incredible designer. You're gonna be famous, Ames. I know it."

"You think I'm beautiful?" She asked in a low voice.

He studied her face. His thumb was still stroking her cheekbone and when it dipped down to rub across her bottom lip, she parted her lips. He made a low groan and his voice was hoarse when he said, "Yeah, I do."

She rubbed her hand across his naked chest. Her nails brushed across his flat nipple, and he made another groan that brought goose bumps to her skin.

"I think you're beautiful too," she whispered.

"Amy, I…"

His gaze dropped to her mouth.

"Mark, please," she whispered.

When he didn't move, she tilted her head and leaned forward. Before she could press her mouth against his, Luke wandered into her bedroom.

"Amy, come downstairs and try the pasta I made at cooking class. It'll blow your – what's going on?" He stared in shocked silence at them for a moment. "Why are you sitting on Mark's lap? Are you crying?"

She squeaked in surprise when Mark abruptly pushed her off his lap and onto the bed. Luke was already storming toward them. She cried out when he grabbed Mark and hauled him to his feet before pushing him up against the wall.

"What the hell, Mark? What are you doing to my sister, you asshole?"

"Luke, I wasn't - "

"She's crying! Why the fuck is she crying? Did you hurt her? Did you fucking touch her?"

"Luke! Stop it!" Amy jumped off the bed and grabbed Luke's arm just as he cocked it back to punch Mark in the face. She held it grimly as Luke tried to shake her loose.

"Stop it, you stupid ass!" She shouted. "He's your best friend!"

"You're my sister," Luke snapped. "If he hurt you or touched you, I'll - "

"He didn't! I was upset, and he was comforting me." She smacked Luke hard on the arm. "Let him go."

He let go of Mark's shoulder, and Mark rubbed it gingerly as Luke gave her a confused look. "Tell me what's wrong."

She sighed and pointed to the letter lying on her bed. "I got my rejection letter from the San Francisco school today."

"I'm sorry," Luke said. "Shit, I'm really sorry."

The sincerity in his voice made her start to cry again. "No, I'm sorry. You – you gave up your dream of culinary school and went into business for me and now – and now…"

She wiped at the tears on her face as Luke hugged her hard. "It's okay, Ames."

"It isn't," she insisted. "Both you and Mark are doing careers that you wouldn't have chosen because of me and my stupid dream. Now I can't even get into goddamn fashion school. I've failed before I even started."

"Not true." Luke glanced at Mark. "Mark was

always going to go into accounting, weren't you?"

"Yes," Mark replied. "I was, Amy, you know I was."

"Yeah, well, you weren't going into business, Lukie," she said dully.

"The plan hasn't changed," Luke said.

Her mouth dropped open and she gave him a look of shock. "Of course it's changed. I can't even get into school for fashion design. I'll never start my own clothing line."

"Yes, you will," Luke said. He led her to the bed and sat her down on it before sitting next to her. After a moment, Mark joined them. He sat next to her but left a good foot of space between their bodies.

"I appreciate the vote of confidence, but no one is going to take a chance on a woman who can't even get accepted into a fashion design school," Amy said. "No company will hire me without an education."

"So, we cut out the part of the plan where you work for another company to gain experience," Luke said with a shrug, "and go directly to starting your own company."

She gaped at him. "Lukie, I love you, but you're delusional."

"No, I just know you're meant to do this, Amy. Listen, both Mark and I graduate next year. We'll work and gain some experience while you work on your designs. Evenings and weekends, we'll work on our business plan together. Okay? You can apply again next year to the schools, but if you don't get in, it doesn't matter. We'll start our own damn company in five years just like we planned, whether you go to school or not."

"And if I fail?" Amy whispered. "Then what?"

"You won't," Luke said. "Will she, Mark?"

Mark gave her a crooked smile. "It's like I said, Ames – you're gonna be famous."

Luke put his arm around her and gave her a rough hug. "Don't worry. It's all going to work out."

She leaned against her brother, feeling a warm flush of love for both of them as Luke said to Mark. "Dude, sorry about earlier. It's just – she's my baby sister, you know?"

"Yeah, I know," Mark said. "But I would never hurt her. I think of Amy as my sister too – you know that."

Amy stiffened, and Luke squeezed her before standing. "Yeah, I know, man. C'mon, let's go downstairs and you guys can try the pasta I made."

"Be right there." Amy wiped her face and as Luke left her bedroom, she called Mark's name.

He stopped in the doorway and gave her a solemn look. "I'm sorry for earlier. I shouldn't have… I think of you as a sister and nothing more. I'm sorry if I gave you the wrong impression just now."

"You didn't." Hurt and a healthy dose of embarrassment flooded though her. "I think of you like a brother and I know what happened wasn't, uh, real. It was just, um, because I was upset."

He wouldn't look at her, and when he turned to leave she called his name a little hysterically. His hand gripped the doorframe as he stared out into the hallway. His back was ramrod straight. Despite what she had just told him, she wanted to run across the room and throw her arms around him. She wanted just one kiss to know if what she was feeling was real. Instead, she wrapped her arms around her own torso as he said, "What is it?"

"Are we – are we good?" She whispered.

For a moment, she thought he was just going to leave without replying but then he turned and gave her his sweet smile. Her heart thudded in her chest and she blinked back fresh tears as he said, "Yeah, Ames, we're good. I'll see you downstairs."

Chapter One

"Hey, Ames? You busy?"

Her heart immediately sped up and she hitched in a shaky breath as Mark Stanford strolled into her office. He was wearing a charcoal coloured suit with a dark red tie. She kept the saliva in her mouth with sheer willpower alone as he dropped into the chair across from her desk.

She tried not to stare at the way his jacket stretched across his broad shoulders. She tried even harder not to imagine how he would look naked and stretched out in her bed. Her cheeks flushed, and she turned back to her computer screen.

There was a knock on the door and her brother's assistant, Elaine, stuck her head into the room. "Amy? Luke wanted me to remind you that you have a meeting with him in half an hour. Hey, Mark."

"Hi, Elaine. How's your mom?"

Elaine's cheerful face fell a little. "She's not great, but the doctors think there's been some improvement. Thanks for asking."

where I don't want anyone in my personal bubble."

He smiled at her. "I get it. Do you have time to look at the reports today?"

"Sure," she said.

He laughed. "Are you going to actually look at them or just pretend you did."

"I told you and my brother that I didn't want anything to do with the business side, remember?" She said with a small smile.

"I remember." He headed toward the door. "Later, Ames. I'll see you on Sunday."

"Bye, Mark."

She waited until he'd left before leaning back in her chair and rubbing at her forehead. She felt like she'd been put through the wringer. She pulled her phone out and sent a quick text to Valerie.

Hey, we still on for this weekend?

She hadn't even put her phone down when it buzzed.

Of course we are, doll! You're going to love it, I promise you! See you Friday!

She shoved her phone into her desk and stared blankly at her computer. She would live out her biggest fantasy this weekend and maybe, just maybe, her obsession with Mark would end.

Chapter Two

"Are you nervous?"

"Terrified," Amy admitted as they approached the large stone house. It was Friday night and she gave Valerie a nervous look before studying the house again. She decided that house wasn't exactly the right word – mansion was more appropriate.

"Don't be," Valerie said. "I told you – it'll be an amazing experience. You won't regret it."

"This isn't exactly my thing," Amy said.

"How do you know? You've never tried it before," Valerie countered. "Besides, you're the one who told me you wanted to try it, remember?"

"I remember." A decision she was starting to regret as Valerie rang the doorbell.

It opened almost immediately, and Amy wondered if her jaw could actually hit the ground if she tried a little harder. The man who opened the door was wearing a bowtie around his neck and a pair of very tight and revealing shorts and nothing else. His body was amazing, all hard muscles and tanned skin, and she swallowed as he smiled at

Valerie.

"Welcome back, Miss Valerie."

"Thank you, Josh."

"Come in, please."

Amy followed Valerie into the house. It opened into a giant foyer with marble floors and cold white walls. A few women and men were wandering the room and Amy suddenly felt extremely overdressed in her winter jacket and jeans.

"Come on, doll." Valerie had a small grin on her face and she took Amy's hand and led her toward a desk that was tucked into one corner. A woman wearing a bustier and short leather skirt was behind the desk and she looked up from the computer with a smile.

"Hello, Valerie."

"Hi, Angie."

The woman typed something into the computer before handing them two plain white key cards. "You're in rooms 234 and 235. Up the stairs and to the left. Enjoy your stay."

"Thank you," Valerie said. Still holding Amy's hand, she walked toward the grand staircase that dominated the foyer. Amy followed her up the stairs, holding her small suitcase in one hand as she studied her surroundings.

The place was lushly decorated and the thick carpet in the upstairs hallway muffled their footsteps as they walked to their rooms.

"What do you think?" Valerie asked as they stopped in front of a door marked with a small metal plaque that had the numbers 234 etched into it.

"There are fewer chains and whips than I thought," Amy said.

Valerie giggled. "Those are downstairs. Upstairs is pure decadence."

"It should be for the amount of money it costs to rent a room here," Amy said.

"Please, you're a friggin millionaire, you can afford it. Besides, it'll be worth it. Trust me."

Valerie opened the door using the key card. "Come into my room for a minute."

"Wow, this is nice," Amy said as she studied the large room with the king bed.

"I splurged and booked us the nicer rooms," Valerie said. She set her suitcase down and sat on the bed, running her hand over the thick duvet. "God, I'm so glad to be here."

"How often do you come here?" Amy asked.

"About twice a month. If I could, I'd be here every weekend," Valerie replied.

"Does your dad know this is how you're spending your trust fund?"

"Hell, no!" Valerie said with a laugh. "Can you imagine what he'd say and do if he knew his little girl was a kink addict?"

"Is that what we are?" Amy asked with a grimace.

"It's what I am," Valerie clarified. "You're just trying a new experience. That you're going to love," she added with an impish grin.

"I'm not sure about that," Amy said.

Valerie shrugged. "Sweetie, you told me yourself that you liked being held down during sex. Liked it a lot. Don't you think it's worth the time to see if you wouldn't like more? There's nothing wrong with being submissive."

Amy blushed. A few weeks ago, after too much wine, she had confessed to Valerie her secret enjoyment of being dominated during sex, as well as her deepest fantasy. Valerie was thrilled with her admittance. Amy was completely blown away by her best friend's immediate admission that she was a card-carrying member of a BDSM club called "Secrets". She'd had instantaneous visions of a dungeon-type atmosphere filled with scantily-clad women and men carrying whips. But after nearly two hours of more wine and talking, Valerie had convinced her that "Secrets" was nothing like she was picturing.

"Ames, if you don't want to do this, you don't have to. You know that, right?" Valerie was giving her a serious look.

"I know. I want to try it, I'm just nervous," Amy said.

"I know you are. Which is why I've booked you a special treat tonight."

"What do you mean?" Amy said.

"Well," Valerie said delicately, "I don't think you're ready to just wander the floor and find a Dom to claim you for the night. So, I booked you in with one of the Dom's in a private room."

Amy's eyes widened. "You did what?"

"Don't freak out," Valerie said. "It's a good thing, I promise. He knows you're a newbie and exactly what you're looking for. He won't go further than what you're comfortable with, and if he does, you can safe word and he'll stop immediately."

"You told him!" Amy dropped her suitcase on the floor and collapsed on the bed next to Valerie. Boldened by the wine, she had told Valerie exactly the type of experience she was looking for, but she had never imagined that Valerie would tell someone else.

"Honey, of course I did," Valerie said. "They can't give you what you want if they don't know exactly what you want."

"He's going to think I'm a freak," Amy said.

Valerie burst into laughter. "Are you kidding me? Being blindfolded, restrained and having sex with an anonymous stranger doesn't even crack the top fifty of freaky requests at this place."

Amy blushed furiously. Having Valerie talk about her deepest fantasy with such candor was making her feel both embarrassed and relieved. Being told she wasn't a freak was oddly comforting, especially after the disaster with her last boyfriend.

"I know what you're thinking, Ames, and stop it."

"No, you don't."

"Of course I do. I'm your best friend. Tom's reaction to your request was stupid and childish."

Amy closed her eyes as Valerie patted her leg. "He said I was sick, Valerie. He said that only women with psychological issues had – had rape fantasies."

Her cheeks were hot, and she felt a little sick to her stomach. Even saying the words sent shame spiraling through her.

"Amy, look at me." Valerie cupped her face

and squeezed gently. "I know I told you this the other night, but I'm going to tell you again. Asking your boyfriend to blindfold you, tie you to the bed and pretend to be a stranger while he's fucking you, is not a rape fantasy. Do you understand?"

Amy nodded as Valerie stroked her blonde hair. "Wanting to be dominated in bed, wanting to be restrained and held down during sex - hell, wanting to have your ass spanked or wondering what it would be like to be in a master/slave relationship – does not equate to a rape fantasy. Don't let some misinformed asshole try and convince you it is. Okay?"

"Okay," Amy said.

"One other thing – even if you did have a rape fantasy, that doesn't make you sick either. Understand?"

"Yes," Amy said.

"Good. Besides, I know of like twenty women alone who have fantasized about having sex with a total stranger. It's a common one, Ames. I'll be right back. I've got to pee like you wouldn't believe."

Amy studied the duvet as she silently thanked God that the wine wasn't enough to completely loosen her inhibitions that night. Yes, she had told Valerie about her fantasy to be fucked by a stranger but if she knew the second part of it...

You mean the true part of it.

She tried to ignore her inner voice as Valerie stood and walked to the bathroom, but it refused to be quiet.

You don't want to be fucked by a stranger. You

want to be fucked by your brother's best friend. Do you really think sleeping with a stranger is the answer to your wish?

The fucked-up thing was – she really did. Being tied down was a kink of its own, she supposed, but asking Tom to blindfold her and pretend to be a stranger was just her way of pretending it was Mark. If she couldn't see Tom, if he stayed quiet and just fucked her, she could sink much more easily into her fantasy that it was Mark between her legs and not him.

She groaned to herself. God, she was awful. Tom was a perfectly good guy, and she was horrible for trying to pretend he was Mark. She needed to grow up and face reality. Every boyfriend she'd had since she was nineteen was nothing more than a poor substitute for Mark.

She couldn't keep doing that to the nice guys she dated. It wasn't fair to them and it really did make her feel horrible. But having sex with an actual stranger and pretending it was Mark... well, that wasn't such a bad thing. Was it?

"Can I give you a piece of advice?" Valerie had returned from the bathroom and she sat next to Amy again. "Don't overthink any of this. Just relax and enjoy the experience tonight, okay? Tomorrow night, if you're interested in trying other things, we can walk the floor. You'll find a Dom that's the right fit for you."

"How can you be so sure?"

"Because this place is amazing, Ames," Valerie replied. "The Doms here are very, very good at what they do. It's a safe place. There are cameras monitoring everything and everyone, and they're diligent about being certain that everyone's experience is safe, sane, and consensual. Now, we have a few hours before we go downstairs. I'm going to have a hot bath and I suggest you go to your room and do the same. Tonight will be a fantastic experience. I promise, doll."

"Okay, but can I ask you a quick question?" Amy asked.

"Sure." Valerie started to unpack her suitcase.

"We've been best friends since high school. Why haven't you ever told me you like this sort of thing? If there's nothing wrong with it, why keep it a secret from me?"

Valerie studied her for a moment. "I wanted to tell you, but I was worried."

"About what?"

"Well, and don't take this the wrong way, but you give off a serious 'missionary only type of girl' vibe. Your friendship is important to me and I didn't want it to end just because I like a little kink in the bedroom."

"I'm sorry," Amy said.

"For what?" Valerie asked.

"That you thought I would stop being your friend over something like this. I obviously come across as a jerk about certain things."

"You don't. This is just my own insecurity rearing its ugly head. I adore you and can't imagine my life without you."

"Same here," Amy said. "I'm glad we can, uh, share this type of experience."

"Whoa, that's a whole other kink," Valerie said.

Amy blushed furiously, and Valerie laughed. "Sorry, I couldn't resist."

"Are you into girls?" Amy asked.

"I've been dominated a few times by female Dommes, but I prefer the male ones," Valerie said. "I've also done a couple of threesomes, but who hasn't, right?"

"Uh, right," Amy said.

Valerie grinned at her. "Go on, doll. Have a bath and relax."

∂∘ ∾∾

"Breathe, Amy."

"I'm breathing."

"Not enough," Valerie said as the elevator doors opened.

They stepped out into a small room with white walls. A man was standing beside a door and Valerie smiled at him. "Just give us a minute."

He nodded, and Valerie led Amy to the far corner. "Take a couple deep breaths, babe."

She breathed deeply before smiling tentatively. "I'm good."

"Better than good," Valerie said. "You're about to have the best experience of your life."

"Right. Are you sure I look okay?"

"No. You look fucking amazing." Valerie eyed her dress before letting her gaze linger on Amy's breasts. "God, I wish I had your tits."

"Be thirty pounds overweight and you can have them too!" Amy said brightly.

"Men love your curves and you know it."

"Yeah, they really do," Amy said, and Valerie

laughed.

"There's my Amy. C'mon, doll, let's go and get you laid by a total stranger."

They approached the man standing at the door and Valerie held out her arm. A plastic blue wristband was around her slender wrist and the man scanned it before turning to Amy. Amy held her own arm out. Her waistband was green, and she had found it on the nightstand in her room. Valerie had explained that the wristbands were required to enter the lower area of the club and that the colour represented her experience in the BDSM world. Green was for a complete novice and she was a little embarrassed by it. The man scanned her bracelet without saying anything, then opened the door and ushered them through the doorway.

Amy stopped immediately and tried to keep a blasé look on her face. Scantily-clad women and men filled the room and her eyes widened when a woman wearing leather pants and a leather bustier walked by. She had a leash in her hand that was clipped to the collar of a man wearing just a pair of tight jean shorts.

It was a large room – large enough that she couldn't see the far end of it through the people milling around – and it was painted a dark red. Dim light shone from sconces hung on the wall, and there were a series of hallways that broke off from the main room.

"What's going on over there?" Amy whispered to Valerie.

There were about seven rows of chairs set up in front of a small stage. Dark curtains were drawn across the stage, but the chairs were already nearly full. Each chair had a cushion beside it and she watched as a blond-haired man sat down. A slender woman wearing a collar and a gorgeous form-fitting dark green dress knelt gracefully on the cushion next to the chair. The man smiled at her and petted her dark hair before gently pushing her head to his thigh. She rested her cheek against his leg and stared adoringly at him as he spoke with the man sitting next to him.

"They're setting up for the show," Valerie said.

"Show?"

Valerie nodded. "They do some public performances."

"Public performances of what?"

"Depends. I think tonight there's a flogging and a forced orgasm scene."

Amy's eyes widened. "Flogging?"

Valerie squeezed her arm. "Stay calm, doll. Remember, everything that happens here is consensual."

The dull sound of a paddle hitting flesh and a sharp squeal of pain came from their left. Amy turned, her hand gripping Valerie's as she stared at the scene. A man, his pale skin glowing in the dim light, was straddling a bench. His chest and stomach rested against the padded upper part of the bench. His arms and legs were placed on the padded arm and leg rests screwed into the sides of the wooden bench. Leather straps were attached just above the rests and they were wrapped around his upper thighs and biceps, holding him firmly in place.

As they watched, a woman wearing a beaded mask and a short red dress, spanked him on the right ass cheek with a wooden paddle. The man jerked and cried out then moaned happily when the woman rubbed his red cheek.

"It's called a spanking bench," Valerie murmured into her ear.

"H-have you ever tried it?" Amy asked.

Valerie nodded. "Yes, but not in public. I always ask my chosen Dom to take me to a private room."

Amy barely heard her. She watched in fascination as the woman set the paddle on a small table before slapping the man's ass repeatedly with her right hand. The man was moaning in pain, but the look of pure bliss on his face was undeniable.

She wondered what it would be like to be strapped to a bench like that. To be vulnerable and helpless while a man spanked her. As the woman gave the man a particularly vicious slap and the man squealed loudly, Amy decided it wasn't for her. She wanted to give up some control but not like that.

What if it was Mark doing the spanking?

The errant thought sent an almost painful cramp of pleasure deep in her belly. She made herself look away from the spanking scene. Mark was the most easy-going man she knew. He wasn't a pushover, but he was always willing to accommodate and compromise both in his work life and personal life. Pretending he was a Dom and pretending he would like to spank her was utterly ridiculous. A man like Mark wouldn't set foot in a place like this and just the thought of him finding out that she did, made her cringe. Despite Valerie's assurances, she was still feeling very much like a freak. She'd die before she'd ever let Mark know that she liked the idea of being dominated.

An image of Mark hovering over her, of his hands clamping around her wrists and holding her still as he pushed between her thighs flickered through her. It sent more pleasure pulsing through her belly and a ridiculous desire to giggle. The thought of sweet, gentle Mark ever holding her down and forcing her to take his cock was so absurd it bordered on surreal.

Still, if it meant having Mark in her bed, she'd gladly give up all of her own timid desires to be dominated. She liked the idea of it, but she wanted Mark. Wanted him exactly as he was – sweet and kind and undoubtedly amazing in bed but not dominant. Not him.

Valerie was pulling on her hand. She wanted to take a quick walk through the room – her initial shock was wearing off and she was fascinated by everything – but Valerie led her to the first hallway.

A woman, holding a tablet in one hand, was standing at the entrance wearing jeans and a golf shirt that said "Secrets" over the right breast. She looked so normal and ordinary that it sent another wave of surreal through Amy.

"Hi, Kori. How are you?" Valerie asked.

"Fine, thanks," the woman said. "You have a private session booked tonight?"

"Not me but my friend. This is Amy. Amy, this is Kori. She works here."

"Right," Dave said.

Mark gave him a look of exasperation. "Where's Selene?"

"She's getting a newbie ready."

"We have a newbie tonight?" Mark asked.

Trent nodded and pointed to the second screen from the left. "Yes, first time at the club. She's in the Blue Room."

Mark only half-glanced at the screen. Selene was standing in front of a tall, curvy blonde who had a truly spectacular body. He looked back at the spreadsheet in front of him. The blonde's body reminded him a little of Amy's, actually. If Amy ditched the flowing skirts and peasant blouses she normally wore and poured herself into a little black dress.

His stomach tightened, and his cock twitched a little against the confines of his jeans. Jesus, just thinking about his best friend's little sister was a mistake. For years, he'd kept his lust for her a secret, kept it firmly hidden under a tight fist of control, but it was becoming more and more difficult to be around her. If he didn't figure out what the hell to do about his inappropriate desire to fuck her, he would have to quit his job at Dawson's Clothing. He made more than enough money from the club, he didn't technically even have to continue with his job as CFO of Amy's clothing company.

If you quit, you won't get to see her anymore.

He scowled at the spreadsheet. That was the fucking idea. He couldn't keep seeing her. It was too difficult and too damn dangerous. Three months ago, he had stopped playing completely with the subs at the club. Stopped when he realized he was deliberately choosing women who looked like Amy. Stopped when he realized that playing with them left him cold and empty.

He glanced at the Blue Room screen again. Of course, this woman's body was making him reconsider –

His eyes widened as he finally took a look at the woman's face. "Fuck me!"

Trent jerked wildly, nearly spilling the cup of his coffee by his right hand as he twisted to stare at Mark. "Boss, what's wrong?"

"It can't be." Mark stood and squinted at the screen. "It can't be her."

"Can't be who?" Dave asked.

Mark clenched his fists and muttered, "Move, Selene. Goddammit."

Selene was partially blocking the blonde's face and all the breath rushed out of him when she stepped away and walked to the wardrobe.

"Holy fuck."

Amy - his sweet Amy - was standing in the Blue Room.

"Boss, what's going on?" Trent asked.

"The newbie, what is she asking for?"

"Uh, I don't know," Trent said.

"Look it up!"

Trent grabbed a tablet and quickly scrolled through it. "Um, she's wanting some sensory deprivation, restraints and vaginal intercourse only."

Mark watched as Selene led Amy to the chair and buckled the cuffs around her wrists. "Who's assigned to her?"

"Brandon's with her tonight."

"No, he isn't," Mark said.

"He isn't?" Trent replied.

"No, goddammit," Mark said.

"We always use him for the newbies," Dave said.

"Not tonight. Let him know he can walk the floor instead."

"Uh, okay, but what do we do with the newbie?"

"She's playing with me," Mark said grimly before stalking from the room.

Trent stared at Dave who grinned. "Guess his break is over."

∾ ∾

Mark stood outside the Blue Room. His goddamn hands were shaking, and he ran one through his dark hair. He had deliberately avoided Selene, ducking into an empty room until she passed by. Trent would tell her about the change in plans for Amy. She would probably find it a little odd, but one look at his face and she'd know something was wrong. The woman was too smart for her own good and if she knew that this was his Amy, she'd stop him from playing with her.

Not that he was going to play with her, he reminded himself immediately. No, he was going to do the right thing. He would walk into that room, take off Amy's blindfold, give her a quick explanation and walk her out of the damn club and back to her room upstairs.

A quick explanation? That's not gonna work, buddy.

No, not long term but it would work long enough to get her out of the club. He would explain more in the hard light of day. When she was dressed like she normally was, and he had better control. He could just explain that he was one of the owners of the club. She didn't need to know that he was dominant. Didn't need to know that he'd had more than one dark fantasy of her chained to his bed, legs spread wide and helpless, as he pumped himself into her over and over until his never-ending need for her was finally satisfied.

His cock was hardening, and he adjusted it roughly. If Amy knew exactly what he wanted to do to her, she'd run screaming. Or worse yet, she'd tell Luke that his best friend was a fucking pervert who wanted to defile her. Luke would kick him out of his life forever and he'd lose not just his best friend, but the family that was so important to him. He could – had to – convince Amy that his involvement in the Club was strictly business.

Uh, Mark, buddy? She's here looking to be dominated, remember? She'd probably like it if she knew the real you.

He grimaced and rubbed his head again. No, she wouldn't. He had looked at the paperwork she'd filled out as he was waiting for Selene to leave. Amy wanted light restraints on her arms only and she was seeking what they called the 'stranger experience'. She wanted to be fucked by someone she didn't know while being lightly restrained. It was a common kink for women and one he had fulfilled many times in the past. Being blindfolded for the entire time was a little strange, but it was one of her requests.

You know, if she's blindfolded she won't know it's you. You could give her what she wants without her knowing.

He pushed that thought out of his head and opened the door to the Blue Room. The lights in the room were soft and dim. But as he closed the door and stared at Amy, he had no trouble seeing the flush in her cheeks or the way her chest rose and fell rapidly. At the sight of her, every good intention he had of telling her the truth flew out the door. His cock grew painfully erect and he wanted to unbutton his jeans and free it. He wanted to wrap Amy's soft hand around it and force her to rub him until the deep-seated ache in his balls was gone.

He wanted her. Had wanted her for years, and this was his only chance to finally take what was his. She would never know it was him, and while the thought made his chest tighten painfully, it was for the best. In the last two years, she had grown more distant with him. The affectionate touches and hugs she had once bestowed so freely had dried up. Now she did everything she could to avoid touching him. A stupid man might have thought her affection had turned to dislike, but he wasn't stupid.

She wanted him as much as he wanted her. He could see it in the subtle way her body stiffened on the rare occasions that he stood too close to her. He could see it in the odd shine in her eyes and the way she crossed her arms over her torso whenever he walked into the room. She utterly refused to be alone with him anymore and while he understood why, he missed her so much it was a constant ache in his chest.

He took a deep breath and walked silently across the room. There was a camera tucked discreetly in the upper corner of the room. For a moment, he considered turning it off but dismissed it almost immediately. No doubt, Trent and Dave had already told Selene about his odd reaction to Amy, but if he shut off the camera, it was over. Every room was monitored, and it was against the club's rules to shut off the camera. Even for him. It had never bothered him before that Trent or any of the Dom's who worked at the club could watch him during a play session with a sub, but this was his Amy. He didn't want anyone seeing her naked but him.

He hesitated for a moment before striding forward. Amy knew there was a camera in the room and obviously she was fine with it. He would do his damn job and fulfill his biggest personal fantasy at the same time.

His cock throbbed and he took another deep breath as he stopped in front of Amy. She tilted her head back. She obviously knew he was there even though she couldn't see him. He studied her mouth before running his thumb across her soft cheek.

She jumped and made a frightened squeak before whispering, "Sorry."

He didn't reply. He moved around behind her and she twisted her head, following his movements. He cupped her head and gently pushed until she was facing forward again. He brushed her hair back and leaned down, pressing his nose into the side of her throat and inhaling deeply. She smelled so good, that subtle scent of flowers that he always associated with her.

She made another nervous squeak before clearing her throat. "Uh, my name is Amy."

He ran the tips of his fingers over her exposed collarbone. She twitched again. "What's your name?"

He leaned down and licked the curve of her ear before whispering, "Sir."

He heard the audible click of her throat when she swallowed. "You want me to call you sir?"

Just hearing her say the word 'sir', made him want to come and his hand tightened on her shoulder. She shivered violently. He made himself release her before whispering. "Yes."

He moved to her front and took her hands. He pulled her to her feet and she stumbled a little when he turned her around so that she was facing the chair. He pressed his hands on her shoulders, and she resisted for a moment before kneeling gracefully. He petted her long hair as he stared at her. How many times had he imagined Amy on her knees in front of him? More than he could count. He resisted his urge to free his cock and guide it past her lips. Instead, he sat down in the chair and made her shuffle forward until she was wedged between his legs with her stomach pressed against the edge of the chair.

She was wearing a skin-tight, short black dress that showed off an intoxicating amount of her magnificent breasts. He traced the top of her breasts and her little gasp made him smile. He cupped the back of her head in a tight grip and leaned forward until his lips were almost touching hers.

"Open," he whispered.

Her mouth parted immediately, and another hot wave of desire washed over him. Fuck, she was so beautiful. He sucked on her bottom lip and she moaned when he flicked his tongue against her upper lip. He curved his arm around her ample waist and drew her up against his chest before kissing her deeply. She responded with hot eagerness but when she tried to put her arms around him, he stopped her. He took both of her wrists just above the leather cuffs and moved them behind her back before holding them firmly with one hand. He didn't think she would recognize him just by touching him, but he sure as hell wasn't taking any chances.

She pulled at his hand and he gripped her even harder. She gasped and wetted her upper lip with the tip of her tongue before relaxing in his grip.

"Good girl," he whispered and smiled when she flushed.

He kissed her again, reminding himself to go slowly as he explored her mouth. She tasted as sweet as he had imagined. He sucked slowly on her tongue as she made soft little sounds in the back of her throat.

When he finally released her mouth, her head swayed on her neck before she blindly leaned forward to search for his mouth. He stopped her with a tight squeeze to the back of her neck and she pouted adorably.

"Please kiss me."

He waited patiently. She was a smart girl – she would figure it out.

She licked her lips and he grinned when she said, "Please kiss me, Sir."

He rewarded her, and she moaned happily and returned his kiss. He loved the way she kissed, loved how soft her lips were and the taste of her mouth. He released the back of her neck and cupped her right breast, squeezing it firmly as she moaned again. Her back arched and he rubbed at her nipple with his thumb. The material of her dress and bra impeded his touch and he released her wrists and stood up. He cupped her elbows and helped her to her feet before taking her hand and leading her toward the bed. She walked hesitantly, and he squeezed her hand as he stopped next to the bed.

He leaned down and tasted the soft skin of her throat. She let her head drop back and he pressed a trail of warm, wet kisses down the column of her throat before licking her collarbone. He reached behind her, and she stiffened when he unzipped her dress. Moving quickly, he pulled her dress down over her arms and pushed it past her full hips and down her legs before making her step out of it. He inhaled sharply. She was wearing a dark red lace bra with matching panties. The bra pushed her full breasts up and he stared hungrily at them.

Nearly desperate to see her breasts, he reached around her again and unclasped her bra, pulling it off her body before she could protest. She crossed her arms protectively over her naked breasts as he dropped her bra to the floor. He made a low noise of disapproval and took her by the wrists, forcing her arms down.

"Beautiful," he whispered.

She flushed with pleasure and he released her wrists before cupping both her breasts. Her nipples were light pink in colour and already hard. He flicked them with his thumbs, liking the way she jerked in response. He bent his head and sucked one nipple into his mouth. She cried out as her back arched and her hands threaded through his dark hair. She pulled restlessly at his hair as he teased her nipple into a hard point. When the pale pink had turned a dark rose, he moved to her left nipple and nipped and licked it until it matched her right in colour. She was pressing her lower body against his rhythmically and he cupped her ass and rubbed his erection against her stomach.

She reached between them and he nearly blew his load right there when she touched his cock through his jeans. He pushed her hand away. She froze and said, "I'm sorry, Sir."

He kissed her briefly before urging her onto her back in the middle of the bed. She went willingly enough and didn't object when he lifted her arms above her head. Small chains were embedded in the headboard and he quickly clipped them to the metal rings on both cuffs. He sat on the side of the bed and admired the way she looked. With her arms stretched above her head, her full breasts were lifted, and he stroked the curve of one as she tested the strength of the chains that held her captive.

He smiled a little when she realized that she wasn't going to get free. He wished he could see her eyes. For a moment he was tempted to remove her blindfold before he got a hold of himself. She had specifically requested to keep the blindfold on the entire time, and she wasn't supposed to know it was him.

He continued to stare at her utterly amazing body, picturing the way she would look with her legs spread and tied down as well. There was a spreader bar in the wardrobe and he was again tempted to go and get it. The thought of Amy locked into a spreader bar, her legs spread wide and unable to stop him from fucking her, made a surge of precum leak from the head of his cock.

"Sir?"

He realized Amy had stopped wiggling and she was turning her head back and forth a bit anxiously. "Sir, are you still there?"

He rested his hand on her stomach, rubbing it lightly before leaning toward the nightstand next to the bed. The top drawer held lube and condoms and he removed a condom package before opening the lower door. A bar fridge was hidden inside the lower half of it and he opened it and removed the shallow bowl from the freezer compartment. It was full of ice cubes and he sat it on the nightstand.

A lot of the Doms at Secrets had their own special methods of driving their subs mad, but he suspected he was the only one who used ice cubes. He knew the others considered it a bit cliché and he supposed it was, but he loved a sub's reaction to them.

He picked up an ice cube and without warning, ran it over Amy's erect right nipple. She squealed and tried to twist away, her arms yanking uselessly at her bonds.

"Cold!" She cried when he ran the ice cube over her side. She tried to wiggle away, and he slapped her lightly on the thigh. She jerked again before falling still. He set the ice cube on her belly button and she gasped but didn't move.

"Good girl," he whispered. He stood and shed his clothes before grabbing a second ice cube and stretching out on the bed beside her. The ice cube on her navel was slowly melting, sending little rivers of water down her skin. He leaned over and licked them away. She moaned at the touch of his warm wet tongue and he traced her navel with the tip of his tongue before straightening.

The ice cube in his hand was starting to melt and he ran it over her nipple again as she squealed and pounded the bed with her feet.

"It's too cold, Sir!" She said desperately as he ran it between her breasts and in a circle around her left nipple.

He ignored her and returned the ice cube to her right nipple. Her nipple was rock hard, and he brushed the cube over it repeatedly as she gasped and cried out.

"Please, Sir! Please!" She said. "Too cold!"

He ran the small chip of ice that was left along the underside of her breast before sucking on her nipple. It was cold, and he warmed it with his tongue as she moaned and pleaded breathlessly.

He grabbed a third ice cube and ran it up and

down her stomach, tracing the waistband of her panties as her pelvis rose and fell. He left the cube on her belly button again before rubbing her thighs with the palm of his hand. Despite her obvious desire, her thighs were closed tightly.

He pressed his mouth against her ear. "Spread your thighs for me."

She didn't do what he asked, and he pinched her right nipple in punishment. She cried out and spread her legs wide. He bent his head and soothed the sting of her pinched nipple with his tongue as he traced her inner thighs with the tips of his fingers before running them over her abdomen.

He could see a wet spot on the crotch of her silk panties and it sent a throb of lust through him. He cupped her left breast and kneaded it as he whispered into her ear, "Are you wet for me, little slave?"

She shuddered violently when he called her slave and her hips bucked. Her reaction sent his lust into overdrive and he couldn't resist rubbing his aching cock against her smooth thigh as he whispered, "Answer me."

"Yes, Sir," she moaned.

"Should I check for myself, little slave?"

Again, that full body shiver that made his cock leak precum all over her thigh.

"Y-yes, Sir," she stuttered.

He pinched her left nipple hard and she gasped with pain.

"Try again," he whispered.

He gave her a few seconds to think before he pinched her nipple again. She twitched and moaned, and he reminded himself to reign it in. Amy hadn't asked for pain or punishment. His gaze drifted to her pussy. Of course, the wet spot on her panties *had* grown significantly in the last few minutes.

"Try again, slave," he repeated in a whisper.

She bit her bottom lip before saying, "Please check to see if I'm wet for you, Sir."

"Such a good girl," he crooned into her ear before nipping her earlobe.

"Thank you, Sir," she panted.

He smiled. She was a fast learner and more submissive than he could ever have hoped for.

He slid his hand into her panties, briefly touching the soft curls at the top of her pussy before touching her swollen lips. She was soaking wet and at the touch of his fingers, her legs widened even more. He rubbed her clit as a reward and she moaned and pumped her hips against his fingers.

Fuck, she was so responsive to his touch. It was driving him mad. He slid one thick finger into her core. She tightened around him and muttered "cold". He rubbed her clit with his thumb as he fucked her with his finger. Her pussy was unbelievably tight, and he muttered a curse of surprise when she suddenly arched upward and climaxed violently. Her pussy squeezed rhythmically around his finger and she didn't make a sound as she shuddered wildly against his hand.

He'd wanted to tease her for a while longer, wanted to draw this moment out for as long as he could but she had surprised him with her sudden climax. His need for her was suddenly overwhelming in its intensity. He withdrew his hand and quickly yanked her panties down her legs and off her feet. She was splayed wide open for him, her chest heaving as she fought to catch her breath. He grabbed the condom and leaned down to press a kiss against her mouth.

"Thank you, Sir," she whispered when he released her mouth. "That was so good."

Good? Jesus, he needed to do a better job next time if all he got was a 'so good'.

There won't be a next time.

He ignored his inner voice as he pressed the condom package against her bound right hand. He could see her forehead wrinkling above the silk blindfold as she felt the package. Her face relaxed in understanding. "Condom. Thank you."

He reached for her nipple but stopped when she said, "I mean, thank you, Sir."

He grinned and studied her naked body for a moment. He wished he could taste her, wished he could bury his face in that soaking wet pussy and lick every inch of her clean, but she had clearly stated no oral sex. He wasn't surprised by it. Most newbies to the club took a while to warm up to oral sex. Sexual intercourse was intimate, but oral sex was even more so. He stared at her pussy with regret before kneeling between her thighs. He smoothed the condom over his cock, hissing a little when even the pressure of his own hand made his balls tighten, before gripping her thighs with both hands.

"Sir?" She suddenly said. "Are you – are you big, Sir?"

He rubbed the head of his cock against her clit and she moaned before biting at her lip. "It's been a while and I'm not used to, uh, big men. If you're big, will you go slowly?"

He rubbed her thighs until she relaxed. God, he wanted to taste her pussy. He cursed inwardly, then guided his cock to her entrance and pushed. He groaned when the head slipped into her wet and extremely tight pussy. He leaned over her, propping himself up on his hands above her as he pushed another few inches into her pussy. He *was* on the larger side and she made a low groan and tensed before muttering, "big," under her breath.

He kissed her mouth before whispering into her ear, "Too big for you, little slave?"

She shook her head and he heard that familiar stubbornness in her voice when she said, "No, Sir."

"Wider, slave," he whispered.

She spread her legs wide and they both groaned when he pushed firmly and sunk his entire length into her warm pussy. For the first time in his life, he was grateful to be wearing a condom. It dulled the sensation just enough that he didn't embarrass himself by coming immediately.

He gritted his teeth and counted backward from twenty as her pussy stretched to accommodate him. When she wiggled under him, he muttered a curse and slapped her breast. She stopped moving immediately and he released his breath in a harsh groan.

He started a slow and steady rhythm, sweat breaking out on his forehead as her pussy gripped him. Her hips were rising to meet his and he marvelled at how quickly they fell into a rhythm together. She was starting to pant again, her head tossing back and forth on the pillow as her bound hands clenched and unclenched.

He thrust harder, his hands digging into the sheets as he stared at her sweet face. Her curvy body provided a soft cushion for his hard one and he drove in and out of her with quick hard thrusts.

He was fucking Amy.

He was inside of her and she was just as warm and tight as he'd dreamed she would be. His balls tightened, and the base of his spine tingled as his orgasm started. He was moving so quickly now that she was bouncing on the mattress, but she didn't complain. She moaned and gasped, and when her body arched and her pussy squeezed him as she climaxed in that oddly silent way of hers, his entire body shuddered and he came with a hoarse howl of pleasure.

He pumped steadily as he came, pressing kisses against her damp chest and shoulders before he shuddered to a stop inside of her. He wanted to stay exactly where he was for the rest of his goddamn life, but he made himself pull out of her. He removed the condom and threw it into the waste basket next to the bed before curling up beside her. He released her cuffs from the chains and turned her limp body onto her side before spooning her tightly. He cupped her breast and kissed the back of her shoulder as she made a soft noise of contentment.

He was oddly nervous that it wasn't good for her but before he could embarrass himself as a Dom by asking, she said, "Thank you, Sir. I enjoyed that very much."

He kissed her shoulder again. She was starting to tense, and she said timidly, "Do I, um, leave now?"

He held her in a firm grip and nuzzled her throat affectionately before whispering, "Quiet, little slave."

She relaxed in his grip. "Yes, Sir."

He held her until her breathing evened out and deepened. He wanted to spend the night with her. Wanted to hold her until she woke, and he could bring her even more pleasure. He sighed inwardly. There was no way in hell he could do that. He had one chance to be with Amy and this was it. He'd never be with her again. The memory of this night would be all he'd have.

A wave of bitterness went through him and he eased away from Amy's warm curves and slid out of the bed. He dressed quickly before tucking the covers around her and kissing her forehead.

"Bye, Ames," he murmured before kissing her forehead again. He left the room without looking back and walked quickly down the hallway. Normally he would stay with a sub, let her sleep for half an hour or so before waking her up and providing aftercare. He felt a moment of guilt that he shook off. He hadn't done anything to Amy that required actual aftercare. If she didn't wake after half an hour or so, one of the other employees would wake her and escort her back to her room upstairs. She'd be fine. In the meantime, he needed to leave before Selene started asking questions.

As if his thoughts had summoned her, she

appeared in the hallway. "We need to talk, Mark."

"Not now, Selene," he said before skirting around her. "Go home. It's your night off, remember?"

"Mark - "

He waved his hand in the air before yanking open the door at the end of the hallway and disappearing.

Chapter Four

Mark checked his watch before moving the flyer on his desk. He set it near the edge of his desk and then covered half of it with a file. He studied it before moving the file so more of the flyer showed. He sat down and checked his watch again. God, he was acting as jittery as a teenage girl on prom night.

He pulled absently on his left earlobe before staring at his computer screen. It was Saturday afternoon. He hadn't needed to come into the office today, but after leaving the club at two, he'd spent a sleepless night staring at the ceiling of his bedroom. The idea had come to him when he was stepping into the shower just before noon. He knew Luke would be at the office today, had spoken with him about it on Thursday. Excitement brewing in his belly, he had showered before grabbing the flyer from his study and heading into the office.

Now, he glanced at the flyer and then his watch again. If Luke didn't show up in his office soon, he'd make up some excuse to get him in here. Another trickle of excitement went through him. If this went well, then maybe he and Amy could finally be together.

You're getting ahead of yourself. Say Luke doesn't think you're a freak. Doesn't mean Amy won't. She's sweet and innocent, remember?

She came to the club last night! He argued inwardly. *She liked what I did to her.*

She had no idea it was you, buddy. Besides, so you pinched her nipples, gave her a few gentle slaps and made her call you Sir. That's only a fraction of what you really want to do to her. Just because she liked a little dominance, doesn't mean she'll be eager for whatever else you want. Her fantasy was only slightly above vanilla, and you know that. Are you sure you want your Amy knowing what you're really like?

He tried to push the doubt down. He didn't have to go full Dom with Amy right away. He could ease her into the lifestyle. A good Dom helped a new submissive learn her likes and dislikes anyway, right? He was positive that Amy had never done anything like this before, and he was just the man to help her navigate these new waters.

What if she doesn't want more than what you gave her last night? What if you two can have a relationship, but she isn't willing to give you what you truly want? Then what?

He stared out the window of his office. Then he would take what she gave him and be happy with that.

You won't be happy with that.

He ignored his inner voice. Yes, he would. If it meant having Amy in his arms and in his bed every night, he would change. He wanted Amy and for the first time in a decade, he could see a glimmer of hope that she could be his. He wouldn't do anything to destroy that chance.

You won't be happy. Eventually your true self will come out and what do you think Amy will say or do then? You need to be honest with her, and if that isn't what she wants then –

"Hey, Mark. What are you doing here?"

Luke was strolling into his office and he pushed away his doubts and smiled at his best friend. "Hey. Just had a couple of finance reports I wanted to finish before Monday."

Luke dropped into the chair and scratched at the stubble on his chin. "I think Elaine's gonna quit."

"What? Why?" Mark tried to keep his gaze on Luke's face and not on the flyer on his desk.

Luke shrugged. "Just a feeling. Her mom isn't doing so hot."

"I thought she said she was doing better," Mark replied.

"A little. But she lives in Florida and Elaine's said a couple of things about retiring to Florida."

"Uh oh."

"Yeah," Luke said. "Elaine's husband works overseas. He just left for a month-long job so I'm pretty sure I'll have her for at least this month but after that, who the hell knows."

He scratched at his chin again. "Elaine's the best PA I've ever had. I'm up shit creek if she leaves. I wonder if I could convince her to…"

Mark dropped his hands below his desk and clenched them into fists as Luke leaned forward and plucked the flyer out from under the file. "What is this?"

He scanned the flyer before staring at Mark. "Why the hell do you have a flyer for a BDSM club on your desk?"

Mark shrugged. "Todd left it on my desk. He's thinking about checking it out."

"Holy shit. Todd's a freak in the bedroom, who knew," Luke said.

Saying a silent apology to Todd, Mark said, "Going to a BDSM club doesn't make Todd a freak."

"Doesn't it?" Luke arched an eyebrow at him. "Do you know what they do there?"

"Do you?" Mark asked.

Luke shrugged. "I know it's full of men who get their rocks off by hurting women. I like control, but I'm not interested in slapping a woman around to get it."

"Pretty sure it's not like that," Mark said as dismay flooded his belly. "Everything that happens there is consensual."

"So, you think it's okay to hurt a woman because she has psychological problems and asks to be hurt?" Luke said.

"I didn't say that," Mark said. "I'm just saying that I think you have a skewed view of what BDSM is."

Luke set the flyer down on the desk. He raised his gaze and Mark almost flinched at the disgust in his eyes. "Mark, you're not thinking of going to this place, are you?"

His stomach in knots, Mark plucked the flyer

off the desk and crumpled it up. "No." He threw the flyer in the garbage can as Luke gave him a look of relief.

"Thank God. You had me worried for a minute there, buddy. Hey, you want to have dinner tonight?"

"I can't," Mark said. "I've got plans."

"All right." Luke stood and stretched before ambling toward the door. "See you at Mom's on Sunday."

"You bet," Mark said.

He waited until he was sure Luke was back in his office before slamming his fist on the desk. It hurt like hell and he muttered a curse before leaning back in his chair. Well, that couldn't have gone any fucking worse if he tried.

He turned and stared out the window of his office. He hadn't realized until this moment just how much he wanted Luke to know about Secrets. He'd kept his life as a Dom hidden from his best friend for almost eight years now and it was wearing on him. Buying the club two years ago had made things worse.

At the time, he didn't think it would make it any more difficult to conceal it from Luke and his family. But it was increasingly difficult to come up with realistic excuses for why he was never available on a Friday or Saturday night.

He wondered bleakly how much longer he would be able to keep this part of his life hidden from his loved ones. The thought that ten years from now, he'd still be hiding his life at the club and still yearning for the one woman he couldn't have, made him shudder.

But the look of disgust on Luke's face, the way he considered BDSM to be hurting women and nothing more, meant he had no choice.

Fine, so you keep your BDSM lifestyle hidden from Luke. Doesn't mean you can't date Amy. You think she's going to tell her brother that you like to restrain her and spank her during sex?

He cursed again before closing his laptop with a snap. It didn't matter anyway. He was a fool to think that Amy would ever accept him for who he was. She might be a little more open-minded than her brother, but she wouldn't want to give him what he craved most from her. He'd had his night with Amy and that was it. He needed to stop dreaming about a life he would never have.

❧ ❧

"Amy, are you sure you're okay?" Valerie asked.

"Yes, why?" Amy checked her reflection in the full-length mirror in her room.

"You've been acting weird all day."

"No, I haven't," she said.

"You kind of have. You did enjoy yourself last night, right?"

She nodded and smoothed her hand over the bustier she was wearing. "I told you I did."

"I know but you're so quiet."

Amy sat next to Valerie on the bed and smiled at her. "It was amazing. Really. If it hadn't been, do you think I would still be here?"

"Well, we did pay for two nights," Valerie said.

Amy laughed. "Yes, but if I hadn't enjoyed myself and wanted to leave, I would."

"Okay. And you're sure you want to walk the floor tonight?" Valerie said.

"Positive."

"Maybe you'll find the same Dom from last night," Valerie said.

Amy shrugged. "Even if he did approach me, I wouldn't know it was him. I was blindfolded the whole time."

"He didn't talk to you?"

"Well, he whispered," she said. "I already told you that."

"Right. Sorry, my brains are still a bit scrambled from my own sex-athon last night," Valerie said. "I've got to run back to my room for a minute and then we'll head downstairs, okay?"

"Sure." Amy's cheerful smile faded away the minute Valerie left her room. She hadn't lied to Valerie, she had enjoyed herself last night.

A little too much.

The mystery man who had made her come harder than she'd ever come in her entire life, had occupied her thoughts way too much today. From the in-room breakfast to the full body massage Valerie had talked her into having at the spa located on the main level of the club, she couldn't get him out of her damn head. She had expected to have a bout of anonymous sex that she could just pretend was Mark. Instead she had some unknown Dom who had refused to let her sink completely into her personal fantasy.

The hell of it was – she hadn't cared in the

moment. It was pretty much impossible to pretend it was Mark. Not with the way the Dom was whispering in her ear, not when he made her call him "Sir" and not when he called her his little slave and doled out punishments that oddly excited her. Mark would never act that way and she couldn't even pretend he would. She shifted on the bed and winced slightly when her breasts brushed against the material of her bustier. Her nipples were still a little tender from being pinched and it sent this weird sort of pride tingling through her.

She sighed and rubbed at her forehead. What was really humiliating was her reaction to being called his little slave. Even with the blindfold obscuring most of her face, she was almost certain he knew exactly what it did to her. Jesus, what was wrong with her?

She pasted the smile on her face when Valerie popped back into her room. "Ready to go?"

"You bet," Valerie said. "Honey, I have the feeling you're going to be approached by a lot of the Doms tonight. Take your time in picking one, okay? They'll know you're a newbie because of your bracelet, but you want to make sure you're very clear with them on what your limits are. Don't lie or play coy. Be straight with them about exactly what you will and won't do. Okay?"

"I will be," Amy said. "Don't worry."

⇛ ⇚

"What are you doing, Mark?"

"Good evening to you too, Selene. If you're going to keep showing up on your nights off, why am I even working the weekends?" Mark scanned the floor on the multiple screens.

Selene sank into the chair next to him, but he refused to look at her. Amy was walking the floor and Peter had just approached her. His hands clenched into fists when Peter picked up a lock of her blonde hair before smiling at her.

Not that he could blame the Dom. Amy looked extremely fuckable in her white bustier and her short black skirt. She was wearing high heels and nylons and he wondered not for the first time if they were stockings. He took a deep breath as Amy smiled hesitantly at Peter. He was the third Dom to approach her in less than an hour. He couldn't hear what Brandon or Joseph had said to her, but she had obviously turned down both. Sooner or later she would find a Dom that she did want to sleep with and it made his stomach churn with nausea. He studied her bare neck, pictured another Dom buckling his collar around it, and pounded the desk in sudden frustration.

"Mark, enough," Selene said.

He pulled at his earlobe. "What do you want, Selene?"

"I know what you've done."

"What have I done?" He said. "I had a play session last night. I would think that would make you happy. You and Richard have been complaining for the last month that I haven't been playing with the subs."

"I know she's your Amy," Selene said.

His anger deflated like a balloon and he glanced again at the screen before swivelling in his chair to face Selene. "I didn't plan it," he said hoarsely. "I had no idea she was going to show up. She – she has no idea I'm an owner here."

"I know," Selene said. She reached out and squeezed his hand. "But you shouldn't have played with her last night."

"I had to," he said.

"What if she finds out it was you?"

"She won't," he said. "I couldn't let her play with another Dom, Selene. You know I couldn't."

"Honey, you can't keep torturing yourself like this," Selene said.

"I talked to Luke earlier this afternoon."

Selene gave him a look of surprise. "You told him about the club?"

"No. I wanted to, but I *accidentally* left a flyer on my desk and as soon as he saw it, he was pretty clear about what he thought of the lifestyle. He was disgusted by it."

"I'm sorry," Selene said. She squeezed his hand again. He stared at their linked fingers. After Luke, Selene was his closest friend.

"I'm not that surprised," Mark replied. "It just means that I was right to stay away from Amy all these years."

"But you haven't stayed away from her." Selene pointed out.

"It was just one night," he said.

"What about tonight?"

"What about it?" He couldn't resist studying Amy on the screen again. He had come in tonight with every intention of allowing Amy to find another Dom to play with. But now, watching her walk the floor, knowing that another man would soon be touching her was driving him insane with jealousy.

"She's walking the floor," Selene said. "Are you going to do the right thing and let her play with another Dom tonight?"

He stood abruptly. "No, I'm not."

"Mark - "

"Enough, Selene. I'm an adult and I don't need you lecturing me."

He stormed toward the door, nearly knocking over Trent when he stepped into the room. He was carrying a sandwich and a cup of coffee and he held it protectively. "Hey, watch out, Boss."

"Sorry," Mark muttered.

He left and Trent gave Selene a questioning look. "What's up with him?"

"It's a long story."

❧ ❦

Amy smiled hesitantly at the man standing in front of her. He was tall and handsome enough, but there was a coldness about him that made her a little nervous.

He gave her breasts an appreciative look before picking up a lock of her hair and rubbing it between his fingers. "Why don't you tell me what your hard limits are, my pet."

She cleared her throat. "Oh, um, thank you but I'm not interested in a play session."

He gave her a look of surprise. "Why are you here then?"

"I'm here with a friend. " She edged away.

"Excuse me, please. I need to find her."

She walked away quickly, wobbling a little on her unfamiliar heels. Valerie had already left for a private session. A short redheaded man had approached her not half an hour after they entered the club. He had whispered into her ear for a few moments and Valerie had nodded happily. The man placed a dark red collar around her slender throat while Valerie spoke quietly to him. He headed toward one of the hallways, stopping and waiting at the entrance as Valerie turned to Amy.

"My favourite Dom asked me to do a play session," she said. "Are you okay if I go with him?"

"Of course," Amy said.

"Are you sure? I can stay on the floor if you're a little nervous."

"I'm not," Amy lied. "I think I'll probably go back to my room soon, anyway."

"No sign of the mystery Dom huh?" Valerie said.

"I don't think so," Amy said. She had been approached by two different men and despite being blindfolded last night, she didn't think either of them were her mystery Dom. She had no basis for that other than a feeling in the pit of her stomach.

"Okay, well if you're sure?" Valerie was bouncing on her feet, her gaze sliding repeatedly to the Dom waiting for her.

"I'm sure," Amy said. "Go and have fun, honey."

"Thanks, babe. See you later!" Valerie kissed her cheek and hurried away.

Now, Amy sighed and began to weave her way through the people toward the entrance. She supposed she could stay and maybe watch the show, but she didn't feel like it. She was one of the few women who wasn't wearing a collar and she was feeling oddly self-conscious about it. She snorted inwardly. Did she really want to wear a collar anyway? It wasn't something that most women –

"Excuse me, Amy?"

She turned around and stared at the woman standing behind her. She was dressed in a short skirt and her upper body was completely bare except for two daisy pasties on her nipples. Amy's face reddened and the woman grinned at her.

"Hi, I'm Daisy."

"Uh, hello, Daisy."

"I work here," Daisy said. "I have a message for you."

"You do?"

"Yes." Daisy was holding a thin black collar. The initials 'MM' were stitched in silver thread on the front of it. "Your Sir wondered if you would wear his collar this evening?"

Amy's mouth dropped open. "I – what?"

"Your Sir," Daisy said. "You had a play session with him last night. He would like it if you wore his collar this evening."

"Oh, I, uh…yes, I guess," Amy said as her heart pounded.

"Good," Daisy said. "Come with me." She led her to the bar and sat Amy down on the bar stool. "Lift your hair, please."

Amy lifted her hair and watched with numb

disbelief as Daisy buckled the collar around her throat. She checked the fit before smiling at her. "It looks lovely on you."

"Thank you." Amy glanced around the crowded room. "Um, is Sir here?"

"Not in the room," Daisy said. "He had another matter to take care of first. He would like to request your presence in the Blue Room in about half an hour. If you're agreeable to it?"

"Yes," Amy said.

"Excellent. He'll be very pleased. Why don't you have a drink and relax for a bit. I'll come back and get you, all right?"

"All right," Amy said.

Daisy walked away, moving quickly despite the six-inch heels she was sporting, and Amy touched the collar around her throat. It felt both odd and comforting at the same time. A man sat down next to her, took one look at her collar and immediately left. She blinked in surprise and touched the collar again. Her body was shaking with excitement and she ordered a drink before drumming her fingers on the smooth bar top. Half an hour couldn't come quickly enough.

❧ ❧

Amy watched as Daisy crossed to the wardrobe and removed a blindfold and leather cuffs. This time the blindfold was a soft blue and Daisy smiled at her. "It matches your eyes."

Amy smiled weakly and allowed Daisy to buckle the cuffs around her wrists.

"Your Sir would like you to be in the slave

position for him. Do you know what that is?" Daisy asked.

"Uh, no," Amy said. "I'm new here,"

Daisy giggled. "Yes, I know. Don't worry, we were all newbies once. Let me show you what it is."

She reached for the hooks on Amy's bustier and Amy batted her hands away. "What are you doing?"

"Your Sir had very specific instructions. You're to be naked in the slave position unless you're wearing stockings. If you are, then they and your heels stay on. Are you wearing stockings?"

"Well, yes, but I'm not sure about this," Amy said.

Daisy gave her a serious look. "Would you like me to tell him you've changed your mind?"

Amy shook her head. "No. I just – I feel a little self conscious."

"Don't be. Your body is amazing," Daisy said.

Feeling a little numb and disconnected from her body, Amy allowed Daisy to remove her bustier. She covered her breasts with her arms as Daisy unzipped her skirt and tugged it down her legs. She stepped out of it and Daisy folded it neatly before putting it and Amy's bustier on the armchair.

"Panties next," she said. Before Amy could react, she had tugged them down to her ankles. She ignored her urge to cover her crotch with one hand and stepped out of her panties. They joined the rest of her clothes and she stood awkwardly as Daisy returned to her.

"Okay, let's get you into position."

She pulled a thick mat from under the bed and set it a few feet away from the bed before urging Amy to her knees on top of the mat. Amy sat back with her bottom resting against her calves and blushed when Daisy made her widen her legs as far as she could. She covered her exposed pussy with her hand as Daisy moved around behind her. She pushed on Amy's lower back.

"Nice straight back, please, Amy. Keep your head up. That's a good girl."

Amy did what she asked. The position felt a little unnatural and when Daisy pushed again on her lower back, forcing her to thrust her breasts out even more, she could feel her cheeks burning with embarrassment.

"Good," Daisy said. "You assume the slave position very well for a newbie."

"Thank you," Amy said as Daisy returned to her front.

She stared at Amy's hands covering her crotch. "Hands resting on your thighs, palms up."

She hesitated, and Daisy smiled at her. "I've seen lots of pussy, Amy. No need to be shy."

Blushing furiously, Amy rested her hands on her thighs with the palms up.

"God, your tits are amazing," Daisy said.

"Um, thank you," Amy said again.

"Widen your legs a little more. You want your Master to see all of your sweet little pussy when he comes into the room."

Her cheeks hot enough to catch fire, Amy widened her legs even more. Daisy stared at her pussy and nodded. "Good. Chest out, hon. Be proud of those tits."

She thrust her chest out a little more as Daisy picked up the blindfold and moved behind her. "You really do look very lovely. I'm not surprised he ended his dry streak to play with you."

"What do you mean?" Amy asked as Daisy placed the blindfold across her eyes.

"Your Master hasn't played with a sub in months," Daisy said. "But like I said, you are lovely, so I'm not surprised he chose you. Now, if you weren't blindfolded, I would remind you to keep your head up, but your gaze lowered when your Master comes in. But since you are blindfolded…"

She kissed Amy's cheek. "Have a good time, hon." She walked across the room and Amy heard the soft click of the door.

She wasn't sure how long she could hold the slave position, but she didn't have to wait long. Less than two minutes later, the door opened. She caught her breath. Her body was vibrating with nerves and anticipation. The door closed, and she heard him approach. He stopped in front of her and she kept her chest thrust out and her legs wide. She felt the brush of his pant leg against her inner thigh when he stepped closer. His hand petted her hair and she shivered all over at just that brief touch.

She felt more than heard him crouch in front of her. She licked her lips as his warm breath washed over her face. He leaned forward and whispered into her ear. "Very nice, little slave."

"Thank you, Sir," she said.

"My collar fits you well," he whispered. "Do

you like wearing it?"

She cocked her head. There was suddenly something very familiar about the low sound of his whisper. Like she recognized it or –

She squealed. He had pinched her left nipple which was already hard and aching and she jerked against the sharp bite of pain.

"I asked you a question, little slave."

"Yes, Sir. I like wearing it, Sir," she replied. She wasn't lying. She did like having his collar around her neck.

"Good."

She moaned with unexpected pleasure when his tongue laved across her aching nipple. He soothed the sting with his tongue. She was itching to touch his hair, but she knew better and kept her hands on her thighs as he lifted his head.

"Are you wet for me, little slave?"

"Yes, Sir." She was. Shamefully, her pussy had become wet the moment he stepped into the room.

His warm hand was suddenly between her spread legs and she moaned again when he cupped her pussy.

"Very wet," he whispered.

The embarrassment she was feeling disappeared when he rubbed her clit.

"Please, Sir," she said when he removed his hand.

He cupped her breast and kissed her hard. She returned his kiss, sucking at his offered tongue and trying to rub her breasts against his chest.

He pulled back and cupped her face before

tracing two fingers across her bottom lip. When he pushed them against the seam of her lips, she parted her mouth and sucked at both fingers, rubbing her tongue against the pads of them. She was thrilled when he made a low groan.

"Do you know what I want, little slave?"

She shook her head, unable to answer with his fingers in her mouth.

"I want my cock in your mouth."

She shivered all over and sucked heavily on his fingers. She had specifically said no to oral sex, but now the thought of having his cock in her mouth was making her nearly dizzy with excitement.

He pulled his fingers from her mouth and whispered, "Would you like that?"

"Yes, Sir," she said. "I want your cock in my mouth, Sir. Please, Sir."

"That's my good girl," he whispered. She smiled happily at the approval in his voice.

He stood and petted her hair again before she heard the low rasp of his zipper. She lifted her head as he whispered, "Keep your hands on your thighs, little slave."

When she felt the velvet skin of his cock brush against her lips, she parted them immediately. He slid his cock into her mouth and she sucked as he groaned harshly. She kept her hands on her thighs and swirled her tongue across the tip. His slightly salty taste heightened her excitement and she licked at him enthusiastically. His hands curled in her hair and held her in a tight grip as he slid more of his cock into her mouth. The head of him touched the back of her throat, but he retreated before her gag reflex kicked in. He pushed in and out of her mouth in a slow rhythm. With her hands on her thighs, she couldn't control how much of his cock she took, but he never gave her more than she could handle.

She sucked and licked at his dick. His low groans were setting her nerves on fire and she wished suddenly that she could see him. She wanted to watch his face as she pleasured him. His cock was swelling in her mouth and she sucked more heavily. He groaned again and pulled his cock out of her mouth. She whined in disappointment.

"Please, Sir. I want more," she said.

He muttered a low curse before lifting her to her feet. He kissed her again and whispered, "You almost made me come in your mouth, little slave."

She licked her bottom lip and he made another harsh groan before pushing her back toward the bed. She stumbled in her heels and he caught her and lowered her to the middle of the bed.

He took her wrists and raised them above her head before chaining her to the headboard. She rubbed her bare ass against the silk sheets. Her pussy was throbbing heavily and when he touched her thigh, she let them drop open immediately. She needed his cock. Needed it badly. She whined again when he didn't touch her, but instead moved away from the bed.

"Please, Sir," she begged. "Please fuck me, Sir."

There was no reply and she could barely control her urge to beg again. She heard the rustle of his clothing as he removed them. The end of the bed dipped down, and she moaned when she felt his lips brush against her nylon clad knee.

"Oh God," she said when he pressed his mouth against her inner thigh and then traced his tongue along the edge of her stocking.

"Oh God, yes, please," she said.

He slapped her thigh hard enough to make it sting and she immediately said, "Please, Sir."

He grunted his approval and she felt his shoulders pushing against both her thighs before his tongue was slicking across the lips of her pussy.

She could barely hold back her scream of pleasure when he licked from her wet entrance to the top of her swollen, throbbing clit. He lingered at her clit, pressing the tip of his tongue delicately against it and she writhed against his mouth. She lifted her hips and dug her feet into the bed as she made an inarticulate sound of need.

"More, please," she begged. "I need more."

He parted her pussy lips and licked her clit with wide, flat strokes. She cried out and bucked wildly as he slid his finger deep into her narrow entrance. He thrust rapidly, and she couldn't hold back her scream when he sucked on her clit. Her orgasm shot through her and she screamed again, her entire body heaving against his as he sucked and licked at her clit.

His warm mouth left her pussy and she could feel him kneeling between her legs before she heard the condom being opened. When the blunt head of his cock pushed at her pussy, she arched immediately. The head sank in and she cried out happily. He was so big and thick, she widened her thighs to accommodate him as he pushed in until his balls pressed against her.

"Legs around my waist," he demanded in a hoarse whisper.

She hooked her legs around his waist, digging the heels of her shoes into his back. He groaned softly but did two hard thrusts that made her quiver with pleasure. His hand touched her wrists and there was a soft clink as he unclipped the chains and her hands were free.

She frowned in disappointment. She didn't want to be free. She wanted to be bound and held captive while he fucked her. Her disappointment disappeared when his hard hands wrapped around her arms and he jerked them over her head again, pinning her to the bed. He fucked her roughly as he held her down.

The sensation of his hands holding her down sent her fantasy of being fucked by Mark flooding through her. She bit her bottom lip and let it take hold. The man above her was Mark. The man pinning her to the bed and fucking her like she wanted to be fucked wasn't some unknown Dom but Mark – the man she'd loved since she was nineteen years old.

She moaned in pleasure as Mark's face flickered through her head. The low rhythmic groans of pleasure were coming from Mark's mouth, the hard chest hovering just inches from her aching breasts was Mark's. Mark was fucking her with a hard and rough pace that was pushing her to another climax with an almost embarrassing quickness.

She was fully absorbed in her fantasy now and

as small flickers of pleasure grew in her pelvis, she moaned, "Oh God, please, Mark. Please."

The man above her ground to a halt and the blindfold was ripped off so quickly that it pulled her hair. She gasped in pain before blinking rapidly. The face above her swam into focus and every muscle in her body froze in shock. Mark was staring down at her and his hands tightened painfully around her arms.

"How did you know?" He rasped.

"M-mark?"

"How did you know it was me?" He squeezed her arms again.

She winced before licking her lips. "I – I didn't. I was pretending, fantasizing that…"

He stared almost wildly at her. "You were fantasizing it was me?"

She nodded. What the fuck was happening?

He shifted against her. His thick cock rubbed against the inner walls of her pussy and a moan slipped out before she could stop it. Her mind may have been in total disbelief, but her body didn't give seem to care who was fucking her. It was on the knife-edge of an orgasm and it wanted release.

"Do you want me to stop, Ames?" He asked hoarsely.

"No!" The needy little cry didn't sound like her at all, but she didn't care. "Please don't stop, Sir!"

His eyes darkened with desire when she called him sir and he thrust hard into her. She cried out with pleasure and met each of his strokes with erratic jabs of her hips.

He leaned down, his hands digging painfully

into the soft flesh of her forearms and kissed her hard on the mouth. She returned his kiss, licking and nipping at his lips as his pace turned brutal in its intensity. She moaned and cried out, panting with exertion as he drove in and out of her.

"Amy," he muttered as his head fell back. "God, Amy, you're so tight, so wet."

She made another sharp cry before her entire body shuddered with the force of her climax. She writhed beneath him and screamed as waves of pleasure rippled through her. He shouted her name and climaxed deep inside of her.

He collapsed against her soft body and she winced before pushing on his shoulders. He rolled off of her and sat up on the side of the bed. He removed the condom and tossed it in the waste basket then stood and walked to the bathroom.

She needed to get up. She needed to get dressed and figure out what the fuck was going on. But her entire body was still trembling, and she felt weak and disoriented from her orgasms. Her pelvis kept twitching uncontrollably and her pulse was pounding so rapidly she felt a little lightheaded.

She watched silently as Mark returned from the bathroom. He reached into the nightstand and weirdly brought out a bottle of water. He sat down next to her before pulling her into a sitting position. She was still twitching and shaking, and he leaned her against his hard chest before opening the bottle of water. He held it to her mouth.

"Drink, Ames."

She drank. The water was cold and soothed her dry throat and parched mouth. He pulled it away and took a large swallow of water before giving her more. He set the bottle on the nightstand and made her lie on her side before curling up behind her. He rubbed her side as she shook, before lifting her arm and examining it closely. There were very clear imprints of his fingers in her pale flesh and he rubbed the red marks gently before placing her arm back on the bed. He rubbed her hip and side until her shivering stopped.

"What just happened?" She whispered.

He sighed and sat up on the side of the bed again, scrubbing his hand through his hair. His jeans were on the floor by the bed and he grabbed them and yanked them over his legs.

"We need to talk," she said. She sat up and clutched the sheets to her body, hiding her nakedness as he sighed again.

"I know. But not here. Go up to your room and get dressed in," he paused, "your normal clothes and then meet me in the lobby."

He buttoned his jeans and put on his t-shirt before walking to the door. He left without looking at her and Amy fell back on the bed. She stared in bewilderment at the ceiling for a few minutes before climbing out of bed and dressing.

❧ ❦

"Evening, folks. What can I get ya?" The waitress was short and chubby with long grey hair and an alarmingly thick moustache. She rubbed absently at it as she pulled the order pad from the pocket of her apron.

"Just a coffee, thank you," Amy said.

"You should eat something," Mark said.

"I'm not hungry."

"Ames - "

"I'm not hungry."

He sighed and ordered a coffee as well.

Mark was waiting for her in the foyer of the club and they had driven to the small all-night diner in complete silence. She and Mark, as well as her brother Luke, had been coming here for years. The three of them spent hours in this very booth when they first started Dawson's Clothing. She sketched design after design while Luke and Mark poured over the business plan, adjusting and tweaking the budget.

She took a deep breath as Mark stared solemnly at her. It helped that he brought her here. It was familiar and welcoming and, away from the club, she could almost believe that he was the same sweet and gentle Mark she had always known.

Is he, though? He put a collar around your neck, he called you his little slave and he fucked you so hard that you screamed when you orgasmed. You never scream, Amy.

She shuddered all over at the memory of Mark's hard cock fucking her into the best orgasm of her life and he gave her a look of concern. "Are you okay, Amy?"

She couldn't stop the small bitter laugh from spilling out of her mouth. "Am I okay? Am I okay? Well, let's see – for the last two nights I've been fucking my brother's best friend and had no goddamn idea."

He winced but she continued before he could

speak. "You can imagine how fucking weird that is, right? I mean, I don't even know who you are."

"You do," he said. "I'm still the same guy. I'm still Mark."

"No," she said, "you aren't. The Mark I know is sweet and gentle and easy going. The Mark I know wouldn't chain me to a bed, put a collar around my neck and make me call him "Sir". He most certainly wouldn't be moonlighting at a goddamn BDSM club as a – a Dom!"

Her voice was rising. She made herself take a deep breath as the waitress returned with their coffees then left. She stared at the steam rising from the dark liquid as Mark cleared his throat. "I can explain, Amy."

"Then start explaining."

"I co-own Secrets with a woman named Selene."

"Mistress Selene?" She said.

"Yes. We bought the club two years ago when the previous owner decided to sell."

"How did you even find out about the place?" She asked.

"I'd been going there for years."

"Because you're a Dom."

He hesitated before nodding.

"I don't believe it," she said. "I'm more of a control freak than you are, Mark. You – you don't care if you're in control or...."

Her face flushed. Jesus, she sounded like an idiot. The things Mark had said and done to her over the past two nights was more than enough proof that he did indeed crave control.

"I like control in the bedroom," Mark said. "Always have and always will. Being a dominant is as much a part of me, as being a designer is a part of you."

"Does Luke know?" She asked. "Does he know you own a BDSM club? Does he know you like to tie up women and – and hurt them?"

He flinched again, and shame crept in at the look of hurt on his face. She muttered a curse and said, "I'm sorry. I know that isn't true. I shouldn't have said that, and I didn't mean it. I'm just – Jesus, Mark, I don't know what to say or think right now."

"I know it's a lot to take in. To answer your question – no, Luke doesn't know about any of this."

"Why not?" She was surprised by his admission. He and her brother were as thick as thieves, and she hadn't thought there were any secrets between them.

"Because he's disgusted by it," he said before running his hands restlessly through his hair.

"How do you know that?"

"It doesn't matter," he said. "I was also worried that he would let it slip to you or your parents."

"I wouldn't have thought differently of you."

"You already do."

Now it was her turn to wince. She wanted to argue but she couldn't. She had already proven to him that she did.

"Mark, I – I was just surprised, that's all."

"I know." Hurt still lingered on his face.

"How often are you at the club?"

85

"Every Friday and Saturday night. Sometimes during the week nights if Selene can't be there. Selene is in charge of the day-to-day running of the Club and I do a lot of the admin and accounting work."

"Daisy said that my – my Master hadn't played with a sub in months," she said. "Is that true?"

He nodded.

"Why?"

"I needed a break. Can I ask you a question?"

"Yes."

"How did you find out about Secrets?"

"My friend Valerie goes there," she said. "One night I drank too much wine and told her some stuff that made her think I should go with her."

"What did you tell her?" He said.

She hesitated, and he said, "Tell me."

A little shiver went down her back. His voice had deepened and there was a note of command to it that made her want to obey him. God, how could she not have seen this side of him before? Was she that stupid?

"Tell me, Amy."

"I told her about Tom," she said.

A look of distaste crossed his face. "Didn't you break up with him?"

"He broke up with me," she said. "I – I asked him to try some, uh, new stuff in the bedroom and he wasn't receptive to it."

"You wanted him to dominate you."

"Well, not exactly. I mean, I asked him to do what you did to me. To blindfold me, restrain me and pretend he was a stranger while we had sex."

She didn't want to say anything else. She was oddly ashamed to tell Mark what Tom had said to her.

"What did he say?" Mark said.

"Does it matter?" She replied. "He didn't want to do it and broke up with me, end of story."

"No, it isn't," Mark said. "You know you can't lie to me so tell me the truth."

She stared at the marks on her arms. She would have bruises from Mark's grip she thought idly. The idea that she would be marked by him sent an unexpected wave of pleasure through her belly.

"Amy," Mark's voice held a warning note and for one crazy minute she thought he was going to go all Dom on her right there in the diner.

Would that be so bad? You like it when he's dominant.

Refusing to look at him, she said, "Tom told me that I was sick. He said he couldn't be with a girl who had – had rape fantasies. So, he dumped me."

Mark cursed. She kept her gaze on the coffee cup in front of her. She jumped when Mark took her hand, but didn't resist when he linked her fingers with his.

"Amy, look at me."

She lifted her gaze and stared at him.

"You're not sick and what you were asking him for is not a rape fantasy. Do you understand that?"

"Yes," she whispered.

"Do you?"

"Yes."

"Good. Having sex with a stranger is a common fantasy for women."

"So I've heard," she said.

"I'm sorry that stupid asshole broke up with you over it."

"It was for the best anyway," she said.

"What do you mean?"

She hesitated and then decided to forge ahead. In for a penny, in for a pound, right? "The reason I wanted to be blindfolded and make Tom pretend to be a stranger was because I wanted to pretend he was someone else. It was much easier to do that if I couldn't see him and he didn't say anything to me."

Mark didn't reply, and she gave him a searching look. "You know who I wanted him to be, don't you?"

"Yes," he said.

He didn't say anything else and she sighed. "That's all you're going to say?"

"Amy, I - "

"Why was it you in the room with me? Valerie booked my private session. Were you just randomly chosen?"

He shook his head. "No. You were supposed to be with a Dom named Brandon. I was in the control room and saw you in the Blue Room. I took Brandon's place."

"Why?" She asked.

"Because," he hesitated, "Brandon wasn't the right Dom for you."

"Why not?"

"He just wasn't."

"But why wasn't he?" She persisted.

He scowled at her. "Just trust me on this."

She shook her head. "No. I want to know why

you took his place. Why you asked me to play with you again tonight. I deserve to know."

"Because I couldn't sit there and watch another man touch you, all right?" Mark said in a low and furious voice. "I couldn't sit in that fucking control room and watch another man undress you, touch you and make you come. Not when I've spent the last ten fucking years wondering what you looked like naked, what you tasted like and how you would sound when you were coming all over my cock."

Another pulse of desire went through her. This one was so strong it made her breathless. She squeezed his hand before smiling at him. Mark wanted her just as much as she wanted him.

Duh, obviously.

She ignored her inner voice. "So, what do we do now?"

"What do you mean?" He asked cautiously.

"Well, obviously we both want the same thing from each other. Do we tell Luke and my parents right away or do we try dating for a few months before we say anything?"

He pulled his hand away from hers with a sharp tug. "Amy, what happened between us is done. We can't do this again."

"What? Why not?" She asked.

"You're Luke's little sister."

"What does that have to do with anything?"

"We can't date. What do you think Luke will say when he finds out that I had sex with you?"

"It's none of his business who I sleep with," she said.

"Ames, we can't," he said softly. "I – I enjoyed

what happened between us, really I did, but it can't go any further."

"Are you serious?" She said.

"Yes. Look, I know we've been, uh, attracted to each other for a long time, but if you hadn't come into the club I would never have…"

She glared at him. "You would never have had sex with me."

"No," he said. "I wouldn't have."

"But you want me, and I want you."

"Yes, and we got to find out what it would be like between us. That has to be enough, Amy."

"Well it fucking isn't," she retorted.

"I'm sorry," he said. "But Luke and your parents are important to me. I don't want to lose them, okay? You can try and deny it all you want, but you know that if Luke found out we were sleeping together, he would fucking lose it. You're his baby sister and he's stupidly protective of you."

"He's my brother and your best friend, but that doesn't give him the right to tell us how to live our lives," she said. "Besides, you don't know he won't be okay with it."

He laughed bitterly. "Are you kidding me? Don't you remember that day in your bedroom when he saw you sitting on my lap? He lost his shit, Amy, and all I was doing was comforting you."

"That was ten years ago. We're adults and I'm more than capable of taking care of myself. I don't need Luke to protect me," Amy said.

"He won't ever believe that. If I date you, things won't be the same with Luke and me. He's been my best friend for over twenty years. My

90

parents are dead, and my brother is an addict who only calls me when he needs money for drugs. You and Luke and your parents are all I have. If we start dating and it doesn't work out, it won't just be you that I lose. I'll lose Luke and your parents as well. I can't lose them just because we happen to be compatible in bed."

"Compatible in bed? Is that all this was to you?"

He cleared his throat. "We had two play sessions, Amy. You wanted to be dominated and I gave you that. It's part of my job at the club."

"You asshole," she said. She blinked rapidly to hold back the hot tears. She wouldn't cry in front of Mark. She wouldn't let him see how badly he had hurt her. Not when he considered her to be nothing more than a goddamn work assignment.

She stood up and yanked on her jacket. "Take me back to the club."

"You're not walking the floor." He tossed some bills on the table before shrugging into his own jacket.

"Your *job* is done, Mark. You don't get to tell me what to do anymore," she said.

"I know you're angry and upset with me but you're not going downstairs," he said. "I will carry you out kicking and screaming if I have to."

"Oh, for fuck's sake," she snapped. "I don't want to go back to your stupid dungeon fucking playground anyway. But my goddamn stuff is still in my room and it's not like I'm going to just leave it there. Take me back so I can get my stuff and leave. I don't ever want to see or think about your fucking club again."

She turned and marched toward the door of the diner. Her face was hot, and her stomach was rolling with nausea. She swallowed down the bile that was rising in her throat. Why she ever thought she was in love with Mark Stanford, she'd never know. She hated him, and he could burn in hell for all she cared.

Chapter Five

Two months later

"You okay, Amy?"

She sighed and turned to smile at her roommate Jane. The petite brunette was giving her a worried look and Amy felt a wave of affection for her. She'd only known Jane a month or so, but she was already very fond of her. "I'm fine. I should be the one asking you that. This is a tough day for you and you need to stop worrying about me."

Jane took a deep breath. "Honestly, it kind of helps to worry about you."

Amy gave her an impulsive hug. Jane wasn't just her roommate, she also worked at the company and was dating Luke. She smiled inwardly. Jane worked in the accounting department of Dawson Clothing before applying for the job to be Luke's personal assistant. Five minutes before the interview, Jane's skirt ripped, and Amy repaired it in the bathroom. Jane's nervousness combined with a pin from her repaired skirt sticking her in the ass during the interview had made her pooch it. Luke wasn't going to hire her, but Amy had intervened and asked him to give her a chance. Luke had grudgingly agreed.

It hadn't taken long before her brother was completely smitten with Jane. Although there were some rocky moments between them the last month, they both finally confessed their love to each other and Jane moved back to the accounting department. As of five days ago, they were officially a couple.

Jane returned her hug before grabbing a mug from the cupboard and pouring herself a cup of coffee. She added some cream to it and sat down at the table. Her simple black dress made her pale skin look even paler and she rubbed at her forehead as Amy sat next to her.

"Where's Lukie?"

"Just getting out of the shower." Jane glanced at her watch. "We need to leave a bit early to meet with the funeral director before the funeral starts."

Her eyes watered and Amy grabbed her hand and squeezed it. Just six days ago, Jane's foster mother, Mama J, had passed away from a brain aneurism. She'd suffered from Alzheimer's for years. Jane had nearly starved to death trying to earn enough money to pay for Mama J's care.

"Will her other foster kids be there?" Amy asked.

Jane nodded and wiped at her eyes with a tissue. "Yeah. A couple of them even offered to help with the funeral costs, but Luke had already paid for everything so…"

Amy squeezed her hand. "Are you angry with

them?"

"A little, I suppose," Jane said. "I'm not resentful that they left me to care for Mama J once she got sick. I loved her so much and would have done anything for her, but I guess I'm angry that they just abandoned her. I know she was different with the Alzheimer's and it was terrible when she couldn't remember who you were, but they all just – just drifted away. It was like they forgot who she was and what she'd done for them once she forgot them. You know?"

"I'm sorry. I wish I could have met her. Luke said she was a wonderful lady."

Jane smiled at her. "I wish you could have met her too."

They sat in silence for a few minutes before Amy said, "So, when are you moving in with Luke?"

Jane gave her a startled look. "I told Luke I wanted to talk to you about that."

"Luke didn't say anything to me," Amy replied. "But I know him and there's no way he's going to let you continue to be my roommate now that he's confessed his love for you. I'm surprised he hasn't moved all of your stuff to his place already."

Jane flushed. "He wanted to, but I was busy with the funeral details and I wanted to make sure you were okay with me leaving."

"Why wouldn't I be?" Amy asked.

"Well, because you hate to live alone and if I leave, you'll have to look for another roommate."

"Oh, right." Amy tried not to look guilty. She'd invited Jane to be her roommate only because

Luke had asked her to do it. The expense of Mama J's care meant that Jane could barely afford groceries, lived in a rough part of town called the Badlands and she had no heat or electricity in her apartment. Worried about her, but too stubborn to admit it to Jane, Luke had convinced Amy to ask her to be her roommate. Not that she had minded. Although she enjoyed living on her own, she and Jane got along very well. It was nice to have someone to hang out with on the weekends.

"I can stay until you find a new roommate," Jane said.

"No, that's fine. I'm going to try living on my own for a while. It'll be good for me."

"Are you sure? I don't mind staying for a while longer," Jane said.

Amy laughed. "You might not but my brother would mind. If you continued to live here, Luke would just move in. Between you and me, I love Lukie but I don't want to live with him."

Jane smiled at her. "Fair enough. But if you change your mind, just tell me, okay?"

"Okay." Amy grabbed her phone and checked her messages as Jane cleared her throat.

"Um, listen I'm not sure if you know this or not, but Luke told me that Mark is planning on coming to the funeral today."

Amy tensed before saying, "That's nice of him."

"I just thought I would give you a heads up."

"Thank you, Jane. I appreciate it," she said as Luke wandered into the kitchen. He was dressed in a dark suit and he tugged absently at his tie.

He kissed Jane's forehead and took a sip of her

coffee before sitting beside her. "You okay?"

She nodded, and he squeezed her hand before smiling at Amy. "Hey, Ames."

"Hi, Lukie."

"Are you driving with us?" He studied her tank top and yoga pants. "Because we need to leave soon."

"No, I'll drive myself. I'll probably go into the office after. I'm going to go have a shower. I'll see you both there, okay?"

"Yes, thanks, Amy," Jane said.

"You're welcome, honey."

&ear; &ear;

Amy pumped the brakes on her car as she approached the red light. A snowstorm last night had left the roads icy and her car slid forward before stopping. She blew her breath out and drummed her fingers on the steering wheel.

She was feeling anxious and unsettled and it had nothing to do with attending a funeral and everything to do with seeing Mark again. She hadn't seen him at all since the family dinner night at her parents' house nearly two weeks ago. Pretty impressive feat considering they worked in the same office.

Sudden heat infused her cheeks. Mark was angry with her that night. She had spent the day before playing tourist guide for their new international investors. Pierre and Julien were both handsome and they'd made it perfectly clear they found her attractive. They shared their woman and while she wasn't a prude, she couldn't sleep with them. She told herself it was because a threesome just wasn't her thing, but she was lying to herself. Despite their attractiveness, despite their obvious interest, she had zero interest in them. Neither of them were Mark.

Stop it! Stop thinking that way! You're going to die alone if you constantly compare every man you meet to Mark. What happened between you is over. Be happy that you at least got to fuck him twice.

She should have been happy about that, but she wondered if it wouldn't have been better to never have been with Mark at all. At least then she wouldn't know how incredible it was to be fucked by him, or the way his need for total control in the bedroom left her wet and aching.

The light turned green and she drove through the intersection. She needed to stop obsessing over Mark. There was nothing between them. Of course, the way he had pinned her against the wall at her childhood home, stuck his hand into her pants and demanded she tell him if she had fucked Pierre and Julien suggested that he didn't want there to be nothing.

She shivered as she remembered the feel of his hot breath in her ear. The rough touch of his fingers as he'd first rubbed her clit then slid two fingers deep inside of her pussy. He'd called her his little slave, made her admit that she hadn't fucked Pierre or Julien, and told her that her pussy belonged to him. She would have gone back to his house and been on her knees and willingly sucking his cock if they hadn't been interrupted by Jane and Luke.

Thankfully, Jane had prevented Luke from

seeing her with Mark, but the close call rattled Mark. He'd immediately backed away from her and when she'd reached for him, he'd pushed her hands away.

"Don't," he said hoarsely. "I – this was a mistake. I'm sorry."

"I'll always be a mistake to you, won't I?"

"Amy, you know we can't do this."

"Then stay away from me!" She said. "Just stop touching me and stay the fuck away from me!"

She'd spoken those words in the heat of the moment, angry over his rejection again, but Mark had taken them to heart. She hadn't seen or spoken to him since. As she approached the next intersection, the light turned yellow and she tapped the brakes. The car slid forward, and she pumped the brakes again until she came to a stop just inches from the car in front of her. She rested her head against the back of the seat. She didn't miss Mark. It was better this way.

There was a sudden loud bang and the car jerked forward, slamming into the car in front of her. Her seat belt locked painfully against her chest as the air bag deployed and she made a muffled scream of surprise.

❧ ❧

Mark leaned against the wall as two women wearing black dresses slipped by him to claim two of the few remaining seats. The funeral home was packed with people, but he didn't see the one person he was looking for.

Knock it off, idiot. Amy doesn't want to see you

and is a funeral really the place to be mooning over her?

His inner voice was right, but it didn't stop him from scanning the crowd of people. Luke hadn't told him specifically that Amy would be at the funeral, but Jane was her friend. Amy would be here. So why didn't he see her? The service started in less than ten minutes and it wasn't like Amy to be late. He could see Jane standing near the front talking with a few other mourners. He scanned the crowd again, frowning when he saw Luke huddled in an empty corner of the room. He was talking on his cell phone and Mark could tell from the look on his face that something was wrong. He made his way over to Luke just as his best friend tucked his cell phone into his pocket.

"What's wrong?" Mark asked.

"Amy," Luke said, "she's been in a car accident."

"What?" Icy cold fear gripped his heart and he grabbed Luke's arm. "Is she okay?"

Luke nodded. "Yes, she was rear ended, and it pushed her car into the one in front of her hard enough to deploy the airbag. She said she doesn't have any injuries, but the car isn't driveable."

"Shit. Where is she now?"

"Still at the accident. The police were just about to take her statement." Luke swept his gaze over the crowd of people. "Do you see Mom and Dad? Amy said she would take a cab home, but I don't think she should do that."

"Give me the address, I'll go," Mark said.

"Are you sure?"

"Yes. Where is she, Luke?" Even he could hear the panic in his voice and he wasn't surprised when Luke gave him an odd look.

"She's okay, Mark. She said she wasn't hurt."

"Yeah, I know," he said. "I'm just worried about her."

Luke clapped him on the back. "Did you and Amy finally make up?"

"I keep telling you, we're not fighting." A complete lie but he couldn't tell Luke the truth.

"Maybe I should send Dad to get her."

"No! It's fine. We're not fighting. Tell me where she is, and I'll take her home."

"Okay, thanks, buddy," Luke said. He recited the address and, panic still clawing at his stomach, Mark hurried out of the funeral home.

❧ ❧

Fifteen minutes later as he parked on the street and jumped out of his car, the panic roared its way up his throat. Amy's car wasn't too badly banged up, but he could see her sitting in the back of an ambulance with a paramedic. He ran past the damaged cars and climbed into the back of the ambulance without a second thought. He cupped the back of her neck, staring at the abrasion on her cheek as she gave him a startled look.

"Hey, buddy, you can't be in here," the paramedic said.

Mark ignored him. "Amy, baby, are you okay?"

"I'm fine." She pulled away from him. "What are you doing here?"

"Luke told me what happened. I said I would

give you a ride home."

"I can take a cab," she said.

He reached for her and she batted his hands away. "Don't."

"You know this guy?" The paramedic asked.

Amy nodded. "Yes, he's my brother's friend."

"You're in my way," the paramedic said. He was young and good looking in a smarmy kind of way. Mark disliked him instantly.

His dislike grew when the paramedic raised one eyebrow at him and said, "Either move back and give me some room or get out of my bus."

He slid over on the bed a little as the paramedic leaned forward and ran his gloved finger over the abrasion on Amy's face. She hissed, and he smiled at her. "Sorry, Amy."

"That's okay," she said.

"Airbags are great, but sometimes they can leave some abrasions and burns," the paramedic said. "You sure you don't have any pain in your chest?"

"No," Amy said.

The paramedic placed his hand on Amy's upper chest and pressed anyway. Mark's dislike turned to hate, and he reached out and grabbed Amy's hand. She tried to tug free and he linked their fingers together.

She rolled her eyes at him before smiling at the paramedic. "It doesn't hurt, Cole."

Mark's jealousy flamed higher. Why the hell did she know his name?

"Okay, good. Let's put some ointment on that abrasion and then I'll set you free." He winked at her and Amy smiled again at him.

"Maybe she should go to the hospital for some x-ray's," Mark said. "Are you really qualified to know nothing is broken just by touch?"

"Mark!" Amy said.

Cole gave him an amused look. "You a doctor, Mark?"

"No," Mark said through gritted teeth.

"Then how about you let me do my job?"

Cole turned away and Amy gave Mark a furious look. He squeezed her hand, but wouldn't release it when she pulled. She huffed out her breath and gave him another murderous look as Cole turned back.

"Hold still, Amy. Okay?" He said.

"Yes." She tilted her face as he spread a layer of ointment on the abrasion on her face.

She winced, and Mark made a low sound of distress as Cole said, "Sorry, I know it stings."

When he was finished, he sat back and removed his gloves before patting Amy on the knee. Mark could barely stop from punching the smug asshole. His hand squeezed Amy's compulsively.

"Mark! Too tight." Amy tried to pull her hand away.

He released her hand and mumbled an apology. Douchebag Cole said, "You'll be pretty sore by tomorrow morning but if you have any type of chest pain or trouble breathing, go to the hospital immediately. Understand?"

She nodded, and he tucked the ointment away. "You probably shouldn't be alone tonight. Do you have someone who can stay with you?"

"I'm staying with her," Mark said.

"No, you're not," Amy said.

"Yes, I am.".

She glared at him as Cole laughed. "Well, make sure someone stays with you. Just to be on the safe side. It was nice to meet you."

"Nice to meet you too." Amy shook his hand and Mark jumped out of the ambulance. He helped her out of the ambulance, giving her an anxious look when she stopped and stretched gingerly.

"You okay?"

"Fine." Her voice was colder than the air around them.

She glanced at Cole before moving out of earshot of the paramedic. She gave Mark a fierce look. "What the hell is going on with you?"

"What do you mean?"

"In the ambulance – I thought you were going to punch Cole."

"How do you know his name?" He asked.

She stared at him blankly. "What?"

"You know his name."

"Yeah, because he introduced himself. Its what normal people do," Amy said in exasperation.

"He was flirting with you."

Amy's mouth dropped open. "Are you crazy? He was not flirting with me."

"Yes, he was."

"He was doing his job. Not every guy who talks to me is flirting, for God's sake," she said. "Besides, even if he was, it's none of your damn business."

Before he could reply, a police officer joined

them. "Ms. Dawson?"

"Yes?"

"Tow trucks are here. Can you let the driver know where you want your car towed?"

She nodded and, shivering in the cold air, headed over to the tow truck driver.

◈ ◈

"Amy, are you sure you don't need to go to the hospital?"

"I'm sure, Mom." Amy shifted her cell phone to her other hand. "But I'm not supposed to stay alone tonight. Could I ask you to - "

"Oh, I know, honey," her mom said. "Mark told me when he called. It's really sweet of him to stay with you tonight. Honestly, I'm glad to hear it. It felt like there was a bit of tension between the two of you during the last family dinner. Did you two have a fight or something?"

"No," Amy said. She thought about asking her mother to stay with her anyway before dismissing it. Her mother would want to know why she didn't want Mark staying with her, and she didn't have the energy or the brain power tonight to think up a viable excuse.

"Honey, I'd better go. The funeral is over but we're still at the reception at Luke's. I want to start cleaning up a bit, so Jane and Luke don't have to do it."

"Okay. I love you, Mom."

"I love you too, Ames."

She hit the end button just as Luke texted her.
You need us to stay with you tonight?

No, I'm good. Mark is staying with me. Take care of Jane and tell her I'm sorry I missed the funeral.

Will do. Glad you and Mark made up.

She sighed and tossed her cell phone on the bed before dropping her towel. Mark had insisted on driving her home and coming into the house with her. He had been upstairs and drawing her a bath before she even had her boots off. She'd lingered in the tub, not just because the hot water felt good against her already aching body, but because she'd hoped that Mark would just leave. Obviously, that wasn't happening.

She studied the silk nightgown in the drawer before snorting and reaching for a plain cotton one. She slipped it over her head, yanked on some underwear and then pulled on her terrycloth robe and belted it securely. She didn't want Mark to think she was trying to seduce him. That ship had sailed.

Then why is he staying with you tonight? Why did he look so freaked out when he climbed into the ambulance?

Because he was a nice guy and he didn't hate her. Just like she didn't hate him, despite telling herself that she did. She wished she hated him. It would make things so much simpler.

She shut the light off and headed downstairs to the kitchen. Mark was stirring some soup on the stove. "How are you feeling, Ames?"

"Fine." She sat down at the island.

"I found some leftover soup in the fridge."

"Luke made it the other day. I called Mom to

ask her to stay with me."

"Oh yeah?" He grabbed two bowls from the cupboard and set them on the counter.

"Turns out that you'd already called and told her you'd be staying with me tonight."

He poured soup into both bowls and carried them to the island before grabbing spoons and napkins. "Eat up, Amy."

He sat down across from her and took a bite of soup. "It's good."

"Of course it is. Luke made it," she said. She picked up her spoon but didn't dip it into her soup. "Why are you here, Mark?"

"Because you need someone to stay with you," he said.

"Mom would have stayed with me."

"I thought Luke and Jane might need her tonight."

"Bullshit," she said. "Why did you come to the accident? Why did you drive me home and tell everyone else you're staying with me?"

He gave her an angry look. "Because I miss you! Is that so hard to believe? We used to be friends. I miss talking to you and hanging out with you. All right?"

"Is that all you miss?" She asked.

He stared into his soup. "Does it matter?"

"It matters to me."

"No," he said. "It isn't all that I miss. I miss kissing you, touching you, listening to your soft cries when you're coming all over my cock. Every single night I think about what it was like to be in your tight pussy. I think about it until my dick is rock hard and I have to masturbate like a fucking teenage boy just to get some sleep. So, yeah, I miss fucking you."

He gave her a look of smoldering need and intensity and, despite the soreness of her body, liquid flooded her panties. Her pulse was thudding, and she was much too warm.

"Mark," she whispered before reaching for his hand.

He pulled away just as her fingers brushed his and stood up, catching the stool when it started to tip over. "Don't, Amy," he rasped.

He staggered over to the counter and gripped the sink, staring out the window into the darkness.

"Mark," she said.

"Give me a minute," he replied. "Eat your soup."

His Dom voice was back, and she was dipping her spoon into the soup and taking a mouthful even as new lust fluttered to life in her belly.

"It's not just the fear of losing you, and your family." Mark continued to stare out the window and she had to strain to hear his low voice. "I like certain things in the bedroom, Ames."

"I know," she said. "You're dominant. I liked the – the way you were with me."

"It's more than that. I was holding back with you, giving you only what you asked for."

That wasn't true. She had asked for a stranger to fuck her. She hadn't asked for him to make her call him Sir, or to pose naked in a slave position, or to punish her when she didn't obey him. Of course, considering that it had sent her lust to a whole other level, she wasn't going to bring up his mistake.

"If you knew what I – I wanted to do to you, Ames, you'd be horrified."

"You don't know that."

He turned and gave her a stark look. "I do."

"Tell me what you like in the bedroom," she said.

He leaned against the counter and closed his eyes for a moment. When he opened them, she could see a weary resignation in them that hurt her heart.

"I like impact play. Do you know what that is?"

"Maybe," she said. "It's spanking, right?"

"Yes, I like to spank," he said. "Not just with my hand, but with other things too."

"Like what?"

"Floggers, paddles, crops," he said. "Hell, sometimes just a plain old wooden ruler."

A fresh surge of liquid soaked her panties. The word ruler had brought on a sudden and twisted little fantasy. An image of her dressed like a school girl and being bent over a desk while Mark lifted her skirt and spanked her with a ruler was playing on a loop in her head. She squeezed her thighs together and pushed her soup away. Who the fuck knew she had a teacher/school girl fantasy?

"I can handle spanking," she said.

Mark sighed. "It's not what you think it is. It's not a fun little game of slap and tickle between two consenting adults. I'll spank you hard enough to leave marks." He hesitated and then said, "I *want* to leave marks, Amy. I only play with women who like pain mixed with their pleasure and want those marks too."

He tugged on the lobe of his left ear, a habit he'd had since he was a kid and one she'd always found slightly endearing. "I'll make you wear my collar and call you my slave. I need total control in the bedroom – always. Your orgasms belong to me and if you have one without my permission, I'll punish you. I'll tie you up and spank you. I'll tease you, fuck you, and make you beg me for your orgasm."

He tugged on his ear again before lapsing into silence. She took a deep breath and said, "I'm okay with those things."

There was a flare of lust in his eyes before he looked away and shook his head. "No, Amy."

"You don't get to just say no," she said.

"Yes, I do," he replied. "You don't understand exactly what I'm saying. You think you do but you don't. It's my fault because I'm not – I can't seem to explain it well enough."

"I don't mind giving up control in the bedroom," she couldn't seem to quite say the word submissive, "and you know that. You've *seen* it."

"Being submissive and enjoying impact play or slave play are different things," Mark said.

"We can find out together if I enjoy it."

"No."

"Stop saying no," she said in frustration.

Mark paced back and forth. "What happens if you don't like it, Amy? I'm not going to change. I don't do vanilla sex, ever."

"I liked what you did to me and I think I would like it a little rougher," she said.

"This isn't the only reason we can't be together. There's still Luke and your parents to consider. They are the only family have and I don't want to lose any of you. If we're more than friends, that might happen."

"I'm not worth the risk, is what you're saying," she said.

His hands clenched into fists before he slumped against the counter. "You can't possibly understand. You have your parents and Luke. You don't know what it's like to lose your entire family. I do, and I can't go through that again."

The pain in his voice tore at the lining of her stomach until she thought she would throw up. "I'm sorry."

"I want to be friends again." He gave her a hopeful look. "Can we?"

"I don't know," she said. "I don't know if I can go back to being just friends."

"We can try."

She studied the smooth granite top of the island. She didn't want to be just friends with him. She'd spent the last decade being just friends and it wasn't enough. But saying no to his request meant losing him forever. The tension between them would force him to eventually drift away from her and her family. His fear of losing her family would come true. She loved him too much to do that to him.

She lifted her head. "Yes, we can try."

His shoulders relaxed, and he sat down across from her before reaching for her hand. She let him take it and he squeezed gently. "Thank you, Amy."

"You're welcome," she said. "But, there's

something you need to know."

Don't, Amy. Don't say it.

He stared silently at her and she said, "What we did – what you *did* to me – I liked it very much. I want to," she paused, "try it again and maybe even try different things. I'm not telling you this to convince you to, uh, play with me, but because I don't want you to think I'm going behind your back when you see me at the club again."

Oh, you dirty little liar.

She was. She was a disgusting liar and she hated herself for it. Still, she held her breath and waited for Mark to immediately tell her she wasn't allowed to play with anyone at the club. That, if she was going to do this, then forget being friends. He would be more than happy to help her fulfill her most depraved fantasies.

Mark's hand tightened on hers and dismay rushed through her when he said, "I understand. Let me know when you're planning on being at the club and I'll make sure the right Dom plays with you."

He pulled his hand free and stood again, grabbing his bowl of soup and turning away to set it on the counter. She stared dumbly at his broad back. Mark really was finished with her.

She had played her hand and lost.

He was willing to let another man touch her, willing to let another man –

She slid off the stool and headed for the hallway.

"Amy?"

She paused in the doorway and without looking

at him, said, "I'm suddenly really tired and a little sore. Do you mind if I call it a night?"

"No, of course not," Mark said. "If you need anything in the night…"

She made her voice light and cheery. "I'm sure I'll be fine, but I'll holler for you if I need help. Good night."

"Good night, Amy."

Chapter Six

"Okay, well that's everything." Jane lugged her suitcase down the stairs and set it in the hallway.

"You should have let me help you carry that down," Amy said as Jane followed her into the kitchen.

"You were in a car accident two days ago. You need to rest."

Amy poured some tea into two mugs before passing one to Jane. "I'm fine. I have some mild bruising from the seat belt and that's it. Where's Luke tonight?"

Jane sat at the island and sipped at her tea. "He's helping your dad fix their washing machine. Luke wanted to just buy him a new one, but your mom refused."

Amy laughed. "That washing machine is older than me. I swear."

"He had dinner with Mark earlier and he invited him to come by your parents," Jane said. "Apparently, your dad has started watching hockey now and wants Mark and Luke to get into it too.

Mark had other plans though."

Amy didn't reply. Her stomach had clenched painfully when Jane mentioned Mark's name. She wondered bleakly if she'd ever stop having such a visceral reaction to hearing his name. God, she was already dreading the family dinner tomorrow night. Before he left Friday morning, Mark had asked her if she was okay with him joining them on Sunday nights again. She had said it was fine. A decision she was regretting immensely. Maybe she could beg off from dinner this weekend, say she was too sore.

"Amy?" Jane's warm hand covered hers. "Please tell me what's wrong."

She pressed her lips together. "Nothing's wrong. Just tired today."

"Are you – is everything okay with Mark now? Luke told me he stayed with you after the accident. Are you, uh…"

"Everything's fine with us. We're not fighting anymore. In fact, we're back to being friends like nothing ever happened. Like we have no idea what each other looks like - "

To her horror and shame, she burst into tears. Jane hurried around the island and put her arm around her shoulder. "I'm sorry, honey."

She rested her head on top of Amy's. "I know you don't want to talk to me about Mark, but if you ever change your mind – I'm here and I'm a good listener."

Amy wiped at her face and stared at Jane for a moment. "I want to tell you."

Jane kissed her forehead and squeezed her

shoulder. "Okay."

❧ ❦

"You can't tell Luke."

It was just over an hour later. After telling Jane everything, little tendrils of regret were already worming their way into her stomach. What had she been thinking? Jane was Luke's girlfriend. Of course, she would tell him. She'd been desperate to tell someone, she was so tired of keeping her love for Mark a secret, but she should have told Valerie.

"Amy?"

She jerked when Jane touched her hand. "What did you say?"

"I said not to look so worried. I won't tell Luke."

"I shouldn't have told you," Amy said. "It's not fair of me to ask you to keep something like this from Luke."

Jane shrugged. "You might be his sister, but that doesn't mean he has the right to know every detail of your life. I'm glad you told me, and I promise I won't say a word to your brother or to anyone."

"Thanks, Janie," Amy said.

"You're welcome. Now, are you sure that Mark really just wants to be friends again?"

"Yes. I told him I would play at the club with someone else and he – he was fine with it. All he said was to tell him, so he could find the right Dom for me. Remember?"

"I remember." Jane tapped one short nail against the island. "But I'm doubtful he meant it.

116

There's only one way to find out."

Amy's mouth dropped open. "You think I should test him?"

"I'm saying it's an option," Jane said. "Unless you really do want to just experiment and want to move on from Mark? In that case, maybe pick a different BDSM club to experiment. It would get weird if Mark walked in on a play session."

"I – how much of this lifestyle do you know?"

"A fair amount, actually," Jane said. "A few of the girls I worked with at Teasers were into BDSM. I don't think they went to Secrets though."

She tapped her chin thoughtfully. "I can't remember the name of the club but I'm pretty sure it wasn't Secrets. Anyway, they weren't shy about sharing what happened and I was curious."

"Have you ever tried it?" Amy asked. "Wait, sorry, that isn't any of my business."

Jane grinned at her. "I don't mind and no, I haven't tried it. It's not really my kink. But that doesn't mean it's weird or sick."

"I know."

"Do you? Because when you were telling me how this all started and what Tom said to you, you looked like you might barf."

Amy groaned and rubbed her hands against her thighs. "I – I don't know. I always knew I was somewhat submissive, you know? I had a couple boyfriends who would kind of pin me down during sex if I asked, and I liked it. One guy even slapped my ass a few times. He didn't do it hard - he couldn't seem to work up the nerve to do it hard - but holy crap, it turned me on. I mean, embarrassingly so. I couldn't hide how much it turned me on, and I think that kind of freaked him out. He broke up with me, like, two weeks later."

She suddenly blushed. "I'm sorry, this is really TMI."

"I don't mind," Jane said. "I know I give off a good girl vibe, but I worked at a strip club for years. Nothing you say can shock me."

"Anyway, I've never had a boyfriend even remotely interested in this kind of thing and I've always thought I was a bit of a freak for even liking the idea of being," she paused, "spanked."

She peeked at Jane, looking for disgust on the woman's face. Jane just smiled and made a go on gesture. Feeling a little more confident, she said, "When Mark said he was into impact play, that he, um, liked to leave marks, it turned me on. A lot. But I don't know if it's only the idea of being spanked that turns me on or the actual act. You know? And Mark made it clear that he doesn't do vanilla sex."

She stood and paced back and forth. "Even if I could convince Mark to try the, uh, more hardcore stuff with me, what if I didn't actually like it? Our chance at a relationship would be over before it even started."

"But what if you did really like it?"

"I still couldn't be with Mark," Amy said. "It's only one of the reasons he won't have a relationship with me, remember? He's convinced himself that we won't work out and he'll lose my parents and Luke. Or, even if we did work out, he'll lose Luke because Luke is so overprotective of me and won't approve of us dating."

"He has a point about the overprotectiveness," Jane said. "Remember when Pierre and Julien were hitting on you?"

She suddenly giggled. "Oh man, I had my hands on both Mark and Luke that night, trying to stop them from killing those poor French boys. They have no idea that they have me to thank for keeping them from being murdered."

Amy dropped into her chair. "It's pointless to even think about being with Mark. I agreed to just be friends with him."

"Okay, well, back to my earlier question – are you interested in seeing if you want more of the BDSM? I mean, you can't have Mark, but that doesn't mean you can't investigate the lifestyle. If you're truly only going to be friends with Mark, then maybe finding a Dom to show you new things isn't a bad idea. It might help you forget about Mark."

"Yeah, maybe."

"But I don't think you should go back to Secrets," Jane said.

"Mark doesn't care," Amy said. "He was so casual about it, like it didn't matter to him at all that I would be with someone else."

"Again – you believe that?"

Amy hesitated before nodding. "Yeah, I think I do. There was this – this almost finality about the conversation, you know? Like, Mark had finally, once and for all, closed down the idea of us being anything more than friends. He had a taste of what we could be together and that was enough for him."

"I still don't think you should go back to Secrets," Jane said. "I can text Candy and ask her the name of the other club."

"Sure," Amy said. "Thanks, Jane."

"You're welcome, honey."

"I'm sorry to dump this all on you."

"You haven't," Jane said. "Honestly, I'm really glad you did. Keeping it bottled up like that isn't healthy. Any time you want to talk about Mark or your feelings, or what it was like getting your butt spanked, you just text me."

Amy gaped at her before laughing. Jane grinned at her and took a sip of tea. "Any time, honey. I mean it."

∂∾ ∾∂

"Amy?"

She glanced up from the mannequin in her office and pasted a smile on her face. "Hey, Mark. Come on in."

"You have a minute?"

"I do." She pinned another piece of fabric to the mannequin's body and tried not to stiffen when Mark stood next to her.

"That looks good."

"Thanks. What's up?"

He lowered his voice. "Are we still good?"

She gave him a quick glance. "What do you mean?"

"You haven't been at the family dinner for two weeks in a row. If it's uncomfortable with there, I can stop going."

"What? No, it's fine," she lied. "I didn't go the

week before last because I was still a little sore from the car accident, and last Sunday I had plans with Valerie."

"It's not because of me?"

"Of course not," she lied again. "I'm glad you're coming to family dinners again."

He studied her for so long that her back started to get sweaty. "So, you'll be at family dinner this week?"

"Sure will," she said. "How about you?"

He nodded, and she smiled until her cheeks hurt. "Awesome."

God, would he please just leave? There was at least two feet between them, but it was still too close for her. She pinned the fabric with an aggressive push. The pin slid through the fabric and into her finger and she winced and yanked her hand away.

"Dammit!"

"Let me see."

"No, it's fine, it's just - "

Her voice died when Mark took her hand and peered at her finger. "Shit, it's really bleeding, Ames."

"It's fine." Her voice was so soft and breathy, you would have thought he was sticking his hand up her skirt. Her need for him was embarrassing in its intensity.

She tried to pull her hand away and bit her bottom lip when he wouldn't let go. "I'm serious. It's really bleeding."

"I have Band-aids in my desk," she said.

She tugged her hand free and hurried over to her

desk. Mark followed her, and he opened the top drawer and grabbed the little packet of Band-aids. He tore the wrapper off before grabbing a tissue from the top of her desk. The blood was already starting to clot but she could feel the pulse in the tip of her finger, throbbing in time with the increasing beat of her heart.

Would she ever not feel this all-encompassing need when she was around Mark? Would she ever have a moment where she didn't stand next to him and wish she could touch him?

Mark wiped away the blood, smiling at her when she winced. "Sorry."

He placed the Band-aid on her finger but didn't immediately let go of her hand. He was standing so close to her now.

She wanted to smooth her hand over that broad chest. She wanted to loosen his tie and taste the skin at the base of his throat. She wanted to slide her hand into his pants and grip the cock that gave her so much pleasure.

She wanted.

"Amy? Are you sure we're good? I know I sound like a broken record, but I - "

"We're good." The lie struggled from her throat like the thin shoots of a plant fighting to push through the dark earth.

She pulled her hand away and returned to the mannequin before Mark could see the way her nipples were poking against her shirt.

There was a knock on her door and the head of HR, Maria, stuck her head into the room. "Hey, Amy? Do you have a minute to...oh good, Mark, you're here too. Can I introduce you to our newest employee?"

"Sure," Amy said. She turned around as Maria stepped into her office. A short redheaded woman followed her. She was wearing a dark green Dawson suit and she tugged self-consciously at the hem of the suit jacket. She was slender with the pale skin of a redhead. Clusters of freckles covered the bridge of her nose and her cheeks.

Maria smiled at the woman. "This is - "

"Chloe?"

The redhead turned toward the sound of Mark's voice. Her eyes widened in recognition, and Amy's stomach knotted when delight crossed her face. "Mark!"

Mark moved toward her and after a moment of awkwardness, he and Chloe hugged. The knots in Amy's stomach would have made a Boy Scout proud. She put her hands behind her back and clenched them into fists as Mark smiled at Chloe.

"You work here now?"

"Yes," Chloe said with a quick glance at Maria. "I was hired last week. I didn't know you worked here."

"Chloe is working on the overhaul of our digital storefront. We're still interviewing for the other half of the team, but I knew Chloe would be perfect the minute I saw her resume," Maria said. "How do you guys know each other?"

The look on both Mark and Chloe's faces confirmed Amy's immediate suspicion. Mark knew her from the club, and the warm intimacy in which he greeted her meant that he'd probably seen her naked.

Mark had probably spanked her and fucked her and made her come.

Bile rose in her throat. She swallowed it down, her nails digging into the palms of her hands.

"Oh, um," Chloe hesitated, her gaze on Mark clearly pleading with him for help.

"We met through mutual friends," Mark said.

He was lying. Amy had known him long enough to recognize it.

"Isn't that nice," Maria said. "Amy, this is Chloe. She's working - "

"I heard," Amy said.

She could hear the edge in her voice. Maria cleared her throat. "Right. Well, Chloe Matthews, this is Amy Dawson. I know you know who she is." She gave Chloe a little grin and the redhead's face turned a pale pink.

She held her hand out and Amy shook it briefly. "Nice to meet you."

"It's really nice to meet you, Ms. Dawson," Chloe said. "I'm a big fan of your work and I - "

"That's nice. If you'll excuse me, I'm very busy," Amy said.

Her stiff smile made Chloe's falter. The redhead took a step back. "Of course, I'm sorry. I didn't mean to interrupt."

Amy didn't reply. Maria touched Chloe's arm. "Okay, let's introduce you to the design team and then I'll take you back to your office. Oh, Mark, Kyla is looking for you. Something about the quarterly reports not on the server."

"What? Shit." Mark hurried out of the office

without saying goodbye.

"See you later, Amy," Maria said.

"Bye." Amy turned back to the mannequin. When she heard the door shut, she crossed the office and nearly fell into one of the beanbag chairs. She felt sick to her stomach and she closed her eyes, pressing her hand against one flame-coloured cheek.

Images of Chloe, her slender, perfect body sitting astride Mark as he held her hands behind her back and fucked her, flooded through her almost immediately. Her eyes flew open, and she dropped both hands to the beanbag chair and dug her fingers into the leather.

"Stop it, Amy!" Her voice was too loud in the quiet. "Even if he does know her from there, it doesn't mean he's been with her. Just, fucking cool it and don't be such a jealous bitch. Even if he has slept with her, it's none of your business. He doesn't belong to you."

Her voice cracked, and hot tears threatened. She blinked them back savagely. She would not cry over Mark. Not today.

ತ್ ⊷

"Ma'am? Your sandwich is ready."

Chloe smiled at the man standing behind the counter at the café and took the sandwich. "Thank you."

She crossed the crowded café and found a seat at a table for two near the door. She opened her bottle of water and took a drink before unwrapping her sandwich and placing the paper napkin in her lap.

It was only her second day at Dawson Clothing and she was feeling a little overwhelmed. The company was large, and she'd met so many new people yesterday, her head was still spinning. She was barely able to contain her excitement at finally meeting her idol, Amy Dawson, but the woman's reaction had been cold and bordering on rude.

She bit into her sandwich and chewed slowly as she watched the people scurrying down the street. Disappointment etched through her. She'd been so excited to meet *the* Amy Dawson. It wasn't the only reason she had applied for the job at Dawson Clothing, but she'd be lying if she didn't say it was a big part of it. Too bad it wasn't exactly like she'd pictured it happening. They were right when they said it was better not to meet your idol.

Maybe if you hadn't pictured you and Ms. Dawson becoming instant friends, it might not have been so disappointing. Did you really believe that you could somehow work into your very first conversation that you loved to design clothes? That you've dreamed of being a designer for Dawson Clothing practically since the company started? You're losing it. You don't even have any schooling for design. You were hired for your marketing skills, remember?

"Chloe?"

She glanced up to see Mark standing next to her table. He held a bottle of water and a wrap in his hand and she smiled at him. "Hi, Mark. Have a seat."

"Thanks." He sat down across from her. "This

place is always swamped. How's your second day going?"

"Good," she said. "Listen, I'm sorry about yesterday and how weird it got in Ms. Dawson's office. I was not expecting to see you there."

He grinned at her. "It was a surprise to me too."

"I didn't even know what to say when Maria asked how we knew each other," Chloe said. "Do you think she noticed my 'deer in the headlights' look?"

Mark's grin turned into a laugh. "Maybe? Maria's a pretty sharp lady."

"Crap," Chloe said.

"It's no big deal."

"Do they know you attend Al-Anon meetings?" Chloe asked.

Mark took a drink of water. "No. But it wouldn't be the end of the world if they found out. Amy knows about my brother, so she wouldn't be surprised, and Maria is in HR. She doesn't gossip."

"That's good. But, uh, I don't want my new coworkers knowing about the Al-Anon thing," Chloe said.

"I won't say anything."

"Thank you. So, you know Ms. Dawson outside of work?"

"Yes. Luke is my best friend and has been since we were kids. I practically grew up with him and Amy. We started Dawson Clothing together."

"That's cool. Amy's a really talented designer."

"She is," Mark said. "She's been designing clothing since she was a teenager."

He ate another bite of his wrap. "So, I haven't

seen you at a meeting in a few weeks."

Chloe could feel her traitorous pale skin turning pink. "Uh, yeah, I've been busy with finding a new job. Have you heard from your brother lately?"

"No, not for a couple months," Mark said. "I drove through the Badlands about three weeks ago and spotted him over by the Dartmouth Motel. I tried to talk to him, but he ducked into a room and wouldn't open the door."

"I'm sorry," Chloe said.

"At least I know he's alive, right? Or at least he was three weeks ago."

Mark pushed the rest of his wrap away. "How is your sister doing in rehab?"

Chloe studied her sandwich. She didn't want to tell Mark about Lori. It made her feel like a failure.

"Chloe? How is Lori doing?"

"She left rehab two weeks ago."

"Shit. I'm sorry."

"Yeah, me too." Chloe ripped thin strips from her paper napkin. "She was doing so well. I even visited her at the rehab place a couple of weeks before that. She looked good, you know? Even just two months without the booze had made a difference. She was talking about her future and how she was going to go back to school and…"

Her voice broke and she dabbed at her eyes with what was left of her napkin.

"I'm sorry, Chloe."

Mark's hand took hers and she held it in a hard grip before glancing up at him. "She's back on the booze. She's staying with my grandma again and – and drinking all day."

Her bottom lip trembled, and she squeezed Mark's hand again. "My grandmother just keeps giving her the alcohol like Lori doesn't have a problem. She doesn't care that - "

She needed to stop talking about this before she wept like a damn baby. Not that Mark hadn't seen her cry over her sister before. But there was a big difference between crying in front of him at an Al-Anon meeting and crying in front of him when he was her new boss.

She sniffed and wiped at her face again. "Sorry."

"It's okay." They were still holding hands and she stared at their linked fingers as he said, "Is that why you haven't been to a meeting lately?"

"Yeah. I'm embarrassed and I feel like it's my fault that she failed again."

"It isn't. You know it isn't," Mark said. "You need to come back to a meeting. No one is judging you for your sister's actions. We've all been there, remember?"

"Yes," she whispered.

Mark reached out and took her other hand. The door to the café opened bringing with it a swirl of cold air that made her shiver. "It's not your fault, Chloe."

"Thanks, Mark. I appreciate that."

She shouldn't have heard the harsh gasp, not over the babble of voices in the crowded café, but she did. She glanced up to see Amy Dawson standing just inside the door. Her cheeks were red from the cold and she was clutching her purse in front of her. She was staring at their linked hands and when she raised her gaze to meet Chloe's, there was something very close to hatred in her eyes.

"Ms. Dawson?" Chloe said.

Mark immediately dropped her hands and twisted in his seat. "Amy? Hey, how are you? You should have told me you were coming here for lunch. I would have waited for you."

Her smile was cold, but the heat in her gaze could have melted a rock. "Hello, Mark. Hello, Ms. Matthews."

"Hi," Chloe said. "Why don't you join us?"

"No, thank you," Amy replied. "I didn't mean to interrupt."

"You didn't," Mark said. "We'll grab another chair and - "

"No. I've changed my mind. I'm not very hungry after all," Amy said.

"Ames, what's wrong?" Mark started to stand, and Amy shook her head before backing away.

"Nothing's wrong. Enjoy your lunch."

She turned and bolted out the door, bending her head against the cold wind as she walked down the street.

Mark sank back into his chair. "Shit."

"Did I do something wrong?" Chloe asked.

"No," Mark said. "Of course not."

Chloe placed her crumpled up napkin on the table. "Ms. Dawson doesn't seem to like me."

"She does. Amy likes everyone." He took a drink of water. "Finish up your sandwich and we'll walk back to the office together. Okay?"

"I'm finished." Chloe pushed the rest of her sandwich away.

"You didn't eat very much."

"Neither did you." She pointed to his barely-touched wrap.

"I guess that's what happens when we start talking about our siblings, huh?"

"Yeah," Chloe said.

"Come to the meeting tonight, Chloe."

She hesitated, and he leaned forward. "They help. You can't do this alone."

"You're right," Chloe said.

"Good. So, I'll see you at seven?"

"Yeah." She stood and picked up her uneaten food. "I'd better get back to the office. Taking a long lunch on my second day isn't exactly professional."

တ

Amy stared at the sketch in front of her. She cursed and tore the piece of paper from the sketch pad with a harsh rip. She crumpled it into a ball and tossed it in the trash.

It was nearly twenty-four hours since she'd seen Mark and Chloe in the café together and she still couldn't get the fucking image out of her head. The way Mark was holding her hands, the tender look he was giving her – he might as well have just ripped Amy's heart from her chest and smeared it onto the dirty floor of the café. The pain would have been the same.

She snapped her pencil in two and tossed it in the trash before grabbing another one. It was bad enough that Mark knew Chloe from the club, bad enough that that he had probably fucked her. But the way he looked at her... like he cared about her, like he...

The second pencil broke between her fingers with the sound of a tree branch snapping in the cold. She tossed it and grabbed a third.

"We need to talk."

The very object of her thoughts strode into her office. She stared at the blank sketch pad in front of her and made her voice light. "Sorry, just heading into a meeting."

"No, you're not." He crossed around her desk and sat on the edge of it. She automatically rolled her chair away. "I checked your schedule. You have no meetings this afternoon. In fact, you had no meetings yesterday afternoon either when I tried to talk to you."

"I'm very busy." She refused to look at him. "Can we talk later?"

"No. Look at me."

Fuck, he was using his Dom voice on her. The urge to obey him was excruciatingly difficult to resist.

"Don't do that," she said.

"Don't do what?"

"Use your Dom voice on me."

There was silence, then, "I'm not."

"Yes, you are."

"I'm sorry. I shouldn't have done that. Sometimes it just...happens."

Her laugh was bitter. "With everyone or just with the women you've put your collar on?"

"Amy - "

"How do you know Chloe? The club, right?

Has she been your little slave too?"

The words fell out of her mouth. Dry and dusty as a tumbleweed in the desert.

"No, Chloe doesn't go to the club."

A weight she hadn't known existed, dropped from her chest. She took her first deep breath in twenty-four hours and stared up at Mark. "Then how?"

His fingers grabbed his left earlobe. Tugged. "I told you, through mutual friends."

The weight returned. Settling back onto her chest with a cheery wave and a have-you-missed-me-old-friend grin.

"You're lying."

"I'm not."

"You are." She lowered her gaze to the pencil clenched between her fingers.

"It's not the club, Amy. Can you just trust me on that?"

"If it isn't the club, then why won't you tell me the truth?"

"I am telling you the truth."

The weight sunk deeper, threatening her ability to breathe, to live.

"Fine. Thank you for clearing that up. Could you leave now? I really am very busy." Her tone was ice cold and she felt more than heard Mark's sigh.

"I don't want to fight with you again."

"We're not fighting," she said. "Everything's good."

"No, it isn't," he said. "You're angry and we need to talk about it."

"I'm not angry." She could almost taste the rage on her tongue. "Why would I be angry?"

"Chloe and I are friends, nothing more," Mark said.

"Good for you."

"Ames, don't - "

"Hey, Amy? I redid the jacket on this design like you asked, but honestly, it still doesn't feel right. Like, the shoulders don't sit right or something. Can you take a look at it? Oh, sorry, I didn't mean to interrupt." Rachel, one of the members of her design team stood in the doorway of her office, sketchbook in hand.

"You're not." Amy stood and pushed past Mark. "Mark was just leaving. Come in and we'll look over the design together."

Mark was still standing at her desk and she said, "Bye, Mark."

"We'll continue our meeting later." Mark headed toward the door of her office, smiling distractedly at Rachel.

"Sure." Her voice was careless as she took the sketchbook from Rachel. "Okay, Rachel, let's see what you've got.

Chapter Seven

"Welcome back, Ms. Dawson."

She gave the man who scanned her green wrist band a startled look. "Um, thank you."

"Enjoy your stay at Secrets this evening." The door to the club opened and Amy stepped inside.

She was surprised at how busy it was for a Thursday night. The club was packed with people and seats were already filling up in front of the small stage. A man walked by her. He was tall and thin, and she stared at the wooden paddle in his hand as he gave her body an appreciative look.

"Would you like to play?" He asked.

"Oh, uh, no thank you."

He shrugged, and she fought the urge to cover her chest with her arms when he studied her cleavage.

"Your tits are incredible."

"Thank you." Her tits were now turning an embarrassingly bright shade of red.

"I'd like to cum on them. Are you sure you don't want to play?" He twirled the paddle in his hands and she took a step back.

"I'm sure."

"Pity." He gave her body a final glance before turning and walking away.

Amy, what are you doing?

She tried to ignore her inner voice as she made her way to the bar in the middle of the club, but the damn thing wouldn't shut up.

Go home. You're angry and upset with Mark, and it's making you do something you shouldn't.

She slid onto the bar stool and smiled at the bartender when he stopped in front of her. "I'll take a whiskey sour, please."

She had left the office as soon as she was finished with Rachel. She'd tried to work at home but after the third text message from Mark, she'd turned her cell to silent and tried to nap. Half an hour later, she was phoning Secrets and booking a room for the night. Half an hour after *that*, she was at the mall and buying a dress that showed so much skin she might as well have been naked.

She glanced down at her chest. The plunging neckline of the dark green dress left her no choice but to go braless. Her nerves had made her nipples rock hard and noticeable against the silk material. The dress covered her ass but sitting made the top of her stockings show. She tugged futilely at the hem of her dress as the bartender returned with her drink.

"Thank you." She sipped at the drink. A woman wearing a schoolgirl outfit drifted past her. Her dark hair was in pigtails and she tugged coyly at one as she smiled up at the man walking next to her.

Her own schoolgirl fantasy flickered on a reel in her head and she immediately took another drink. Maybe she could find a Dom here tonight who would play out that fantasy with her.

Do you really want someone other than Mark to be the first man to spank you?

What she wanted was to forget that Mark existed.

What she wanted was to take control of her own damn sex life.

What she wanted was to find someone to make her forget all about Mark and the way he made her feel.

"Good evening."

She smiled at the man who sat on the barstool next to her. He was tall with thick, sand coloured hair and dark brown eyes. She knew immediately that he was a Dom, and she stared at the scar that was slashed across the right side of his neck.

Goose bumps prickled her skin.

"Hello."

"What's your name, sweetness?"

"Amy." Her voice was nervous and thin.

"Hello, Amy. My name is Wallace." He studied her bare throat before his gaze dipped to her cleavage. Her hands reached to adjust her neckline and he caught both of them in a firm grip.

"No, don't. They're lovely. Let me admire them."

She dropped one hand to her lap and wrapped the other around her drink as Wallace studied her tits for a few minutes longer. His gaze drifted to the green wrist band.

"Is this your first time at the club, Amy?"

"No. Um, my third."

He took her hand, his thumb stroking the pulse at her wrist. "Are you looking for a Dom this evening?"

Tell him no and go back to your room.

"I am."

His smile widened, and she stared at his even white teeth. He was a very handsome man, not as handsome as Mark, but maybe if she closed her eyes, maybe if she pretended…

"What type of play are you looking for?" Wallace asked.

"Oh, um, I was thinking I might want to try, uh, impact play." She took a drink of her whiskey sour. "Do you, um, do that kind of play?"

"I can," he said. "My speciality is Shibari, but I am well-practiced with impact play."

"What's Shibari?"

"Shibari means 'to tie' in Japanese," Wallace said. "It is the art of rope bondage."

Her stomach muscles clenched. "Oh, uh, I don't think I'm into that."

"Are you certain? It is a beautiful experience. Those of us who are skilled at Shibari know how to bring pleasure to our canvas."

"Canvas?"

"You, Amy. You would be my canvas." His long fingers stroked along her collarbone before dipping down to stroke the soft skin between her breasts. "The ropes would make such beautiful patterns on your lovely skin."

His voice was low, hypnotic. She'd never had any interest in being tied up but the Dom in front of her was oddly persuasive.

She drained her glass and set it on the bar as Wallace cupped the back of her neck and drew her closer. "I would like to play with you tonight, Amy."

❧ ❦

The elevator doors opened and the man standing at the door of the club made a twitch of surprise before smoothing his tie. "Mr. Stanford, I wasn't expecting to see you this evening."

"Hello, Karl." Mark stepped out of the elevator. Karl opened the door to the club, and Mark scanned the room as the door closed behind him. It was busy for a Thursday night and he muttered a curse as he searched for her.

He'd spent the last two weeks waiting for Amy to tell him she was returning to the club. He had told her he would find her another Dom to teach her the art of submission and he'd regretted it instantly. As the days went on, he'd begun to hope that she was bluffing. The thought of another man – *another Dom* – touching her, made him sick to his stomach.

The text from Selene had dropped his heart to his goddamn feet. He barely remembered the drive from the office to the club. He was lucky he hadn't gotten into an accident.

He scanned the club again, hoping like hell that she hadn't already picked another Dom. The idea that someone else might be seeing his Amy naked, someone else might be making her beg to come, someone else might be spanking his little slave's ass, had him contemplating a murderous rampage.

He made his way through the crowds of people and caught a flash of her hair. She was at the bar and Wallace was sitting next to her. Anger lit up his insides when Wallace cupped the back of her neck and drew her closer. He stalked toward them, his hands clenching into fists.

രം ഏ

"What do you think, Amy?" Wallace's gaze never left her mouth. "Would you like to wear my collar this evening?"

She should say yes. This was what she was here for. So, why was she hesitating?

"Leave, Wallace."

Mark's low voice behind her nearly made her fall off the stool. She pulled away from Wallace's grip, hating the guilt that she felt, and stood. Wallace stood next to her as she turned to face Mark. He was wearing the dark suit he'd wore at the office today and she glared at him. He didn't notice. He was staring at Wallace and the other man studied his face.

"Whatever you say, Mark."

"No, not whatever he says." Amy hooked her hand around Wallace's arm. "We were talking."

Wallace smiled at her and plucked her hand from his arm before pressing a kiss against her knuckles. "Good night, Miss Amy."

He walked away without a second look and Amy spun to face Mark again. "Seriously?"

"What are you doing here?"

"What are you doing here?" She retorted. "It's Thursday night. You don't come here on Thursdays. Don't you have some work to finish at the office?"

"I *was* working," he said, "until I got the text from Selene telling me you were here."

"She narked on me?" Amy said. "That's so not cool."

"You need to leave," Mark said.

"I'm paid for the night. You can't kick me out."

"Like hell I can't." He took her arm. "Let's go, Amy."

She yanked her arm free. "No. I told you I would come here again, and you were fine with it. Remember? In fact, you said you would find another Dom for me. Wallace seemed perfectly nice and he said he knew about impact play. I want to play with him."

His face turned an alarming shade of red. "You are not playing with Wallace."

"You don't get to make that decision," she said.

"My club, my rules. Let's go."

He reached for her arm and she said, "I'll tell Luke and my parents about the club, Mark."

She tried not to wince at the look on his face. She was being such a bitch, but she couldn't seem to stop. "I'll tell them all about it and what you do here."

"You wouldn't," he said.

"Wouldn't I? I have every right to be here. Just because you don't like the thought of someone else tying me up and – and screwing me, that isn't my problem. I want to have fun tonight. I want to," she glanced at the stage, "watch the show and maybe get inspired to try new things."

Amy, stop! You're hurting him!

Yeah, she was. But hell, he'd hurt her badly and it didn't seem to bother him.

"Fine."

She blinked at him. "W-what?"

"I said fine. You can stay and watch the show. But you wear this."

He pulled the thin black collar from his jacket pocket and her pulse raced. He rubbed his thumb over the MM stitched into the front of it. "Turn around, Amy."

"I don't want to wear your collar. If I'm wearing it, none of the other Doms will come near me."

"Tough shit. You can wear my collar and stay for the show, or you can be escorted from the premises and run home to mommy and daddy and tell them all about your new little fetish."

She glared at him. Dammit, why did he have to call her bluff?

He smiled at her. "Make your decision, Amy."

"You're such an asshole." She whipped around and lifted her hair.

He stepped closer and she ignored his warm breath on the back of her neck as he buckled the collar in place around her throat.

She hated how right it felt to be wearing it.

His arm wrapped around her waist and he held her against his body as he slipped his finger between the collar and her throat. "Is it too tight, little slave?"

She jerked against him. "Don't call me that. I – I'm not your slave."

"You're wearing my collar." He tugged on it. "That makes you mine and I'll do with you as I wish."

Well, fuck. Her panties were suddenly soaking wet. "That wasn't part of the deal."

"Of course it was." His voice had deepened to his Dom voice. It sent a shiver of need through her whole body. "Just because you didn't think through your decision, doesn't make it my problem."

"You're still an asshole," she said.

She squealed loudly when his hand connected with her right ass cheek. It sent pain throbbing through her and she glared up at him. "That fucking hurt!"

"It was meant to," he said. "Keep speaking so disrespectfully to me and I'll put you over my knee and spank you right here."

"You wouldn't dare," she whispered.

"Wouldn't I?"

He slapped her left ass cheek this time and she squealed again. The people closest to them turned to stare at her and she flushed with embarrassment. The Dom who had tried to get her to play with him the last time she was here, approached them and grinned at Mark.

"Your subbie is feisty tonight."

He gave her body a slow perusal and she pressed back against Mark as his hand tightened around her waist.

"Nothing I can't handle, Peter," Mark said.

"Well, if you require assistance later with her punishment, I'm more than happy to help."

She made a low sound of protest. Peter and his hard grin made her nervous.

Mark just smiled at him. After a moment, Peter turned and walked away.

"I don't want him touching me," she said.

"No one touches you but me."

She breathed a sigh of relief as Mark tugged again at her collar. "What do you say?"

She stared blankly at him, and he said, "I'm giving you what you want, little slave. What do you say?"

"Thank you," she retorted.

The third slap to her ass was the hardest yet. It sent another stinging wave of pain through her lower body and she jerked against Mark. But, oh, under that pain there was a pleasure that she couldn't seem to deny.

"Try again, little slave."

"Thank you, *Sir*," she said.

Her tone was undeniably sarcastic. She tensed and waited for his slap, but he just smiled at her. "You're welcome. Follow me, please."

He released her and walked toward the stage. After a moment, she followed him. Most of the chairs were already full but there were two empty chairs at the end of the second row from the back. Mark sat down on the chair at the end. When she tried to slide by to sit in the empty chair next to him, he shook his head and pointed to the cushion that was resting on the floor next to the chair.

"You have got to be kidding me," she said.

"I'm not," he said. "Sit on the floor beside me."

She glared at him but sank to her knees on the cushion. She yanked her skirt down and rested her hands on her lap as Mark reached down and petted her long blonde hair. She refused to look at him, staring instead at the people sitting in the chairs.

A petite blonde woman leading a man twice her size on a leash, sat in the chair next to Mark. The man knelt on the cushion next to her and rested his head on her lap. He was gagged with a bright red ball gag and his hands were cuffed behind his back. She stroked his upper back and shoulders absentmindedly as she smiled at Mark.

"Good evening, Master Mark."

"Hello, Mistress Trina. How are you?"

"Very well." She peered around him to study Amy. "I see you have a new pet."

Mark nodded before running his fingers through her hair. "I do."

"She's a pretty little thing."

"Thank you," Mark said.

"Will you be doing any public shows with her?" Trina asked.

Amy stiffened in alarm, but Mark shook his head. "No."

"Pity. It's been forever since you've done a show, and I always enjoy when you're on stage with your pet."

"She's new and a little shy," Mark replied.

"Perhaps with more training, she'll be open to the idea," Trina said.

"Perhaps." Mark petted Amy's hair again and grinned at her when she mouthed an emphatic 'no fucking way' at him.

He leaned down and whispered into her ear, "That's 'no fucking way, *Sir*'."

She glared at him and he tugged on her hair again before staring at the stage. His hand drifted to the back of her neck and she shifted a little closer to him when he pulled lightly. He urged her to rest her cheek on his thigh and when she resisted, his hand tightened. She gave up and pressed her cheek against his leg. He kneaded her neck before running his fingers over her upper back. She shivered with pleasure and he rubbed the top of her shoulders.

She closed her eyes, reminded herself that she hated him and tried to pretend that she hadn't been craving his touch for the last two months.

"Who's doing the show tonight?" Trina asked.

"Richard," Mark replied.

"Excellent. He always puts on a good show. Who's his pet tonight?"

"Mandy, I believe," Mark said.

Trina laughed. "Well, I'm thankful that I'm sitting near the back. She's wonderfully responsive, especially with Richard, but she's a squirter."

"Perhaps we should start providing towels for those who sit in the front row?" Mark said with a laugh.

Trina grinned at him. "Might be a good idea. What's he doing to her tonight?"

"Spanking bench and the St. Andrew's Cross."

"Delightful. Oh good, the show is beginning."

Mark released her, and Amy lifted her head. She strained to see over the people in front of her.

She was tall but not nearly tall enough to see over their heads, and she frowned in frustration. What was the point of watching the show if she couldn't see a damn thing?

Mark tugged on her hair. "Stand up, little slave."

She stood and he pulled her into his lap. She tried to sit forward and he pressed her back against his broad chest. He pushed her thighs apart until her legs were spread wide and resting on the outside of his knees. She tried to close them, and he slapped her thigh.

"No, leave your legs open for me."

He cupped her throat above the collar and held her in a firm grip. Not strong enough to break free and stupidly turned on by being trapped against him, she relaxed. Her head rested against his shoulder and she watched as the curtain drew back.

A tall man with thick grey hair was standing next to a large wooden structure in the shape of an X.

"That is Master Richard and that's St. Andrew's Cross," Mark breathed into her ear.

A spanking bench was next to the cross. The man picked up the flogger that was resting on the padded bench and held it loosely in one hand before holding out his other hand. A woman walked onto the stage. She had short red hair and she was completely naked. Her small breasts were topped with large pink nipples that were already erect. Her pussy was waxed bare, and she smiled at the man before taking his hand and kissing it.

He returned her smile before leading her to the

spanking bench. She climbed onto it, and Richard smoothed his hand over her ass before quickly buckling the restraints around her slender thighs and upper arms.

The woman was nearly vibrating with excitement, and she moaned happily when Richard reached between her legs and stroked her pussy. Amy watched in utter fascination as Richard slapped her right ass cheek and then her left one. The woman jerked and cried out as bright red handprints appeared on her pale flesh. He slapped her again, moving from cheek to cheek in a steady rhythm as she moaned and wriggled against her restraints.

Amy tried not to squirm. Her pulse was pounding, and her nipples were hard as glass against her dress. As Richard continued to spank the redhead, her pussy grew wetter. What would it be like to be spanked like that by Mark? To be strapped down and helpless?

God help her, she wanted to find out. She shifted on Mark's lap and moaned when his erection pushed against her ass. He laughed into her ear and adjusted her so that his cock was pressing against the crack of her ass. She clenched her hands into fists and tried to focus on the show as Mark's hand drifted to her right thigh and rubbed.

The redhead was squealing loudly now with each slap of Richard's hand. Her entire ass was covered in bright red handprints. Amy gasped when Richard brought the flogger in his right hand down sharply against her skin. She winced with every blow that landed on the redhead's ass and

Mark squeezed her thigh.

"She likes it, little slave. I promise you."

"It looks painful," she whispered.

"It is," he said. "But there is pleasure in it as well."

She licked her lips as he rubbed her thigh again. "I never actually asked if you've been spanked before, little slave. Have you? Have you had a man put you over his knee for a proper spanking?"

"No," she said.

He slapped her thigh. She twitched. "No, Sir, I haven't been spanked properly."

"Would you like to be?"

"I – I don't know, Sir."

He dropped the hand around her neck to her left thigh and held it firmly. Before she could stop him, his right hand dipped between her legs and touched the soaked crotch of her panties. She closed her right leg, but his left hand prevented her from moving her other thigh. He slapped her thigh again.

"Legs open, I said."

"Sir, please," she said.

"Open," he repeated.

Squirming with both embarrassment and pleasure she moved her right thigh until she was spread wide open on his lap again. He rubbed her through her panties and she tried to hold in her low moan.

"If your wet panties are any indication, you would like to be spanked, little slave," he said. There was amusement in his voice and she blushed. He cupped her pussy with warm familiarity before staring at the stage.

The people surrounding them made her self-conscious and she squirmed. "Sir, will you please move your hand?"

"No."

"Please, Sir?"

He brushed his mouth across her earlobe. "Your pussy belongs to me, little slave. When I want to touch it, I will. Do you understand?"

Lust throbbed in her belly. "Yes, Sir."

"Say it."

"My pussy belongs to you, Sir."

"That's my good girl." He gave her clit a quick rub through her panties and nuzzled her throat when her pelvis arched. The tip of his finger probed against her entrance, pushing the fabric of her panties into it. This time there was no holding back her moan and he pressed his mouth to her ear again.

"Someone needs to be fucked. Isn't that right, slave?"

She refused to answer, and he pressed again. "Answer me."

She shook her head in denial. He made a low noise of disapproval and quickly slipped his fingers under her panties. His finger slid into her to the last knuckle and her pussy immediately clenched around it.

"Oh God," she moaned. She tried to relax but her pussy squeezed him again as his warm laugh washed over her.

"My little slave's pussy is so greedy tonight," he breathed into her ear. "Have you allowed anyone else to fuck your pussy in the last two months?"

She shook her head no as he slid his finger in

and out of her wet pussy.

"Good," he said. "No one is allowed to touch, taste or fuck your pussy but me. Is that clear?"

"Yes, Sir."

"Why?"

"Because it belongs to you, Sir."

"Good." He pressed a kiss against her cheek. His finger stopped its slow movement and she whined in protest.

"Shh, watch the show," he said. "If you're a good girl, perhaps later I'll give you the fucking you so desperately seem to need."

His thumb was resting against her swollen clit and she moved her hips a little, trying to rub her throbbing clit against his rough skin.

"Stop that," he said. "I'll decide when and if you get your clit rubbed."

She twisted her head and pouted at him. He grinned. "Pouting won't get you what you want."

She didn't reply. Her mouth had dropped open and he followed her gaze. Trina was reclining in her chair, staring intently at the stage. The ball gag that used to be in her slave's mouth was dangling from one slender finger. Amy swallowed, her eyes widening in astonishment and mild disbelief. Trina's slave's head was beneath her long skirt. She couldn't see his face, but it was obviously buried between his Mistress' thighs. Trina's right hand was pressing rhythmically on his head as she watched the show.

"Shit," Amy whispered. She could practically feel her pussy dripping with fresh wetness. The grin on Mark's face sent another wave of embarrassment through her.

He sucked on her earlobe. "You're soaking my hand. My little slave wishes I was eating her pussy right now. Doesn't she?"

"Yes, Sir," she moaned. She tried to move her hips and he bit her earlobe until she gasped.

"I told you to sit still and watch the show," he said. "Move again without my permission and your delightfully firm ass will be spanked tonight."

An image of Mark spanking her flickered through her head and she thrust helplessly against his finger before freezing in place.

"I'm sorry, Sir," she said immediately. "It was an accident, Sir."

"Too late, little slave," he whispered. "After the show is over, you're getting your first spanking."

That sent another wave of intense pleasure through her and she barely managed to keep herself still on his lap.

"Watch the show," he said again.

She didn't want to watch the show anymore. She wanted Mark to take her somewhere private and give her the spanking he said he would. The need to know if she would actually like it, if the pain would heighten her pleasure was unbelievably powerful.

"Sir, please," she whispered.

"Watch the show," he said. "Do as your Master says, slave."

"Yes, Sir," she replied.

She turned her attention to the show. While Mark was teasing her, Richard had moved the redhead from the spanking bench to the cross. She was strapped firmly in place with the restraints around her wrists and ankles. Richard was lightly flogging her breasts and abdomen. The flogger left red marks on her pale skin that Amy found to be almost pretty. She took a deep breath as Richard lowered the flogger. He whispered into the redhead's ear as he cupped one breast and flicked at her nipple with his thumb. Her back arched, and she moaned in pleasure when he trailed his hand down her flat abdomen and cupped her pussy. His thumb rubbed at her clit.

Amy's low cry of pleasure was drowned out by the bound woman's louder shriek of delight. The moment Richard rubbed his slave's clit, Mark had rubbed hers. She dug her hands into his firm thighs, panting harshly and trying not to bring attention to herself as Mark circled her clit before pressing on it.

Richard moved his hand away and Mark immediately stopped rubbing her clit. Amy muttered a curse and then jerked when Mark slapped her pussy.

"Quiet, little slave."

She bit at her bottom lip, her eyes widening when Richard flogged his slave's tiny breasts before flicking the leather straps directly against her exposed pussy. The woman shrieked, her tiny body straining against the restraints. Richard immediately cupped her pussy again, rubbing her clit with slow strokes.

"Oh God, yes, please," Amy whimpered as Mark rubbed her swollen clit. She barely heard the redhead's cries of pleasure. Her concentration had narrowed to a singular thought. She needed to come. She would go crazy if she didn't. Mark was still rubbing her clit and her belly tightened as her orgasm started deep in her pelvis.

When he stopped abruptly, she pounded on his thighs in frustration. He captured her wrists in one large hand and squeezed before slapping her pussy again with his other hand.

The jolt of pain almost threw her over the edge and she couldn't stop her hips from bucking against his hand. He pressed warm kisses against her neck and continued to hold her wrists in a hard grip as she stared glassy-eyed at the stage.

Richard was flogging his slave again. From the top of her breasts to the middle of her thighs, red streaks covered her flesh. With every blow, the woman cried out but even from where she was sitting, Amy could see the wetness that coated her pussy and inner thighs.

Please, oh, please, she thought. *Please touch her. Please touch her.*

The gentle pressure of Mark's hand cupping her pussy was driving her insane. She wanted to come so badly that she was almost crying. All she needed was one more stroke, one more touch to bring her to orgasm. Her pussy was pulsing with a weird combination of pleasure and pain, and she could hear the harsh sound of her rapid breathing in her ears.

"Please touch her," she whispered.

As if he'd heard her, Richard dropped the flogger to the floor. He slid his hand between the redhead's thighs and shoved two fingers deep into her pussy. He fucked her hard with his fingers as she screamed.

Amy made a muffled noise of surprise when Mark dropped her wrists and his hand clamped over her mouth. His other hand rubbed her clit with hard, fast, and just-exactly-what-she-fucking-needed, strokes. She arched, screaming against his hand as her orgasm roared through her like a freight train. Her body shook and she screamed again, the sound muffled by Mark's hand.

She collapsed against him, panting and moaning as he dropped his hand from her mouth and slid his other hand out from under her skirt. He rubbed her thigh and kissed her neck.

"My God, Mark. You really must do a show with her."

Amy stared blearily at Trina. She'd forgotten completely about the people surrounding them and embarrassment crept in as Trina smiled at her. Her slave was kneeling on his cushion again, and his mouth and face were soaked with moisture and, oddly, glitter.

"She's magnificent when she climaxes," Trina said. "I missed the end of Richard's show because I was watching your little pet come all over your hand."

Amy groaned and buried her face in Mark's neck. Her whole body was still trembling, and a hot blush was rising from her chest. Mark continued to rub her thigh as he said, "She is delightfully responsive."

"Would you consider a play session together tonight?" Trina asked eagerly. "I'd love to play with her."

She could feel Mark tensing beneath her. "No."

"Are you sure?" Trina said. "There are so many lovely things I'd like to do to her."

"I said no," Mark said.

Trina recoiled a bit. "Forgive me. I've overstepped."

Mark waited as Trina and her slave left. On the stage, Richard had released the redhead from the cross. She was shaking and wobbling on her feet and he quickly wrapped a blanket around her before picking her up and carrying her off the stage.

"Where is he taking her?" Amy asked.

"Aftercare." Mark eased her off his lap and stood. He held her arm in a tight grip as he studied her face. "Can you walk, baby?"

"Yes, I think so," she replied. "I might have to take my heels off though." She was feeling a little off-kilter.

"Do you need an escort back to your room upstairs?" He asked.

"I don't want to go back to my room," she said. "You can't make me, Mark. You promised you would - "

He pulled her up against his body and gave her ass a light slap. She shuddered as fresh throbbing started in her pussy. Jesus, what was wrong with her? She'd just had an unbelievable orgasm in a roomful of people and she still wanted more.

"When you get to your room, remove all of your clothing. You're to be in the slave position when I get there," Mark said into her ear. "If you're not, your punishment will be more severe. Do you understand?"

"Yes, Sir," she whispered.

"I won't be long, so you might want to get moving." He squeezed her ass before pressing his erection against her stomach. "Unless," he whispered, "you want more than just a spanking."

She moaned, and he grinned before pressing a quick, light kiss against her mouth. "Go, little slave."

Chapter Eight

Amy straightened her back, pushing her breasts out a little further when the door handle turned. Her entire body was shaking with excitement and nerves and she stared at Mark when he entered the room. He was still wearing his suit from the office and she studied the lean length of his thighs as he walked to the bed. He was carrying a small leather bag in one hand and he set it on the bed before moving to her.

He studied her, and she tried not to blush. She thought she was doing the position correctly, but he nudged her knee with his foot and said, "Wider."

She spread her legs until her thigh muscles were straining from the effort. The cool air washed over her pussy. She was incredibly turned on and she hoped desperately that she wasn't dripping all over the fucking carpet.

"Well done, little slave." Mark petted her hair and an absurd tingle of pride went through. It disappeared when he said, "But when I ask you to assume the slave position, you will keep your gaze lowered until I give you permission to look at me."

"I'm sorry, Sir," she said.

"You're doing very well," he stroked her hair again. She watched as he returned to the bed and sat on the side of it. "Come here."

She started to stand. He shook his head. "No. Crawl to me."

She gave him a look of disbelief. He simply smiled at her and waited patiently. She bit at her bottom lip. She wanted Mark to spank her. More importantly, she wanted him to fuck her. He wouldn't do either if she didn't obey him.

Are you really going to crawl to him, Amy? Jesus, being spanked is one thing but this –

She cut off her inner thought grimly. She was wearing his collar, and she was naked on her knees with her legs spread simply for his pleasure. Was crawling really that much worse?

She leaned forward and planted her hands in the carpet before crawling toward Mark. She thought she would feel shame and humiliation, but Mark's gaze dropped immediately to her gently swaying breasts. His nostrils flared as his hands gripped his knees, and the look of pure lust on his face sent an answering call through her own body.

A little ripple of power went through her and she forgot her awkwardness about crawling. She slowed, moving with deliberate leisureliness as she arched her back and exaggerated the sway of her hips. She kept her eyes on his face, a small smile crossing her lips when his mouth parted, and a low groan slipped out.

She straightened into the slave position again when she was between his legs and kept her gaze lowered. His hands were clenching and unclenching against his knees and she smiled again. He placed his finger under her chin and tipped her head up.

"Very good, little slave." His voice was decidedly hoarse, and she moaned when he kissed her. She loved how he kissed. She loved the way he took control and made her forget everything but how much she wanted him.

He sucked hard on her tongue before cupping both her breasts. He tugged at her nipples, rolling them between his forefingers and thumbs until she gasped with pleasure. "Please, Sir."

"Please, what?"

"Please suck on my nipples, Sir," she begged.

He shook his head. "You're here for punishment, remember? If I suck on your nipples, next you'll ask me to eat your pussy and then you'll beg me to fuck you."

He gave her breasts one last squeeze before opening the bag next to him. She watched as he withdrew a small bottle of liquid and placed it on the nightstand before delving into the bag again. This time he withdrew a leather contraption and held it in front of her. It was some type of arm restraint that had both laces and buckles. It was longer and wider than cuffs and once she was in it, she'd be bound from her wrists to her elbows.

Panic threaded through her. Confused and suddenly afraid, she unconsciously leaned back as she hid her arms behind her back. She wanted to be spanked but the idea of being in the arm restraint was sending her brain into a frenzy of anxiety.

What if he really hurt her? What if he tied her up with the restraints and didn't stop spanking her when she asked him to? What if –

"Amy, sweetheart, look at me."

She raised her gaze to Mark, deeply afraid of what she might see, but his face had changed. It was no longer Dom Mark staring at her but only her familiar, sweet Mark.

The boy she'd grown up with and the man she would always love.

"Mark," she whispered. "I don't - "

He tossed the restraint on the bed before helping her stand and sitting her on his lap. She flung her arms around him and buried her face in his throat as he rubbed her back with his warm hands.

"Shh, it's all right. Everything's fine, Ames."

"I'm sorry," she whispered. "I'm so sorry."

"You have nothing to be sorry about. We can stop the play session."

"No!" She lifted her head to stare at him. "No, I don't want to stop. I just – I don't think I'm ready for – for," she glanced at the restraint, "something like that."

He cupped her face and stroked her cheekbone with his thumb. "Amy, do you understand that you have the power here?"

"I – what? No, I'm submissive." Her cheeks burned at her first direct admission of her submissiveness.

"Yes," he said. "Which is why you have the power. Anything that happens in this room is because you want it to happen. I cannot and will not do anything to you that you don't want. Your submissiveness is a gift of trust that is incredibly important to me, and I will never break that trust. If something I introduce in a play session is a hard limit for you, simply say so and we won't use it. If I do something you don't like, use your safe word and I stop immediately. I will *always* stop. Do you understand?"

"Yes," she whispered.

"Tell me your safe word again."

"Magnolia," she replied.

He hugged her and she kissed his thick neck. "I'm sorry for being so dumb about this."

"You're not being dumb," he said. "Don't say that, Ames. You're just learning something new."

They sat quietly for a few moments before he said, "Are you sure you want to continue?"

"Yes," she said. "I – I want you to spank me."

She gathered her courage and sat up, giving him an anxious look. "Do you, um, still want to spank me?"

That hard look of need returned to his eyes. "Amy, you have no idea how badly I want to spank you."

She tried to kiss him. He stopped her with a gentle hand on the back of her neck. "Before we do this, there's one more thing."

"What?" She asked.

He kneaded her neck and smiled at her. "Sometimes a new submissive is so eager to please her master that she'll let things go too far. She'll allow a punishment to continue when she should have said her safe word, just to try and please or impress him. Don't do that, Amy. If you've had enough, say your safe word. I don't want you trying to take more than you can handle because you think it's what I want. Is that clear?"

"Yes."

"Good." He kissed her again. He nipped and sucked at her bottom lip as she moaned quietly. His warm hand cupped her breast and he plucked at her nipple as his other hand curled around her hip. She leaned against him, returning his kiss as he toyed with her nipples. When his hand moved to her pussy, she spread her legs eagerly. He rubbed her clit before sliding two fingers into her and pumping them in and out. She rocked her pelvis against his fingers as her excitement and desire returned in a rush that left her breathless.

She whimpered in disappointment when he moved his hand away. He smiled and kissed her throat. "Stand up, little slave."

She stood, and he rubbed her ass with his warm hand before patting the mattress on his right side. "Kneel here and then lie across my lap."

Feeling awkward and uncoordinated, she kneeled on the bed and stretched out across his thighs. Her stomach and pelvis rested on his thighs, and her knees were pressed into the mattress next to him. His cock was hard against her stomach, and she twitched when he ran his hand over her raised ass. "You look beautiful."

"Thank you, Sir."

"Put your hands on the bed," he demanded.

She did as he asked. He pressed her head down until her cheek was resting on the bed as well. "Do not move your hands from the bed. Do you understand?"

"Yes, Sir," she said.

She tensed again when his hand smoothed over her lower back. She waited anxiously for him to spank her and squeaked in surprise when his hand dipped between her thighs again. He rubbed her clit, making her writhe against his lap and her hands dig into the quilt.

"Did you enjoy Master Wallace's touch earlier?"

She tried to concentrate past the touch of his fingers on her clit. "I – what?"

"When I came into the club, Master Wallace was touching you. Did you enjoy it?" He stopped touching her clit and rubbed the curve of her ass.

"No," she said.

The sound of his hand slapping her ass registered a split second before the pain. She squealed at the shocking amount it hurt and lifted her hands off the bed. Another hard slap to her right ass cheek made her cry out again.

"Hands on the bed, slave."

She flattened her hands to the bed, flinching when Mark rubbed his hand over her ass. "Do you see what happens when you lie to me?"

"Yes, Sir."

"I'll ask you again. Did you enjoy Master Wallace's touch?"

"I didn't hate it."

She waited for his slap, but he dipped his hand between her legs and rubbed at her clit. "Would you have played with him tonight?"

"I - no." She didn't mean to lie to him. It just

slipped out.

The repercussion was swift and painful. Mark spanked her in a hard and unforgiving rhythm. She cried out and after only a few spanks, tried to use her hands to cover her throbbing ass.

Mark's hand wrapped around her wrists and pinned them in the middle of her back. She squirmed and pleaded, kicking her feet, and trying to free herself as he spanked her without mercy.

When she gave up and rested against his thighs, he stopped spanking her and pushed his hand between her legs again. She was dripping wet, she could feel moisture sliding down her thighs. When Mark pinched her clit, the pain in her ass was immediately forgotten.

"Please!" She screamed.

She wanted to come.

She needed to come.

"Please what?" Mark said.

"I want to come. Please!" She begged shamelessly.

"No." He spanked her again and she shrieked, her hands tightening into fists.

"Would you have played with him?" His voice demanded an answer.

Tears running down her cheeks, her ass throbbing with pain and her pussy a fiery ache of pure need, she sobbed, "I would have tried."

His fingers pushed into her pussy and her sob turned to a moan. She pushed back against his fingers as his other hand curled into her hair and lifted her head. "I am your Master and you belong to me. Say it, slave."

"You're my Master," she cried. "I belong to you."

"You will not play with another without your Master's permission. Is that understood?"

"Yes."

His fingers left her pussy and he slapped her ass hard.

"Yes, Master!"

"Good." He rubbed her ass. "Kneel on the bed on your hands and knees."

"Please," she moaned. "Please fuck me, Sir."

He didn't reply. She scrambled to get off his lap and onto the bed. Her arms were shaking, and she could barely hold herself up. Mark pressed on her upper back.

"Rest your cheek on the bed and stretch your arms forward."

She did as he asked, feeling only a slight trickle of embarrassment when he pushed her thighs wide. She was head down and ass up and she felt terribly exposed. But as Mark stood next to the bed, more embarrassment creeped into her.

"You look beautiful, little slave." Mark's voice was a low, hungry rasp, and she clenched her hands into tight fists.

"Please, Sir."

"Please what?"

"Please fuck me, Sir."

"Stay in that position, little slave."

She stayed perfectly still, feeling the cool air wash over her exposed pussy as she listened to Mark strip. There was the sound of the foil of the condom and then Mark was kneeling behind her on the bed. Without speaking, he thrust into her. She screamed with pleasure and pressed her ass against his pelvis.

"Enough!" He slapped her ass and she squealed and clenched around his hard dick.

"Five more spanks as punishment for wanting to play with Master Wallace."

"What? No!" She craned her head to stare at him. "No, please, I don't want to be spanked anymore. I want to be fucked."

"Eight," he said.

"Stop it! I don't want - "

"Ten."

She shut her mouth with a snap and buried her face in the bed covers.

"Good girl," Mark said. "Don't come, little slave."

"Like I'm going to come from being spanked." Her voice was surly, and he reached under her and pinched her nipple.

"Do you want to make it twenty?"

"Ouch! No! I'm sorry, Sir. Please, Sir!"

"Better," he said as he released her nipple. "Be still."

"Yes, Sir."

The first slap burned like fire against her painful ass. She moaned into the covers and clenched around Mark's dick. He groaned and slapped her four more times in quick succession. Each one hurt worse than the previous. She moaned with relief when he stopped and rubbed her clit.

"Oh God," she gasped. "Oh fuck, oh God, that's so good, that... no!"

Mark had stopped touching her and her entire body screamed for relief. She was on the precipice of an orgasm and she writhed frantically beneath him. He pushed in deeper, pinning her to the bed with his cock and one heavy hand on her lower back.

Without speaking he spanked her five more times. Her wails of pain turned into moans of pure delight when he held her hips and fucked her with hard and heavy thrusts.

"Fuck, you're so goddamn fucking tight." Her Master's voice held only a thread of control.

His hand slipped beneath them and the moment the pads of his fingers rubbed across her clit, she climaxed. Her scream was muffled by the bed covers as her body shook and her pussy tightened around Mark's dick. The pleasure rolled through her, blotting out the pain in her ass as Mark drove in and out of her pussy.

He thrust deep, pinning her to the bed and she was only vaguely aware of his hoarse shout as he came deep inside of her. When he collapsed on her, she made a moan of discomfort and he pulled out of her before rolling to her side. She kept her face buried in the covers, heaving air in and out of her lungs. Mark sat up and she flinched when she felt the cold liquid on her ass.

"Ouch," she muttered into the covers.

His warm hand rubbed her lower back. "It'll help, Ames."

She relaxed into the bed, letting him rub the cool liquid all over her stinging ass before he urged her onto her side. She was shaking and weak as a kitten and she could barely help Mark when he tugged the covers out from under her body. He climbed in beside her, and she muttered in annoyance when he made her sit up.

"Drink some water, baby."

He placed a water bottle to her lips and she drank nearly half the bottle before he pulled it away.

"Okay?" He asked.

"Yes."

She wanted to lie down. She wanted to sleep. She was so tired and the intensity of the spanking and the orgasm had wrung every last inch of strength from her. "Tired."

"I know, baby. Lie down."

She collapsed on her side and he pulled the covers up around them before spooning her.

"Mark?" Her voice was thick with sleep.

"Yeah?"

"I liked it."

"Good. I liked it too. Go to sleep now."

❧ ❦

When her alarm went off on her cell phone, she groped for it and shut it off. The warmth of Mark's body was no longer against her back. She was alone in the bed. Disappointed but not surprised, she sat up and rubbed her hand through her hair. She had packed her work clothes in her small suitcase. If she hurried, she might actually have time to go to Starbucks before driving to the office. She slid naked from the bed and winced and grabbed her ass.

"Ouch! Shit, that hurts."

There was a full-length mirror attached to the far wall. She stood with her back to it and stared over her shoulder. Her ass wasn't red anymore, but it was tender and sore. She shuffled backwards to get a closer look. Holy crap, there was a bruise on the bottom of her left ass cheek. It was light, and the shape wasn't perfect, but it was a handprint.

Mark's handprint.

The muscles in her stomach and pussy clenched in perfect harmony. Mark's handprint was bruised onto her ass and not only did it not upset her - it was turning her on.

She walked into the attached bathroom and used it before brushing her teeth and showering. She stood in the steamy bathroom, wrapped in a towel and staring at herself in the fogged-up mirror.

"You liked it." She told her reflection.

The words made her feel a little ashamed. She straightened her back and said, "You liked it when Mark spanked you and there's nothing wrong with that."

She repeated the phrase twice more before leaving the bedroom. She thought she would like to be spanked but the level at which it turned her on was a little shocking. Even though Mark's spanking was more painful than she thought it would be. Despite what he'd told her, there was still a small part of her that believed he would never be able to spank her hard.

Tell that to the bruise on your ass.

She grinned a little as she pulled on her clothes then packed her suitcase with her toiletries and the clothes she wore to the club last night. She'd been completely wrong, and she didn't mind a bit. Mark's spanking had hurt like hell, but she hadn't even been close to saying her safe word. It hadn't even entered her head to say it. She liked the way it felt when she was bent over his lap, helpless against him and having to bend to his will. She liked it a lot.

You know, normal women don't like being spanked. They don't call the guy they're fucking 'Master' or 'Sir', and get wet when they're called a slave. They don't wonder how hard of a spanking they can take. They don't assume a slave position or crawl to –

The knock at the door was a welcome relief from her inner thoughts. She didn't need to be reminded that she had weird tastes in bed. She was well aware of it.

She opened the door. Mark was standing in the hallway and he handed her the Starbucks cup in his hand. "Morning."

"Hi." She was suddenly feeling shy and she sipped at the coffee as Mark stepped into the room. "Thank you for this."

"You're welcome."

There was a moment of awkward silence. Mark tugged on his earlobe. "How do you feel?"

"Good. Uh, my butt is a little sore." She had the sudden urge to lift up her skirt and show him the bruise on her ass. She squelched it down fiercely.

She wondered if he would apologize for spanking her and was relieved when he didn't. "I tucked a bottle of lotion in your purse. Rub it into your skin in the morning and before bed."

"Okay. Thanks."

He just nodded, his hand inching up to tug at his earlobe again.

"This is it for us, isn't it?" She said.

"Nothing has changed, Amy."

"It has," she argued. "We found out I like to be spanked."

"We still can't have a relationship."

Tired of the same argument, she admitted defeat. "Yeah, I know. Thanks for the coffee. I need to get to the office." She crossed the room to get her suitcase and purse.

"Wait."

His Dom voice made her stop immediately. Fuck, would it ever not work on her?

"Are you going to come back to the club?"

"Maybe." She studied the coffee cup in her hand. "I liked last night a lot. I want to try other things. I want to be spanked again, I want to explore the master/slave roleplaying. I want to learn how to," her cheeks flamed red, "please my Master."

"I don't want you playing with another Dom." His voice was hard and tight.

"That's not really your decision to make." She swung her purse over her shoulder.

"Let me be your teacher," he said.

Her head lifted, and she stared at him. "You don't want to have a relationship with me."

"No, I *can't* have a relationship with you," he corrected. "But I can teach you the art of submission. There's a lot to learn and I don't want an inexperienced Dom trying to teach you."

"And once you've taught me how to be submissive?" She asked. "Then what?"

"You'll know what to expect from a Dom and can find one that you're compatible with," he said. "If you enjoy being a submissive."

"You think I won't? I thought it was pretty clear last night that I enjoyed it."

His gaze drifted to her pelvis then back to her face. "Enjoying a spanking doesn't mean that you'll enjoy giving up total control in the bedroom all the time."

"Fair enough. So, let's see," she walked toward him, stopping when she was only a few inches away from him, "you're offering me the chance to be with you but only in a Dom/sub relationship. Once you've taught me how to be a good little submissive, you'll hand me over to another Dom. Is that right?"

He flinched, and she immediately regretted her harsh tone. "Mark, I - "

"This is the best I can offer you, Ames," he said. "I know how it makes me look."

"Then why offer it?"

"Because I want to be with you and it's the only way."

"No, it isn't the only way." Her voice was gentle. "But I understand why you think it is."

A muscle in his jaw ticked, ticked, ticked.

"Do you ever have vanilla sex?" She wanted to reach out and touch that ticking muscle.

"Yes. But not with a...slave."

"When was the last time you had vanilla sex?"

"Francine."

"Your University girlfriend?" She couldn't keep the surprise out of her voice.

"Yes."

"So, we wouldn't ever have vanilla sex?"

"No. If you agree to this, you're my slave, not my girlfriend. This is strictly me teaching you about this lifestyle and nothing more."

His brutal honesty clawed at her insides but there was a part of her that was grateful for his honesty.

"The master/slave thing is only in the bedroom?"

"Yes, bedroom only," he replied.

"Can I think about it?"

The muscle ticked more rapidly. "Of course."

"Okay. Thank you again for last night and for the coffee."

"I'll carry your suitcase to your car." Mark moved past her and picked up her suitcase.

This was the Mark she knew and loved. Thoughtful and considerate and a gentleman.

You love the other Mark too. In fact, the Mark who spanks you and collars you and makes you call him Sir is just as appealing. Admit it.

Yes, she supposed that was true. Still, it didn't mean she should just accept what he was offering.

"Ready?" He was already standing at the door.

"Yes." She followed him out into the hallway.

Chapter Nine

"Why do you keep flinching when you sit down?" Luke asked.

"I'm not." Amy said.

"You are."

"I'm not."

"You are."

She made a sigh of exasperation as Luke nudged Jane. "She flinches. Am I right?"

Before Jane could answer, Luke's cell phone rang. He fished it from his pocket and glanced at the number. "I gotta take this. Be right back."

He left the kitchen and Amy smiled at Jane. "Thanks for having me over for dinner."

"You're welcome." She studied the mess of pots and dishes scattered across the counter. "Your brother is an incredible cook but messy. So messy."

"He really is. I'll help you clean up."

"Don't be silly," Jane said. "I'll clean it up in the morning."

She sipped at her wine. "So, why *are* you flinching every time you sit down?"

Amy flushed bright red. "I'm not."

Jane just stared at her. When Amy drank the rest of her wine in three large swallows, Jane filled her glass again before topping off her own.

Amy glanced at the doorway to the kitchen before lowering her voice. "I – I went to Mark's club last night."

"By yourself?" Jane said.

"Yeah. I went because I wanted to find another Dom to, um, play with."

"I thought you were going to try the club I told you about."

"Well, I knew Mark wouldn't be there. He doesn't work at the club on Thursday nights. Only, his business partner Selene, texted him and told him I was there."

"Uh oh."

"Yeah, he came to the club right away. He was pissed with me."

Jane stood up and went to the doorway of the kitchen. She wandered into the hallway and returned a few seconds later. "Luke's in his office and from the sounds of it, he's going to be there for a while. Tell me what happened."

෧ ෨

"Well," Jane said ten minutes later, "I guess the question is – would you be fine with being his, uh, slave and not his girlfriend?"

Amy groaned. "God, when you say the word slave, it makes me feel like a freak."

"I'm sorry. I don't think you are. You know that, right?"

"I know, it's just... I shouldn't like this master/slave thing. Normal women don't like it."

"What's normal?" Jane challenged. "What's normal to one person could be completely strange to another. My friend Candy likes to have her toes sucked on during sex. I think that's weirder than the master/slave thing. You said your best friend is into the BDSM scene. What does she think of this?"

"I haven't told Valerie anything," Amy said. "I want to, I just – I would have to explain why I'd never told her about my crush on Mark. It just seems like it's too late to tell her, you know? She'd be hurt that I didn't tell her earlier."

"All right. Well, again, the question is – would you be happy just having him teach you how to be submissive?"

"I want to be in a relationship with him. I love him, and I always will. But his fear about losing Luke and our parents is heartbreaking and so real for him. I can't fully understand that fear, but I have to respect his feelings about it."

She traced her finger over the rim of the wine glass. "I'm going to say yes."

"Do you think that's a good idea?" Jane said. "You love him and the more you're with him, the harder it will be when it ends."

"I know. But it's the only way I can be with him, and who knows, maybe this will be enough for me. Maybe having Mark keep this strictly as a Dom/sub thing, will help. Maybe once we're finished, I can move on with my life."

"Do you really believe that?" Jane asked.

"I have to."

"What are you two whispering about?" Luke wandered back into the kitchen.

"Girl stuff," Amy said. "Thanks for dinner. It was really good."

"You're welcome." Luke sat next to Jane and put his arm around her. "You going to family dinner on Sunday?"

"Yes."

"Cool." Luke rubbed Jane's arm and pulled her a little closer.

Amy finished her wine and stood. "I'm gonna head home. Thanks again for dinner."

"Any time," Jane said.

"Bye, Lukie." Amy poked Luke in the shoulder.

"Later, Ames."

❧ ❦

Mark's car was parked on the street when she pulled into the driveway of her parents' home on Sunday night. Heat immediately wormed its way into her belly and she gripped the steering wheel.

Saturday night she'd texted Mark one word, "Yes". He hadn't replied to her text but an hour later, she'd received an email from him. Within the email was a written agreement for their master/slave relationship, a copy of his medical records and a request for her medical records as well as proof she was on birth control.

Her mouth had dropped open. He wanted her to sign an agreement for their proposed master/slave relationship. She had read through it three times.

There was a place for her to fill in her list of hard limits and soft limits and a spot for her signature at the bottom.

The written agreement had thrown her for a loop. She supposed a small part of her hoped that she'd be so good in bed that Mark couldn't help but ask for more – the relationship she wanted. Seeing what he wanted from her in writing had killed that part of her. She'd managed not to cry over it but hadn't yet been able to sign the agreement, and not just because she wasn't even sure what her hard and soft limits were.

She shut the car off and climbed out. She couldn't sit in her damn car all night. The front door opened just as she reached for it and she smiled at her dad.

"Hey, Dad."

"Hey, sweetie. Come in out of the cold." He kissed her cheek, took her jacket, and sent her toward the kitchen.

Her brother, Jane and Mark were already sitting at the table. She took the seat across from Mark as her mother smiled at her. "Hi, honey."

"Hi, Mom. Sorry I'm late."

"It's fine. I love your outfit. Did you design and sew the skirt yourself?" Her mother asked.

"Yes."

"It's so pretty. You really should look at creating this kind of stuff for the business."

"Our clients like work attire," Luke said.

"I bet they would like the other stuff Amy makes too." Her mother gave her a supportive smile.

"Maybe," Luke shrugged, "but right now we're concentrating on expanding internationally with the business attire. Maybe next year we'll look at doing a casual wear line."

Her father joined them, grabbing his seat at the head of the table. Amy stole a quick glance at Mark. He was staring at her and the heat in his gaze made her body buzz with need and anticipation. She quickly looked away, afraid the lust on her face would be apparent to everyone if she didn't stop staring at him.

"Dig in," her mom said.

Her mother was an amazing cook. The smell of the food should have been making her mouth water and her stomach growl. Instead, all she could think about was Mark. About the way it felt when he spanked her and fucked her and called her his little slave. Her pussy clenched around nothing and she squirmed in her seat as she took the dish of green beans from her father.

"Honey, what's wrong?" Her mother said.

"What?" Amy glanced up. "Nothing - nothing's wrong."

"Are you sure? Your cheeks are flushed. Are you coming down with the flu that's been going around? Mrs. Nemeth next door has a terrible case of it. She's been in bed since Thursday."

"No, I don't have the flu," Amy said. "It's just warm in here."

Luke leaned around Jane and studied Amy's face. "If you're getting sick, go sit in the living room. I don't want your germs."

"Shut up. I'm not sick."

Luke passed Jane the platter of roast beef. "I'm sure that's what Typhoid Mary said too."

"Jane, dear, how are you doing?" Clara asked. "Have you started your accounting classes yet?"

"Not yet," Jane replied. "I start them in the spring."

"Lovely," Clara said. "Are you enjoying working for Mark again."

"I am." Jane smiled at Mark. "He's a much nicer boss than my previous one."

"Hey," Luke said, "I'm just as nice as Mark."

There was silence around the table. Luke laughed. "Someone agree with me for God's sake. Mom?"

"I'm sure you have many other excellent qualities as a boss, dearest," Clara said.

Everyone laughed, and Amy stole another glance at Mark. He was still staring at her with pure hunger, and she licked her lips before pushing the potatoes around on her plate with her fork.

"Pass the butter, please, Amy."

Her hand reached for the butter dish before Mark even finished speaking. He was using his Dom voice and it had the same affect on her it always did. Jane's hand grazed hers as she reached for the butter and the smaller woman made a sound of apology. Jane's face was flushed, and she was staring at Mark with a mixture of confusion and disbelief.

If she hadn't been so damn horny, Amy would have laughed. It was almost comforting to know she wasn't the only one being affected by Mark and his damn Dom voice. Her mother seemed entirely unaffected – Christ, how awkward would it be if she wasn't - but Jane obviously wasn't immune to it despite her love for Luke.

She handed the butter to Mark, goose bumps popping up on her arm when his fingers brushed against hers.

"Thank you, Amy."

Oh God. That damn voice.

"You're welcome."

Could the others hear the lust in her voice? Her family seemed oblivious, but Jane's cheeks grew even more flushed.

"Oh goodness, now Jane's face is red." Clara's voice was tinged with worry. "Are you feeling all right?"

"I knew you were Typhoid Mary." Luke pressed his hand against Jane's forehead.

"I'm not sick," Jane said. "It's really warm in here."

"Mark, dearest, open the window, would you?" Clara said.

Mark stood and opened the window over the sink. Amy stared at his ass before dragging her gaze away. She held her fork with grim doggedness and poked at the roast beef on her plate.

She'd be lucky if she survived dinner.

❧ ❦

Amy slipped into her childhood bedroom and shut the door. Her parents had converted her room to her mother's sewing room, but she still took comfort in being in here. There was a long wooden table against the far wall and she crossed the room to it. Neat squares of fabric were lined up on the far end of the table, right next to the sewing machine.

She picked up one of the pieces and smiled a little. Seeing the piles of fabric brought back so many childhood memories. Playing on the floor of the sunroom with pieces of fabric as her mother sewed on her sewing machine and sang under her breath. She had five quilts given to her by her mother and she cherished each of them.

The door opened, and she didn't have to turn around to know it was him. Of course it was him. She could tell herself that she had slipped out of the living room as the others watched TV so she could have a moment to herself, but it was a lie.

"Hello, Amy."

Goosebumps poked to life on her skin. "You have to stop doing that."

"Stop doing what?" He was directly behind her now and she closed her lips against the moan when his arm slid around her waist and gripped her hip. His erection pressed against her ass.

"Using your damn Dom voice at the dinner table. Looking at me that way."

"What way am I looking at you?" His other hand brushed her hair away from her neck. His tongue licked the fluttering pulse at the base of her throat.

"Like you – oh god," his hand cupped her breast and squeezed, "like you want to have sex with me."

"I do want to have sex with you." He pulled her tight against him and she ground her ass against his cock. "But you haven't signed the agreement."

"It surprised me," she admitted.

"I just want to be clear about what this is. It's standard for a master/slave relationship."

"Right," she said.

"Have you changed your mind?" His fingers which had been pulling her nipple into a hard bud through her clothing, stilled.

"No. I just – I wasn't sure what to put down for hard and soft limits," she said.

"We can talk about it together, if you'd like."

"I – yeah, I would like that."

He kissed her throat and she relaxed against him, staring at the far wall where posters of Michael Jackson – her favourite singer when she was a teen – used to hang.

"When did you start seeing me as more than Luke's bratty little sister?"

"It was in the summer. A Tuesday. Michael had been arrested for selling drugs the week before and I was still pissed and upset. I went to your place and you were the only one home. You knew I was upset, but I refused to talk about it. Your mom's macaroni and cheese was my favourite food, and you decided to make it for me to cheer me up. It tasted so bad."

"I remember that day. The pasta *was* gross. I really can't cook at all."

His low laugh warmed her. "We watched TV together on the couch and you didn't push me to talk. You just snuggled up to me and rubbed my back while we watched TV. I looked at you and I just…"

"Just what?"

"Realized you were super hot and got an immediate boner."

She laughed. "That's romantic."

"What? I had a hot girl rubbing my back. What do you expect?"

He nuzzled her neck. "I felt guilty as hell."

"Why?"

"Because you were Luke's baby sister. Because you were only seventeen."

"I turned eighteen like a week later."

"When did you realize you were attracted to me?" He asked.

"The summer I applied for design school."

He didn't reply, and she pressed her ass against his still-hard cock. "Do you remember how often you slept over at our place? Even when you were in your twenties?"

"Yeah. Michael was living at home again and I was trying to avoid him. He got mean when he was high."

"I'm sorry." She rubbed his hand that was gripping her hip.

"It was a long time ago. Finish what you were saying."

There was just a hint of his Dom side in his voice, but she could feel wetness dampening her panties.

"When you slept over, I used to lie in my bed at night after everyone had gone to sleep and pretend that you snuck into my room."

His fingers traced her collarbone before slipping under the neckline of her shirt and into her bra cup. He pinched her nipple and she moaned, her back arching.

"Keep going, little slave."

"Even as a teenager and a virgin I knew I – I liked things a little different," she whispered. "In my fantasy, you would climb into my bed and tell me that I was a bad girl and you were going to punish me."

"How did I punish you?" His hand switched to her other breast and toyed with her nipple.

"You said I had to have sex with you. I would pretend that I didn't want to. I told you that I was a virgin and wanted to wait. That I wasn't attracted to you."

The hand around her hip slid inside her skirt. "Open your legs, little slave."

She spread her legs and moaned when he cupped her pussy through her panties.

"What did I do then?" His finger rubbed her clit through the wet material and she dug her nails into his arm.

"You pinned my arms above my head and used your other hand to pull my legs apart. I would struggle but you were much stronger than me. You'd slide your hand up my nightgown and touch my pussy. Then you'd show me how wet I was for you. You'd make me suck your fingers clean. Then you'd strip off my nightgown and touch my breasts and my pussy until I was begging for you to fuck me."

She arched her hips into his hand. "I would masturbate to that fantasy every time you spent the night."

She moaned in disappointment when he pulled

his hand out from under her skirt. His fingers weaved into her hair and he pulled her head back before biting her neck. "You've been a bad girl, little slave."

Every muscle in her body clenched in pleasure and she could barely form words. "I – no, I haven't."

"You have." His other hand was still teasing her nipple and he gave it a hard pinch. "You've taken much too long to sign the agreement, you didn't send me your medical records and you haven't given me an adequate explanation for failing to do so."

"I," she moaned when he pinched her nipple again, "I'm clean and I'm on birth control."

"Good," he said. "Because I'm going to fuck you right here and I don't want anything between my cock and my slave's tight pussy."

"Mark, we can't. Everyone's just – oh, fuck, ouch!"

He had pulled her hair hard. Even as pain tingled along her scalp, she could feel her pussy grow wetter.

"Try again, slave."

"I'm sorry, Sir."

"Better." He released her and stepped back. She twisted her head to stare at him in confusion.

"Mar – Sir, what are you doing?"

"Bend over the table." His hands were unbuttoning his jeans.

Amy! You can't do this! Your family is downstairs. What if your mom decides to look for you? You know the TV will only distract her for so

—

"Bend over. I won't ask you again."

She bent over the table immediately, placing her hands flat against the table as Mark tugged her skirt up over her hips. She was wearing a thong and he rubbed his hand over her ass cheeks. The light bruise had already faded, and the tenderness had disappeared.

"Are you wet for me, little slave?"

"Yes, Sir."

"Show me."

She spread her legs wide. He rubbed the wet fabric that covered her pussy and she moaned quietly and arched her back.

"Hold your panties to the side so your Master can fuck you."

A hot blush rising in her cheeks, she pulled her panties to the side. The head of Mark's cock brushed against the back of her hand and then it was sliding into her wet pussy, stretching her walls, and making her want to cry out like a cat in heat.

She gripped the table with her free hand as he sheathed himself completely within her hot core. His hands took her hips and lifted her until she was on her tiptoes.

"Good." His voice was hoarse, and his hand smoothed along her ass for a moment. "Listen very carefully to me, little slave."

"Yes, Master."

"You are not allowed to come."

She froze and lifted her head to glare at him over her shoulder. "What? No, that's not fair!"

"You're being punished, remember?"

"Then just spank me for God's sake."

"No. If you're a good girl and don't come, I will consider allowing you to come the next time we're together."

"The next time... no. No fucking way am I waiting until the next time." She glared at him and tried to straighten. "Let me up. If you think I'm going to...oh god!"

Mark had pushed her back down to the table. He held her there with one heavy hand in the middle of her back and made two deep, hard thrusts into her pussy.

"Oh, oh fuck, that's good," she moaned.

He slid in and out of her with long, smooth strokes. Her anger forgotten, she met each of his strokes with eagerness. When he stopped, she made a low cry of need.

"Please, Master!"

"No," he said. He pulled out until just the head of his cock was in her. She whined in disappointment and tried to thrust back, but his hand kept her pinned to the table. "You are not allowed to come. Do you understand, slave?"

"Please, please let me come," she whispered.

"No." His voice was stern, loving, cruel. "Tell me you'll be my good girl, or I'll stop fucking you right now."

Her pussy clenched around him at the thought. She needed to be fucked. She needed to come but if she couldn't have that, she'd at least take the fucking. She'd spent years dreaming about Mark fucking her in her bedroom. She wanted it to be a reality.

"Will you be my good girl?" He asked.

"Yes, Master." She wrapped her fingers tighter around the fabric of her panties. The urge to rub her clit was nearly overwhelming in its intensity. She ignored it and gripped the edge of the table with her other hand as Mark fucked her with a hard and deep rhythm.

She was unbelievably grateful when after only a few minutes, he stiffened behind her, pushed in deep and came with a low moan of pleasure. Her pussy milked his cock eagerly even as it ached for relief.

He pulled out and helped her straighten up from the table. She moved her panties back into place as he pulled her skirt down. She stared mutely at him as he buttoned and zipped his jeans.

He smiled at her. "Well done, little slave."

She didn't reply. She was already trying to determine how quickly she could get the fuck out of here and go home. She was planning on having a very long session with her goddamn vibrator.

Mark reached out and cupped her face, tipping her head up until she was staring at him. "Your orgasms belong to me. You are not allowed to have one unless I'm there."

Her mouth dropped open. "I – what?"

"No masturbating tonight, little slave."

"Mark, no! That's not fair. I can't - "

"Keep arguing with me and I won't let you come the next three times I fuck you."

She shut her mouth immediately. He was telling the truth, she could see it in his face.

"Good girl." He pressed a fleeting kiss against

her mouth. "You go downstairs first."

Her legs trembling, she slipped out of the room.

Chapter Ten

He hadn't planned on fucking Amy in her childhood bedroom. Just like he hadn't planned to leave her parents' house and drive straight to hers. But, here he was, sitting at her kitchen table and waiting for her to get home. He had a key to her place, just like she had one to his, but he'd never used the key without at least texting her first.

He shifted in the chair and rubbed at his cock. He was hard and throbbing despite fucking her earlier. God, the way she had sounded when she told him about her fantasy. He hadn't worked up the nerve to tell her he'd had similar fantasies. Maybe because her fantasy about him sounded light and sweet and his fantasies about her were just... dark.

He told himself to avoid touching her until she'd signed the agreement. He'd fucked that up royally, but he'd spent most of Sunday in a state of weird anxiety as he checked his email repeatedly. As the hours passed, his anxiety had turned to panic. Even now, he could feel that panic lurking just below the surface of his skin. What if she didn't sign the agreement? What if she changed her mind? He would go crazy if she showed up at the club and played with another Dom. Hell, he'd go crazy if she went to another club. Amy was his and he wasn't –

Stop it! She's not yours. She's not yours and she never can be. You need to stop this madness. Do you really think you can treat Amy like she's a toy to play with? You love her and -

He shut down his inner voice. It was just a desperate attempt to keep Amy from the wrong Dom that had made him offer her the master/slave thing. Well, maybe not just desperation. He wanted Amy to be his slave, he wanted Amy tied to his bed moaning and crying out for him to fuck her. He wanted to spank her and collar her and teach her the art of submission. He wanted all of those things. He wanted more.

He tugged at his earlobe before pulling his cell phone out of his pocket. This was all he could have with Amy and he would enjoy it for as long as she agreed to it. Maybe after a month or two, they would be satisfied and the attraction would end. Maybe it wasn't really love he felt but a lust so intense it only masqueraded as love.

You're an idiot. You know that, right?

He was saved from answering by the sound of Amy's key in the door. He stared at his cell phone, his heart bang, bang, banging in his chest. It had nearly killed him not to let Amy come earlier but she needed to learn to obey him. Still, he couldn't stand the thought of making her wait to orgasm.

So, here he was. Sitting in her kitchen like he belonged there, staring at his phone with an air of indifference while his heart threatened to beat right out of his damn chest.

"Mark?" Her voice was tinged with surprise. "What are you doing here?"

"In your bedroom, slave position." He didn't look up from his phone, scrolling across the screen without seeing anything on it.

She walked out of the kitchen immediately. He gave her a few extra minutes, knowing the objects he'd placed on her bed would make her pause. After an agonizing ten minutes, he stood and walked to her bedroom. She had left the door open and it was almost impossible to keep the impassive look on his face as he entered the room.

She was naked and kneeling next to the bed. Her lush, smooth thighs were spread wide, giving him a gorgeous view of her pussy. He studied the short patch of light blonde curls above her mound before raising his gaze to her tits. Fuck, he loved her tits. Her pink nipples were hard, and he could barely control his urge to drop to his knees in front of her and suck on them. His erection was huge, his cock pressing against the denim with painful intensity.

He stood in front of her. Her hands rested against her thighs, palms up, and she held her head up but kept her eyes lowered. She was a fast learner. He was almost disappointed by that. The longer it took her to learn how to be submissive, the longer he had with her.

Her cheeks were red, but she didn't move when

he reached out and petted her hair. "Very good, little slave."

She had a vanity in the far corner with a wooden chair. Leaving Amy on her knees, he crossed the room and picked up the chair, carrying it over and setting it about five feet away from her. He picked up his collar and the paddle from the bed. The paddle was round and made of leather with a short handle. He returned to her and held it where he knew her downcast gaze could see it. Her cheeks pinked more, and his cock protested the confinement of his jeans.

Just thinking about the way her ass would look when he was finished made his dick throb and his balls tightened. He petted her hair again before moving to the chair and sitting down. He was antsy with anticipation and need, and he made himself take a few deep breaths to calm down. He needed to keep his control. Just because he was in Amy's bedroom, just because she was naked and on her knees and every part of him was screaming to fuck her perfect, pink, pussy, he couldn't lose control.

He was living out one of his biggest fantasies, but he also had a job to do. He had done this countless times before with new submissives. This wasn't any different.

Bullshit. This isn't some random submissive. This is Amy. The woman you love.

He shoved aside his inner voice. "Look at me, slave."

She raised her gaze to him. Her blue eyes held anticipation, fear, desire.

"Come."

She started to stand, and he shook his head. She hesitated and then dropped to her hands and knees and crawled towards him. He stared at her breasts and the seductive sway of her hips. The pressure in his groin was unbearable and he had to adjust his jeans. A quick, smug smile crossed her face and he almost laughed. God, she would be a handful as a submissive. He was more than up to the challenge of taming her.

She stopped in front of him and assumed the slave position, staring fixedly at his chest as he tapped the paddle against his own thigh. Her gaze flickered to the paddle and he could see her body tense.

He held the paddle out to her. "Hold this, little slave."

She took it from him gingerly, almost as if it would burn her. Relief crossed her face. The paddle was light in weight and he knew she thought it meant it would hurt less. She wasn't completely wrong. A wooden paddle would hurt more but the leather one she held in her hands would still deliver a satisfying sting.

He leaned forward, groaning at the pressure it put on his dick, and buckled the collar around her neck. The moment it was fastened, some of his tension ease. Amy was wearing his collar. She belonged to him and any Dom who saw her would know she was taken.

"Are you ready for your punishment?"

She stared up at him without invitation, but he let it slide. "I've already been punished, Sir."

He mentally added five spanks to her

punishment. "Have you?"

"Yes. Earlier. You wouldn't let me come, remember, Sir?"

Her tone made him itch to push her over his knee and start spanking her immediately, but he said, "That was punishment for not signing the agreement in a timely manner."

"I haven't done anything else to deserve punishment."

Another five spanks were added.

He leaned forward. Her blonde hair was in a clip and he released the clip and tossed it aside. He slid his hand into her silky hair and pulled her head back with a sharp and painful tug. She winced but he saw a flash of desire in her eyes before she gave him an impudent look.

"What were you going to do when you came home, slave?"

"I – nothing, Sir."

He tugged on her hair again. "You weren't going to masturbate?"

"No." She cast her eyes to the left and he cupped her breast with his other hand and squeezed.

"Look at me, little slave."

She dragged her gaze back to his.

"Are you telling me that you weren't going to touch your perfect, little pussy – which belongs to me, by the way – with your soft fingers until you came all over them?"

"No, Sir."

He pinched her nipple. She winced and gave him a defiant look. "I was going to use my vibrator, Sir."

His snort of laughter escaped before he could stop it. Her cheeky and way-too-adorable grin dropped from her face when he said, "In the last two minutes, you've added ten spanks to your punishment. That just got you another ten."

Her lips pressed together and the defiance in her eyes faded. He rubbed his thumb across her cheekbone. "Time for your punishment, slave. Lie across my lap."

She hesitated. "Will you kiss me first, Mark? I mean…Sir?"

Without speaking, he shifted forward on the chair until she was wedged between his legs. He took the paddle from her and tucked it under his thigh before brushing her hair away from her face. He bent his head and pressed his mouth against hers. She moaned and returned his kiss, licking at his mouth with her soft tongue. He sucked on her tongue when she pushed it into his mouth. She rubbed her tits against his chest and he cupped her breast, pulling and tugging on her nipple as he tasted every part of her sweet mouth. He put his arms around her and reached down to rub and massage her ass, increasing the blood flow in preparation for his spanking. When she was clutching at his thighs and making low groans of need, he pulled away. He ran his fingers over her mouth before sitting back in the chair and patting his lap.

This time there was no hesitation. She stood and draped her body over his lap. Her head hung down and he threaded his hand around her collar and tugged. "Look at the mirror, little slave."

He had deliberately placed the chair near the full-length mirror in her room. She shook her head. "No, I don't want to."

He spanked her left cheek with his hand. She squealed, and he tugged on her collar again. "Look."

She turned her head and stared at their images. Her face flushed red, but he smiled at her and smoothed his hand over her ass. "You're beautiful."

"Thank you, Sir," she whispered.

"You're welcome." He kept his hand around her collar, keeping her head twisted toward the mirror as he spanked her again. She squeaked out another cry but watched in the mirror as he spanked her a third time. When he released her collar and pressed his hand against her lower back to steady her on her lap, she continued to stare into the mirror.

"Good girl," he praised before spanking her again. He spanked each cheek five times, reveling in her little squeals of pain and the way her body twitched. He continued to spank her until her ass was a warm, rosy red. He stopped and pushed his hand between her legs.

"Oh, oh please, Sir" she immediately begged.

She was soaking wet and he thumbed her clit before sliding his finger into her pussy. She squeezed around him and he gave her a few hard strokes with his finger before pulling it away.

"No! Please, Sir!" She cried.

"What's your safe word, little slave?"

"Magnolia, Sir." Her eyes grew round when he

pulled the paddle out from under his thigh.

He ran it over the backs of her thighs as she stiffened.

"Sir?"

"Twenty strokes with the paddle," he said. "You're going to count

"Sir, I - "

"You will count out loud, little slave. If you miss one, another will be added to your punishment. Do you understand?"

"Yes, Sir."

"Very good." He spanked her left cheek with the paddle. It made a low thud against her flesh that made his cock twitch with anticipation.

She cried out, her back arching before she moaned, "One, Sir."

"Very good, little slave," he praised before spanking her again.

"Two, Sir!"

He spanked her again and again, each one driving his need for her higher. He kept the spanking lighter than he normally would. The paddle produced a harder, deeper pain than spanking with his hand and he didn't want to bruise her. Spanking Amy was a huge turn on for him and he'd rather spank her lightly and more often, than harder and be forced to wait until the bruises abated. He had debated whether she was even ready for the paddle. In the end, unable to resist, he had decided to use it. Staring at the bright red blotches the paddle left on her ass sent fresh excitement through him. He spanked her again.

"Ten!" He could hear the waver in her voice

and he pushed his hand between her legs and rubbed at her pussy.

She moaned and squirmed against his hand. She was so wet, she was leaving a damp spot on his jeans. He groaned inwardly. Fuck, he needed to finish spanking her before he came in his pants like a fucking teenager.

"You're doing very well, little slave," he said as he brushed his hand over her bright red ass. "Only ten more."

"Please, Sir," she begged.

Her head was hanging down and he used her collar to gently tug it up to study her face in the mirror. Her eyes were bright with tears and he could see the wet tracks on her cheeks.

Worried that she was trying to take too much, he did something he never did during a play session.

He broke it.

"Amy, baby, do you need to stop?"

"No, I – no, I don't want to stop yet."

He rubbed her lower back. "Are you sure?"

"Yes. I didn't say my safe word. I can take more." He could hear the impatience in her voice.

God, she was so fucking beautiful and strong.

He spanked her again, letting the rhythm take over as she counted out each spank with increasing urgency. At thirteen, she reached behind her to try and protect her ass. He pinned her wrists against her lower back with one hard hand, relishing the power over her as she kicked her feet and shouted out the fourteenth spank.

By the twentieth spank she was slumped against his lap, shuddering and panting heavily. He dropped the paddle and rubbed her ass, giving her some time to catch her breath. She winced and tried to pull away and he switched to rubbing the back of her thighs.

"Stand up, little slave," he said.

"I can't."

"You can. Just for a minute," he said.

She moaned her displeasure as he helped her stand. Her legs were trembling, and she swayed like she was standing on the deck of a ship. "Please, Sir."

She clutched at his shoulders for balance as he unbuttoned and unzipped his jeans. He shoved them and his briefs down his legs and kicked them off before pulling his shirt over his head.

"Please, Sir," Amy whispered. Her hand was inching toward her pussy and he pulled it away before sitting on the chair again.

"Straddle me."

She did what he asked, and he helped steady her with one hand on her hip as the other held the base of his cock. He guided it into her pussy as she eased down. She moaned in sheer delight as he filled her. He clenched his teeth against the groan that wanted to escape. Her pussy was smooth, warm and oh-so-fucking tight.

He was sheathed completely in her and he made a few thrusts. She cried out and, despite how badly she was shaking, used her legs to bounce up and down on him.

"Oh fuck," he moaned. "Stop moving, slave."

She made a noise of frustration but obeyed him. He closed his eyes and thought about spreadsheets, numbers, the weird noise coming from his furnace that he really needed to have someone look at.

When he had a little more control, he opened his eyes. Amy's hand was sliding toward her pussy again and he grabbed both of her hands and yanked them behind her back. He held them with one hard hand and pulled until her back arched.

"Mark, please!"

He spanked her ass with his other hand and she squealed in pain and clenched around him so tightly that he nearly shot his load into her.

"Master! I'm sorry!" She cried out.

He bent his head and sucked one hard nipple into his mouth. Her cries of pleasure and the way her pussy squeezed and released him were pushing him toward his orgasm, even though neither of them were moving.

He raised his head and tightened his hand around her wrists before cupping her pussy with his other hand. He let his fingers rest against her clit but didn't move them. "Your pussy belongs to me."

"Yes, Sir," she moaned.

"You are not to touch it unless I give you permission. Do you understand, little slave?"

"Please!" She rubbed herself against his hand and he pinched her clit hard between his fingertips. She cried out and froze against him.

"Look at me."

She bit her bottom lip before opening her eyes. Her magnificent breasts were heaving for air, her cheeks were bright red, and a tear was sliding down her face. "Please, Master, I need to come."

"Whose pussy is this?"

"My Master's."

"Louder, little slave."

"My Master's!" She shouted. "It's my Master's pussy!"

"Good girl." He released her clit and she cried out with a combination of relief and pure need.

He thrust back and forth. Her pussy clenched around him like a vise and he stared at her bouncing breasts as he fucked her. Christ, he couldn't last a goddamn second longer. He reached for her clit again and whispered, "Come for me, little slave."

He gave her clit two hard strokes with his thumb. She screamed and came immediately, her pussy clamping around his dick in a stranglehold. He released her wrists and grabbed her hips, holding her still as he fucked her twice more before climaxing with a primal roar of hunger and lust.

She collapsed against him, resting her head against his shoulder as he pumped in and out of her with slow strokes. He rubbed her back and kissed her neck. "Stand up, Ames."

"Can't," she mumbled into his shoulder.

He grinned and hooked his hands under her thighs before standing. She squealed and clung to his thick neck. "Mark! Put me down."

"You said you couldn't stand, remember?"

"I'm too heavy to be carried. You're going to hurt yourself."

He nipped at her shoulder. "Say that again and I'll spank you."

She winced. "Please don't. My butt is on fire right now."

He carried her to the bed and set her next to it.

She held on to the bed post as he pulled the quilt and sheets back. "Get in, Ames."

She climbed gingerly into the bed, lying on her side with her back to him. She was shaking, and he pulled the leather bag he'd brought from the car closer to the bed and opened it. There was a bottle of aloe vera gel and a couple of bottles of water. He opened the water.

"Sit up."

She propped her upper half up on her hip, trying to keep pressure off her ass. He held the bottle to her mouth. "Drink."

She drank almost half of it and he smoothed the strands of hair away from her face. She was still trembling, and he debated for a moment before reaching back into the bag. She hadn't gone into subspace, but it wouldn't hurt to give her chocolate. He produced a plastic bag of small pieces of dark chocolate. He handed her a square.

"Eat this."

She gave him a quizzical look and he said, "Eat, Amy."

As she popped the chocolate into her mouth, he poured some Aloe Vera gel onto his hands and smoothed it over her red ass. She winced and returned to lying on her side. When he was finished, he drank some water and rubbed her lower back before shutting off the light and climbing into the bed behind her. He caressed her hip and her side, keeping his touch gentle.

"Are you leaving now?" Her voice was low.

He needed to say yes. He didn't sleep with the slaves he trained. He had a play session, provided aftercare and then left. But the thought of leaving Amy, of getting dressed and driving home in the cold and the dark, made his insides clench. He wrapped his arm around her waist and pressed up against her.

She winced at the pressure on her butt but didn't move away. He nuzzled the back of her shoulder. "Do you want me to?"

"You know I don't."

"Then I'll stay."

She relaxed into him. He thought she'd fallen asleep when her voice drifted out of the dark. "What are your hard limits?"

"Incest play, and blood play are the top two," he said.

She shuddered against him. "Gross."

I have a more detailed list that I can give you to look at," he said. "I can explain what each one is."

"Okay. I can do some research on my own as well."

"I'll send you some links to a few BDSM sites that have good information." He kissed the back of her shoulder. "There's a lot to sift through."

"Right. Can I ask you something else?"

"Of course."

"That night that I was at the club, when we, uh, watched the show together. Do you remember?"

"Anytime you come all over my hand, I'm gonna remember."

He could almost feel the heat of her blush. "Anyway, the lady beside us - "

"Mistress Trina."

"Yeah. Her, um, slave had glitter on his mouth

after he went down on her. Why?"

He rubbed her smooth hip. "Some mistresses put glitter on their pussies. When their slave eats their pussy, the glitter gets all over their mouth and face. People know what he's done, and they know he belongs to her."

She started to giggle, and he squeezed her hip. "What?"

"You're not going to put glitter on your dick, are you?"

"No. Definitely not."

"Good. Because I hate glitter. It's like the STD of the art world. Once you have it, you never get rid of it."

He laughed so hard the bed shook. "Where did you come up with that?"

She grinned over her shoulder at him. "I don't know. Internet probably."

He wanted to kiss her. He wanted to make her come again. He wanted to fuck her.

No, he wanted to make love to her.

For the first time in years, he wanted vanilla sex. Panic settled in his stomach like a brick. He must have stiffened because her smile died. "What's wrong?"

"We should talk about what nights we play together."

"Can't we just figure it out as we go?"

"No." He needed to keep this professional, needed to remember that this wasn't a relationship. "I have a busy schedule and I'm sure you do as well."

His voice had turned colder than he meant, but

he was rattled by his urge to have normal sex with Amy. She heard the coldness and scooted away from him, wrapping the covers around her body like a shield.

"Amy, - "

"It's fine," she said. "I guess probably just a couple nights a week, right? So, we don't interrupt our busy schedules."

"I don't mean to - "

"My ass probably can't take more than a couple spankings a week anyway," she continued as if he hadn't spoken. "You work at the club Friday and Saturday nights, and Sunday nights probably don't really work because of family dinner. I have pottery on Monday nights. So, what about Tuesday and Wednesday?"

Her tone was brisk and business like, but he could hear the hurt lurking beneath it.

"Tuesdays work but Wednesdays don't."

"Thursday?"

"Sure." She hadn't asked why he couldn't make Wednesday, but he told her anyway. Maybe revealing something personal would ease the coldness that was now in *her* voice. "I have an Al-Anon meeting every Wednesday night."

"I didn't know you went to Al-Anon meetings," she said.

"I've been going for a few years," he said. "Luke knows but I asked him not to tell anyone."

"Does it help?"

"A surprising amount."

"Good," she said. "I'm glad that it helps."

There was silence between them for a few

minutes before she said, "So, Tuesday and Thursday then?"

"Sure."

"My place or yours?"

"Tuesday at my place and Thursday at yours." He lived downtown, and parking was a bitch, but he still wanted Amy at his place. If only to have her scent in his sheets.

"All right."

Another beat of silence and he was just about to move closer to her when she said, "I'm sorry, but I think I've changed my mind about you staying the night. I have a busy day tomorrow and I need to sleep well. I'm not used to someone in my bed with me so..."

"Oh, uh, sure," he said.

"Do you mind?"

"No, of course not. I understand."

Feeling sick to his stomach, he climbed out of bed and turned on the lamp on her nightstand. He dressed quickly and stuffed the paddle and the aloe vera gel into his bag. She had taken off his collar and, without looking at him, held it out.

"Don't forget this."

He took it and stuffed it into the bag. Fuck, he had screwed up already. "Amy, I'm sorry."

She turned and gave him a too-big-too-bright smile. "You have nothing to be sorry about. I really enjoyed tonight."

"No, I mean - "

"Do you need me to walk you out?" She said.

"No. Stay in bed."

"Thanks." She turned away and pulled the

covers to her shoulders. "Good night. I'll see you at the office tomorrow."

Chapter Eleven

"Mark?"

He looked up from his computer. Chloe was standing in his doorway.

"Hey. Come on in."

"Thanks." She sat down and gave him a curious look. "You feeling okay?"

"Fine," he said. He tugged at his earlobe and then cracked his neck. After Amy had kicked him out of her bed last night, he'd gone home and tossed and turned until morning. He was exhausted and already wishing he would be back in Amy's bed tonight. This time he would keep his fucking idiot mouth shut and maybe she'd let him spend the night.

It's Monday, asshole. You won't even see her tonight.

"Mark?"

He shook away the cobwebs and reached for his mug. The coffee was cold, but he drank down a gulp of it anyway. "Sorry. Didn't sleep well last night."

"That's okay."

"How's the new job going?"

"Good, I think," she said. "I've started on my marketing plan for how we're going to debut the new digital storefront. I've been going over inventory and making a list of our best sellers. I need to talk to Ms. Dawson about the new line coming up. I was thinking we could debut the new digital storefront at the same time as the new line. It'll give us extra bang for our buck, you know?"

He nodded, only half listening. He'd sent Amy some BDSM sites by email this morning. She had replied with a short 'thanks' and nothing else. He wondered if she'd looked at them yet.

"I'll come by later."

He jolted in his seat and drank another swallow of bitter coffee. "Chloe, wait. Sorry, my head isn't in the game today."

"That's okay." She hesitated. "I came here to ask you for a personal favour anyway, not talk about work."

"What do you need?"

"A ride to the meeting on Wednesday night," she said. "My car is in the shop and I think you live downtown, right? I'm downtown too so if you don't mind giving me a ride, I'd really appreciate it."

"I don't," he said. "I'll pick you up around 6:30. Text me your address."

"Thanks so much," she said. "I didn't want to miss the meeting."

"It's no problem at all." He hesitated and then said, "I told Amy about going to Al-Anon."

Chloe gave him a puzzled look. "Um, okay."

Shit, what was wrong with him? He couldn't talk to Chloe about Amy. He was losing his fucking mind.

"Sir! Sir, you cannot go in there! Sir!"

Chloe swung around in her seat and stared at the man who stumbled into Mark's office. Brenda, their receptionist, was right behind them and she gave Mark a flustered look. "Mark, this man insists on seeing you. He wouldn't wait for me to call you. Should I call security?"

"No," Mark said. "It's fine, Brenda."

"Yeah, Brenda," the man said. "I told you it was fine. He's my goddamn brother."

"Michael! Lower your voice," Mark said.

"Sure, Mark. Sure. Hey, I need to talk to you."

Brenda walked away, giving Mark one last uncertain look. Chloe stood up as Michael looked her up and down.

"Well, hey there, pretty lady."

"Michael, enough," Mark said.

Michael held up his hands. "Whoa, okay, little brother. Is this your lady? Is that why you don't want me talkin' to her? Afraid big brother's gonna steal her away like I stole your girlfriends when we was kids?"

He burst into loud laughter and Mark winced before moving around his desk. As he drew closer to his brother, the smell washed over him. A combination of stale cigarette smoke, sweat and old pepperoni. He tried not to gag and was impressed by Chloe's stoicism when Michael moved even closer to her. Her small nose wrinkled a little, but she smiled at Michael when he stood in front of her.

"My baby brother gets real touchy about me goin' after his women. Mom always said I had the looks in the family and Mark had the brains." Michael grinned at Chloe and Mark winced again.

At some point in the last two months, he'd lost his front teeth. Either all the drugs had rotted them out or he'd lost them in a fight. His pupils were blown out and his too-thin face was covered in scabs. At one point, he had been a handsome man but that was years ago. Before the drugs took control.

"It's nice to meet you, Michael," Chloe said. She held out her hand and Michael studied it before shaking it with his dirty one. "My name is Chloe. I'm not Mark's girlfriend. I work with him."

"Oh. Nice to meetcha'. I like your hair."

"Thank you."

Michael reached out to touch a lock of her hair. Mark hurried toward them and grabbed his wrist in a hard grip. "Don't touch her, Michael."

He gave Mark a hurt look and yanked out of his grip. "Jesus, ya asshole, that fucking hurt."

"Chloe, can we talk later?" Mark asked.

"Of course, I - "

"No, stay!" Michael bellowed. "I ain't gonna be long and I hate to interrupt your meeting."

He grinned again at Chloe. "You're real pretty."

"Michael." Mark gave his brother a warning look.

"Fine." His voice was petulant. "I just need to borrow some cash."

"No."

"C'mon," Michael whined. "I just need like six hundred to get me through the next week. My rent is due and I ain't got no food. You want your brother to starve?"

Mark shook his head. "Any money I give you will go straight up your nose or into your veins. I told you the last time that I wouldn't give you cash for drugs anymore."

"It ain't for drugs," Michael protested. His tone turned wheedling, "I swear it ain't for drugs, Mark. C'mon, man. You want your big brother freezing to death on the streets? I know you got the cash, you're swimming in it. Loan me some and I'll pay you back next month. Swear to God."

His stomach churning, Mark said, "No, Michael. I'm done supporting your habit."

Michael's face twisted, turned dark and ugly. "This how you gonna treat your brother? The guy who looked after you when mom and dad died? I quit school and the football team to take care of you, didn't I? Got a job to keep a roof over your head so you could be somebody. And this is how you pay me back."

What Michael was saying was a distortion of the truth, but it still sent a hot blade of guilt through Mark's stomach. He took a deep breath. "I want to help you. Let me get you into that rehab facility. They can help you to - "

"I don't want to hear about the fuckin' rehab facility no more!" Michael shouted. "Jesus Christ, are you gonna give me some cash or not, ya big fuckin' crybaby?"

"No, I'm not."

"Asshole!" Michael's hands clenched into fists. Mark stepped between his brother and Chloe, keeping Chloe tucked behind his broad body.

"Leave, Michael."

"Dad was right about you," Michael said. "You're a big whiney ass bitch who ain't never cared for his family."

"It's time for you to go." He took Michael's arm and steered him toward the door.

His brother stumbled over his own feet before yanking his arm out of his hand. "I don't need you to fucking hold onto me."

He stormed out of the office. Mark followed him to reception and pushed the elevator button. Thank Christ, the doors opened immediately. Michael staggered into the elevator, but when Mark went to follow him in, he shoved him hard in the chest.

"Fuck off! I don't need your fucking help! Stay in your office with your little redheaded fuck doll, you asshole!"

The doors shut on his brother's livid face and Mark rubbed at his chest before turning around. "I'm sorry, Brenda."

"Uh, that's okay," she said.

Embarrassment creeping into him, he headed down the hall and back to his office. Chloe was still standing there. She gave him a small smile. "So, that was Michael."

"I'm so sorry," he rasped out. Shame and embarrassment pulsed a hard beat in his chest. "Are you okay?"

"I'm fine," Chloe said. "Are you okay?"

"Yeah, I'm fine," he lied. "What Michael said wasn't true. He had problems with drugs before mom and dad died. He was kicked off the football team two weeks before the car crash, and the house was paid for by the life insurance. He didn't – he didn't give up his dreams for me. This isn't my fault."

"Hey." Chloe hurried over to him and hesitated before putting her thin arms around him. He stiffened and then wrapped his arms around her waist and buried his face in her neck.

"It's okay, you don't have to explain," she said as she patted his back. "You're right. None of this is your fault, honey. None of it. Michael makes his own choices."

"I can't keep giving him money. I can't keep enabling him." His voice was muffled against her skin.

"You did and said all the right things," she said.

He lifted his head and she reached up and cupped his face. "You did the right thing, Mark."

"Holy hell! What is that smell? Did you kill something in here... oh shit."

Luke, followed by Amy, had walked into his office. Mark immediately pushed away from Chloe, but it was too late. Her face pale, Amy turned around and walked out of his office.

"Ames! Hey, Ames – where are you going?" Luke called after her.

He couldn't hear Amy's reply, but Luke nodded. "Yeah, okay."

Chloe was already slipping by him and Luke

said, "I can come back if I'm interrupting something."

"You're not," Mark said.

"No, seriously, it's fine," Luke said.

"I need to get back to work," Chloe said. "Nice to see you again, Mr. Dawson."

"Bye, uh," Luke hesitated.

"Chloe. Chloe Matthews."

"Of course. Bye, Ms. Matthews."

Luke waited until she was gone and then closed the door. He grinned at him. "Guess I'm not the only one banging an employee, huh?"

"I'm not having sex with Chloe," Mark said.

He returned to his chair and dropped into it as Luke sat in one of the other chairs. "She's pretty."

"I'm not having sex with her."

"So you just randomly hug female employees in your office? Seems a little dangerous to me."

"I know Chloe from outside of work," he said.

"Oh. But you're not dating her?"

"No. I don't want her."

"Why not? She's hot and seems into you."

"I said I don't want her!"

"Okay, chill out," Luke said. "Still doesn't explain why you were hugging her. Or why your office smells so fucking bad."

"Michael was just here."

Luke gave him a sympathetic look. "Shit. That sucks."

"He was high and demanding money. He scared the hell out of Brenda and he kept trying to touch Chloe. He looked so bad, Luke. So old and, I don't know, faded, maybe? Like there's nothing left of the Michael I knew when we were kids. He's just gone."

Luke leaned forward and rested his elbows on his knees. "I think the old Michael has been gone for a really long time."

"Yeah, probably." Mark glanced at his watch. He needed to talk to Amy. To somehow explain why he was hugging Chloe, without breaking his promise to Chloe to keep the Al-Anon thing between them.

"Do you need to skip out on the meeting? I can come up with an excuse."

He stared blankly at Luke. "Meeting?"

"With Macy's," Luke said. "It's been on our calendars for weeks. We're going to discuss the new line."

"Right," Mark said. "Sorry, I forgot."

"It's fine. Why don't you go home? I'll cover the meeting on my own."

"I appreciate that, but no. I need to be at the meeting and we both know it."

"True," Luke said, "but – and don't take this the wrong way – if you can't concentrate on the meeting then there's no point in you going."

"I can do my job," Mark said.

"All right. C'mon, we're meeting them at their office. I'll drive."

∂∾ ∾∫

Amy stared out the window of her office. Her mind replayed the scene in Mark's office until she wanted to scream. Mark's arms around Chloe's slender waist. Her hand cupping his face. The way she looked at him.

It was only three, but she couldn't stay in the office a minute longer. Mark would be here any minute to try and explain what she had seen, she knew he would, and she wasn't interested. She was a fool for thinking that –

"Ms. Dawson?"

She whirled around and stared at the redhead standing in her doorway. "Now isn't a good time."

"We have a meeting at three." Chloe stepped into her office and shut the door. "To go over the designs you want to showcase with the new digital storefront."

Amy bit the inside of her cheek. "Reschedule it."

"Sure, I can do that," Chloe said.

She turned to leave and Amy said, "So sorry I interrupted your moment with Mark."

Amy! Stop it! You sound like a jealous little bitch.

She did. She totally did. But, hell, she *was* a jealous little bitch.

Chloe was studying her silently and Amy flushed. "Is there anything else? Because I'm very busy and I'm sure you want to get back to Mark's office."

Amy!

She could almost see the light turn on in Chloe's face and she groaned inwardly. Fuck, Mark was going to kill her. He didn't want a relationship with her, it was just sex between them. If he was thinking of trying to have a relationship with Chloe, her acting like a jealous girlfriend was a real shit thing to do.

It's a real shit thing for him to fuck you and date Chloe at the same time.

"My sister is an alcoholic, Ms. Dawson."

She jerked and stared at Chloe. "What?"

"My sister is an alcoholic. I go to an Al-Anon meeting every week. Specifically, I go to a Wednesday night meeting. That's how I know Mark. I asked him not to say anything to my new coworkers. But, Mark and I are just friends."

Dismay and relief ran through her at once. She groped for her chair and sank into it as Chloe moved closer to her desk. She eyed the beanbag chair then settled for leaning her hip against the desk. "I'm not romantically interested in Mark."

"Oh God," Amy buried her face in her hands, "I am such an idiot."

"I don't think so," Chloe said. "Just in love."

"You can't say anything to anyone," Amy said. "Especially not to my brother."

"I won't. Does Mark know you love him?"

"Yes."

"And he loves you?"

"I don't – no, he doesn't," Amy said.

"Are you sure?"

"Positive," Amy replied. "Fuck. I'm so sorry for what I said and the way I acted. I swear I'm not usually like this."

"It's fine. What you saw – it was just me comforting Mark from one sibling of an addict to another. I was in Mark's office when Michael showed up. He was high, and he demanded money. Mark said no, and Michael said some terrible things to him."

"Oh God. Poor Mark." She rubbed at her temples. "Is your sister doing better?"

"She was in rehab but left and relapsed."

"I really am sorry. You must think I'm a terrible person."

"I don't," Chloe said. "Actually, I'm a really big fan of yours."

"You are?"

"Yes." Chloe hesitated, "I'm in marketing, obviously, but I love design. I spent most of my childhood drawing and creating dresses for my Barbie dolls out of fabric."

"Me too," Amy said.

"Yeah?" Chloe gave her a look of delight. "Anyway, I applied to a few of the design school but never got accepted. I needed a degree, so I went into marketing. It's been good and I like it, but it's not my passion, you know?"

"I do," Amy said.

"I was really excited to get the job here. Not that I'm involved in the design or anything, but just working at Dawson Clothing and getting to meet my idol has been incredible."

She stopped as her cheeks went pink. "Oh God, I sound like a crazed stalker. I'm not, I swear."

Amy laughed. "I don't think you sound like a stalker. Do you still design?"

"I do," Chloe said. "Just like, for fun."

"Bring your sketches in and I'll look at them."

"What? Oh God, no. No." Chloe backed away from the desk. "No, they're not good enough for anyone, let alone *you*, to look at."

"How do you know that?"

"I was rejected from five different design schools," Chloe said. "I know."

"So was I," Amy said.

"What?"

"I never went to design school. Couldn't get into one if my life depended on it."

"Holy shit!" Chloe went pink again and covered her mouth. "Sorry, that was unprofessional."

"Cursing is allowed in my office," Amy said with a small grin. "I know the feeling of rejection well, believe me. My day is busy tomorrow, but bring your sketches in on Wednesday and I'll look at them. Okay?"

"I don't know…"

"What's the harm in letting me look at them?"

"I'll die of shame if you think they're terrible?" Chloe said.

"I doubt I'll think they're terrible, and if I do, I'll keep it to myself. I have a fantastic poker face," Amy said.

"Um, okay," Chloe said.

"Great." Amy pointed to the beanbag chairs. "Have a seat – they're super comfortable, I swear - and we can talk about the digital store."

Chapter Twelve

Amy stood in the lobby of Mark's building, trying to work up the nerve to hit the elevator button. She'd been to Mark's apartment plenty of times, but this time it would be different. This time she'd be at his apartment and fucking him.

Will you be, though? You still haven't signed the agreement and after the research you did last night, you're not going to. You think Mark will keep fucking you if you don't sign the agreement?

Probably not. But after the things she'd read – the things she'd *seen* – on the internet last night, she was one hundred percent positive that a slave/master relationship wasn't for her.

Mark hasn't made you do any of those awful things.

Not yet he hadn't, but she was a newbie. What if that's what he was training her to do, training her to *become*?

She shuddered all over and Paul stood up from behind the security desk. "Ms. Dawson, you okay?"

"Fine, thanks, Paul." Her voice was so high-pitched she was surprised dogs didn't start howling. She pushed the elevator button. When the doors opened, she stepped into the elevator with dread in her belly.

Less than two minutes later, she was knocking on Mark's door. He opened it almost immediately. "Hi, Ames."

He was wearing jeans, a faded blue t-shirt that hugged his lean abdomen and he was barefoot. Lust mixed with the dread. "Hey."

"Come in."

He took her coat and hung it in the closet. She took off her boots and lined them up next to Mark's. She had come straight from work, debating only a few minutes about going home to change her clothes before deciding not to. If she did, she might be tempted to pack an overnight bag and a few toiletries. Stupid idea. She couldn't stay the night after they had sex.

If you even have sex.

"Come in to the kitchen."

She followed him toward the kitchen. Mark didn't have the penthouse, but his apartment was high enough to give stunning views of the city. His apartment was a one-bedroom loft. It had an open floor plan with soaring ceilings, exposed pipes overhead, brick on the walls and floor-to-ceiling windows.

They passed by his bedroom and another trickle of lust seeped into her belly. The bedroom was walled off, although the walls didn't go to the ceiling, and there was a sliding door for privacy.

The door was closed, and she trailed her fingers along the smooth wood as they passed it. Before she stopped being alone with him, she'd come to his place plenty of times, but she'd never been in the bedroom.

"The kitchen looks good," she said.

"Thanks. I guess you haven't seen it since I redid it," Mark replied.

She sat gingerly on the stool that was tucked under the granite covered island. Her ass had bruises on it from the paddle. It was less sore today than it was even yesterday, but it still stung if she sat down too hard. "No. You redid it last year and I haven't been here for - "

"Two years, one month and three days." Mark took a sip from the bottle of beer that was sitting on the counter.

She cleared her throat. "Yeah, well, the kitchen looks good."

He opened the fridge and pulled out a bottle of her favourite wine. Before he could open it, she said, "I'd better not. I haven't eaten dinner yet and if I drink wine on an empty stomach, I'll be drunk in no time."

She tapped her fingers against the island. Driving over, her plan had seemed simple enough. She would tell Mark she was no longer interested in a master/slave relationship, but she still wanted to explore impact play. If he was fine with it, great, they'd have sex and she'd go home. If he wasn't, well... she'd go home.

But now, being in his apartment, being close enough to him to smell his aftershave, her resolve was wavering. Maybe they could have sex first and then she'd tell him she wasn't interested in a master/slave thing. After all, what were the odds of him using her as a damn footstool tonight?

Slim to none, she decided. She would have sex with Mark and then talk to him. She'd give him a really good blowjob. Maybe he'd be distracted enough that he would agree to just impact play.

Smart. Way to think outside the box, Ames.

"So, uh, could we get started with tonight's lesson?" She said.

"Dinner first." Mark was reaching for the handle on the oven door.

"Oh, no, I don't need food. I didn't say that because I wanted you to feed me. I'll eat later."

"We both need to eat." Mark opened the oven door and her stomach growled when the scent of the food drifted to her.

He pulled out two large brown bags and set them on the counter. "I picked up Thai on the way home."

"That's my favourite," she said stupidly.

"I know."

"You didn't have to do that."

"I wanted to," he said. "We have to eat, right? Can you grab the plates and silverware?"

"Sure."

She set the island for two as Mark poured her a glass of wine before setting the food on the island. They sat down across from each other and he smiled at her. "Dig in."

"Thanks." She scooped out some Pad Thai and some Pad Pak before adding a scoop of the chicken and rice to her plate.

They ate in silence for a few minutes before Mark set his fork down and said, "I swear there isn't anything going on with Chloe and me."

"I know," she said. "Didn't you get my text yesterday?"

"I did. I'm glad that Chloe told you how I know her, but you're still upset. I can tell. Chloe was just being a friend when she hugged me."

"I know," she repeated. "I'm not upset about it and I really should apologize to you for my reaction. It isn't any of my business if you're dating someone."

"I wouldn't do that." His scowl was as deep as the Grand Canyon.

"We're not actually dating. So, I wouldn't expect exclusivity."

"Well, I do." He dropped his fork onto his plate. "I don't want you fucking someone else while you belong to me, little slave."

Shit. He had referred to her as slave outside of the bedroom. He *was* planning on using her as a footstool.

"The slave thing is only in the bedroom." Her voice was sharper than she intended, but she kept seeing the images from her computer last night. The woman on all fours on the floor while the man –

"I'm sorry," Mark said. "I didn't mean to say that. It's just – I don't want you sleeping with other men while you're, uh…

"In training?"

He winced, and she pushed her plate of half-eaten food away before reaching for her wine. "Mark, I can't sign the agreement."

"Why?"

"I – I just can't. I know that means this is over but - "

"It doesn't mean it's over. But tell me why you can't sign it," Mark said.

"I can't do the master/slave thing anymore. I want to – to explore impact play but I don't want to be a slave."

"You seemed to enjoy it before. What changed your mind?"

"I just don't think it's for me, okay?" She took a sip of wine.

"Why not?"

"It just isn't."

"Why?" Mark's voice was calm.

Unnerved by how calm he was being, she blurted, "Because I don't want to be a footstool!"

Mark stared at her in stunned silence. She slid off the stool. "I should go."

She hadn't taken two steps before his voice stopped her in her tracks. "Wait."

She both hated and loved how he could control her.

His arm snaked around her waist and he pressed her spine against his chest. He kissed the side of her neck. "Explain, please."

She stared at their reflection in the windows that lined the living room. "I – I did some research last night after pottery class. I looked at the sites you sent me, and I looked at some other ones. There were these pictures and these rules for master/slave relationships. The master made his slave learn all these different rules and positions and – and it's like she's his pet dog, Mark. He makes her heel and park and walk two feet behind him at all times. He taught her a damn fetch command. She has to let him inspect her daily, and he allows other dominants to look at her when she's naked."

Her hands clenched into fists. "He makes her be a footstool for him. A goddamn footstool! There were pictures of her on her hands and knees and he's got his feet propped up on her while he watches fucking TV like he's some - "

"Baby, stop." Mark's arm squeezed her tight.

She had run out of breath anyway.

"I'm not going to ask you to do any of those things."

She sucked in some oxygen. "You aren't?"

"No. Do you really think I would make you walk behind me or let another man look at you naked? I always play with my slaves at the club. Do you know why we're not there now?"

She shook her head and he kissed her neck again. "Because the club has cameras in every room. I don't want anyone seeing you naked but me."

He slipped his hand under her shirt and rubbed her belly with his warm hand. "I swear I only want you to be my slave in the bedroom, Ames. I'm not going to make you learn a bunch of different positions other than the one I've already taught you. Think of what we're doing as more of a," he paused, "PG13 version of a master/slave relationship. Does that make sense?"

He turned her to face him, his hand sliding around to rub at her lower back. She searched his face. "So, no footstool?"

"No footstool."

He bent his head and rested his forehead against hers. She sighed. "I'm an idiot."

"You're not," he said. "There are all different types of master/slave relationships and I should have warned you about that before you did your research."

"Do you - I mean have you ever had a more R rated, master/slave relationship? Like, one where you made them do all those things?"

"Once," he said. "Because she wanted it."

"Did you enjoy it?"

"No, I didn't. Which is why after a few weeks, I found her a more suitable Dom to play with at the club. I couldn't give her what she needed."

She stared at his chest. "I like when you take control in the bedroom. I like when you make me call you Master, but I'm also embarrassed that I like it. Does that make sense?"

"Yes." He pressed a kiss against her forehead. "It's a normal reaction."

"If someone found out that I – I liked being put over your knee and spanked, that I liked being your slave and wearing a collar, I'd be humiliated. But I still want it. Crave it. It's a," she huffed out a small laugh, "weird feeling."

"I know. But you're new to all of this and I promise it gets less weird. What you want is maybe not normal by most people's standards, but it doesn't make it wrong or bad. You think I didn't struggle with being a Dom? Hell, I did therapy over it."

"Really?"

"Yes. You think you feel weird for enjoying being spanked? Consider how it would be if you liked spanking someone, liked causing someone pain, liked calling them your little slave."

"Good point. Especially since you're the complete opposite outside of the bedroom."

"So are you," he pointed out.

"I'm not."

He laughed and kissed her forehead again. "So, if Luke and I tried to tell you what to design, or told you that you had to come to every business meeting, you'd…"

"Tell you to stuff it where the sun doesn't shine."

He laughed again, the sound vibrating against her chest and belly. "Like I said, complete opposite. C'mon, let's finish dinner."

She dug in her heels when he tried to tug her back to the island. "I'm full."

"You hardly ate anything."

She just shrugged. Now that she knew Mark didn't intend to make her act like a goddamn footstool, her horniness far outweighed her hunger.

She could see that Mark was going to argue and she pressed a kiss against his mouth, licking his lips but pulling back when he opened his mouth. "I want you, Master. Don't make me wait."

His nostrils flared and just like that, she could feel his erection against her belly. It sent ripples of need through her entire body. She loved how quickly she could make him hard. She reached down and rubbed his dick through his jeans. "You want me too. Take me to your bedroom, please?"

He took her hand and led her to the bedroom. He pulled back the sliding door and she peered curiously inside. Like the rest of his place, the bedroom had a minimalistic design to it. There was just a king-sized bed, two nightstands and a small armchair in the corner next to a reading lamp. She stared at the photography on the walls before glancing at Mark.

"Aren't you worried that someone will see these?"

"Like who?"

"I don't know - Luke or my parents."

Mark laughed. "Neither your parents nor your brother are ever invited into my bedroom."

She blushed before moving closer to study the photographs. On the wall closest to them there was a black and white picture of a man sitting in a chair. Only his lap and his legs were visible in the picture. A naked woman knelt at his feet, her head resting on the man's thigh, and a thick collar around her neck with a leather leash attached to it. The end of the leash was clasped loosely in the man's left hand. His other hand rested on top of the woman's head in a gentle caress. The woman's eyes were closed, and Amy envied the peace on her face.

The photo on the opposite wall was also in black and white. It showed a man wearing a suit and relaxing in a chair again. This time a naked woman sat cradled on his lap. Her face was buried in his neck and her arms wrapped around his shoulders. One of his hands cupped a smooth naked thigh, the other rested against her ass. Despite the lack of colour, Amy could see the tell-tale marks of a spanking across the pale flesh of her ass and back of her thighs.

"What are those marks from?" She asked.

"A strap," Mark replied.

"Oh." She turned her attention back to the other picture, staring fixedly at the leash. She thought she would feel repulsion or anger. Instead, staring at the way the leash was wrapped around the man's hand made her feel a little hot and breathless.

What would it be like to have a leash clipped to her collar? To have Mark's hand wrapped around it, pulling her closer, tugging her to her knees and using it to guide her mouth to his dick?

"Do you like this picture, little slave?" Mark's breath ruffled her hair.

"Yes."

"What do you like about it?"

"I – I like how peaceful and happy she looks. The way his hand rests on her head."

"What else?"

"I like..."

Oh God, she couldn't say it. She had just lost her shit in the kitchen about being treated like a dog.

"Tell me."

She couldn't resist him, not when he spoke to her that way.

"I like the leash," she whispered.

He brushed aside her hair and kissed her neck. The shadow on his jaw prickled her skin and heightened her need.

"Your collar is on the bed. Bring it to me."

She walked unsteadily to the bed. Her collar was lying on the bed but that was it. No paddle, no crop or strap like she thought there might be. No leash either. She ignored her weird disappointment. She picked up the collar and rubbed her thumb along the 'MM' stitched into it.

"The MM stands for Master Mark?" She brought it back to him and held it out.

He nodded and unbuckled the collar. She lifted her hair and he buckled the collar snug around her neck. She had missed its weight.

The tension around his eyes eased as he stared at the collar. She touched his chest. "You'd make me wear this all the time if you could. Wouldn't you?"

"Yes." His intensity made her a little uneasy.

"Well," she tried to joke, "the leather collar look doesn't exactly go with my hippie wardrobe."

He touched her shirt. "Time to get you naked, little slave."

He helped her undress, unbuttoning her shirt and unhooking her bra for her. She shimmied out of her skirt, her tights, and her panties. When she was naked, he pulled her into his embrace and kissed her.

His kisses drove any doubts and worries from her mind and she lost herself in his taste and his touch. When he reached down and squeezed her ass, she tried not to wince and failed miserably.

He broke their kiss. "Turn around."

"It's fine, Sir. It's just -"

He spanked the back of her thigh. "Turn around."

She turned, and he studied her ass before rubbing his hand across the light bruises.

"It doesn't hurt that much," she said. "It looks more painful than it is."

"No spanking tonight, little slave."

She scowled over her shoulder at him. "I'm fine. I don't need to be babied or -"

He gave her right ass cheek a hard spank and she couldn't stop her cry of pain. Fuck it hurt more than she thought.

He turned her around and pulled her back into his embrace. "No spanking tonight. Arguing with your Master will result in punishment."

She couldn't resist sassing him. "If I'm not being spanked, do I really need to worry about punishment?"

His hand was between her legs and cupping her pussy before she could react. She gasped and then moaned when his thumb rubbed her clit. He bent his head and bit her neck before sucking on her earlobe. "You and I both know there are other ways to punish you, little slave."

Already his rough touch on her clit was bringing her close. She rubbed against his fingers as he kissed the spot below her ear. "Do you want to come tonight?"

"Yes," she whispered.

"Then behave yourself and do as I say."

"Yes, Sir."

He moved his hand and she whined her disappointment. His hand tugged on her collar.

"On your knees."

She dropped to her knees, thankful for the plush rug Mark had next to the bed. She stared up at him. He pulled off his t-shirt and stroked her hair back from her face. "Suck your Master's cock."

"Yes, Master."

She unbuttoned and unzipped his jeans and yanked down the front of his briefs. His cock popped out and she slid her mouth over the head of him and sucked hard. His groan filled her with satisfaction and she traced her tongue around the ridge. He groaned again, his hands sliding into her hair in a tight grip.

"More," he rasped. "Take more of my cock into your mouth."

She took as much as she could, sucking hard as she bobbed her head back and forth. The head of his cock bumped against the back of her throat. She tried to pull back, but he kept her where she was.

She squeezed his hips and stared up at him before making a muffled sound of protest.

"No, relax your throat and breathe through your nose," he said.

She tried to do what he said, struggling not to panic. He pulled back and she gulped in air as he petted her hair. "Try again, little slave."

"Sir, I can't breathe and I - "

"Enough talking." He gave her hair a sharp tug. "Your mouth belongs to me and I'm going to fuck it with my cock. Open."

His harsh command made her pussy gush wetness. She opened her mouth wide and tried to relax as he fed her inch after inch of his thick cock.

Her lips stretched around his width and her eyes watered as he pushed further and harder. He pulled back, allowed her to take a breath, and pushed in again. He repeated the motion, his hand cupping the back of her head to hold her still. When he increased the speed and the intensity, she tried to suck and lick his cock as best she could with every stroke.

"Fuck, that's so good," he panted. "You're such a good girl. You suck my cock so well, good girl."

An absurd amount of pride filled her chest. Saliva ran down her chin, but she leaned into his thrusts, sucking eagerly as he continued to praise her. He moaned and tightened his hand in her hair.

"I'm going to come in your mouth and you're going to swallow all of it. Do you understand?"

She nodded, unable to speak with his cock in her mouth. He petted her hair. "Good girl."

He thrust again and again. She swallowed eagerly when his body stiffened, and he shoved his cock deep into her mouth. He tasted delicious to her and she licked her lips and then the head of his cock when he pulled out of her mouth.

He shuddered all over, breathing harshly and petting her hair almost compulsively before he helped her stand. "Good girl. Such a good girl."

"Thank you, Sir."

He picked up his shirt and cleaned away the mixture of saliva and come that coated her lips.

"Thank you, Sir."

"You're welcome." He kissed her hard, pushing her lips apart with his tongue and tasting every part of her mouth. "I love tasting myself in your mouth, slave."

She clung to him as he cupped her breast and played with her nipple.

"Please, Sir," she moaned.

"Lie on the middle of the bed."

She did what he asked. He undressed, and she admired his lean body as he sat on the bed beside her. He reached under the mattress and she stared at the fabric cuff he produced. It was connected to a thick strap and she didn't resist when he took her arm and strapped the cuff around her wrist.

"It's an under-the-bed restraint system," he said as he secured the cuff.

"Well, isn't that handy," she said.

He laughed and leaned over to suck her nipple into a hard peak. She arched her back and weaved the fingers of her free hand into his thick hair.

He pulled away and she pouted at him. He just grinned before moving to the other side of the bed and pulling out the cuff from under the mattress. When her wrist was secured, she tested her ability to get free. She couldn't. Not without Mark.

More liquid dripped out of her pussy and she squirmed on the bed. Mark leaned over her and sucked on her other nipple until it was as hard as the first one. She moaned and twitched and arched her back, digging her toes into the mattress.

"Comfortable?" He asked.

"Yes, Sir," she replied.

"Good." He kissed between her breasts before kissing his way down her stomach. He nibbled at her hips as she twisted and turned. When his mouth hovered over her pussy, she made a pleading noise.

He kissed the soft curls.

"Not yet, little slave."

"Please, Master."

"Not yet."

He kissed the top of her thigh before licking a path to her knee. He circled it with his tongue and she yanked futilely at her bonds. "Sir! Please!"

He kissed her shin as he pulled her legs apart. She didn't even feel the cuff around her ankle until he pressed the Velcro down firmly.

She tugged at the restraint and frowned at him. "Sir, I don't want my legs restrained."

He smiled at her and kissed her shin again. "Your Master does."

She licked her lips and tried to ignore the way her pussy throbbed as he moved to the other side of the bed. She tried to pull her leg away, but he was too strong. He spread her leg to the edge of the bed and quickly restrained it before stepping back to admire his work.

"Sir."

"Shh, little slave." He stared at her body as she squirmed and wiggled. Her legs were spread so wide she could feel the ache in her thighs and the cool air on her pussy. She was on display for him and she felt vulnerable and exposed.

As he moved to the end of the bed and knelt between her thighs, she said, "Mark, I mean Sir, I don't like this. I'm not comfortable being completely restrained. I don't – oh my God!"

Mark's tongue slicked across her pussy lips and she jerked her hips against his mouth. He licked her exposed clit and then stiffened his tongue and pushed it into her narrow entrance.

"Fuck!"

He licked and nibbled at her pussy, swiping his tongue across her clit every few seconds until she was begging and pleading shamelessly.

He lifted his head and smiled at her. "Still want me to let you go, little slave?"

"No! Pease make me come, Master."

"Not yet."

She moaned again as he sucked and licked at her clit. He pushed two thick fingers inside of her and stroked her roughly as he sucked on her swollen clit. He brought her to the brink repeatedly and then stopped as she begged him to let her come.

He sucked on her clit, while he curled his fingers and rubbed them against the front wall of her pussy. She screamed as pleasure so intense, it made light burst behind her screwed-shut eyelids, exploded through her entire body. She screamed again, her body shaking violently against her restraints before she collapsed.

Her chest heaving, she stared in a daze at Mark as he slipped his fingers out of her pussy and sat up. His lower jaw was covered in liquid and he wiped it on the sheet. His cock was hard again, and he knelt between her thighs and guided his cock into her pussy. She was so wet, he slid in easily despite his large size.

Without speaking, he propped himself up on his hands and fucked her hard and rough. He drove in and out of her body, staring at her tits as he moved faster. Her pussy clenched rhythmically around him, and he groaned with every pump of his hips.

She couldn't come this way, it was too rough and the angle wasn't quite right, but she was happy about that. Another orgasm like that last one and her head would explode.

As it was, she was so weak from her climax she could only lie there as Mark used her for his own pleasure. That thought – the idea that her body was meant for her Master's gratification and nothing more – made her pussy tighten around him. He shouted her name, his head falling back as he plunged deep and stayed there. His body shook, and wetness flooded her already soaked pussy. He thrust a few more times before collapsing against her body.

He was heavy, but she didn't ask him to move as he shuddered repeatedly and kissed the damp skin of her neck.

"Fuck, Amy," he muttered before finally rolling off of her.

He reached up and freed one hand before reaching across her and freeing the other. She rubbed her wrists as he sat up and quickly released her ankles. His body was shaking and when he tried to stand, he immediately fell back on his ass on the bed.

"Mark, lie down."

"Aftercare," he mumbled. "You need water and - "

"Lie down," she repeated.

He collapsed on his back and she curled on her side, resting her head on his chest. His heart was thudding heavily against her ear and she rubbed his warm skin. "I think you're the one who needs aftercare."

"Did I hurt you?" He asked. "I was rough at the end and I - "

"You didn't hurt me. It was the best orgasm of my life."

"Good." He curved his arm around her and rubbed her back. "For me too."

He was quiet for a few minutes. "Thank you, Amy."

"For what?"

"That was one of my biggest fantasies about you."

"Giving me a g-spot orgasm was your biggest fantasy?"

He laughed. "Not exactly, although that *was* a happy bonus."

She traced circles on his chest and he squeezed her hip. "You wearing my collar and tied to my bed. Helpless to stop me while I fucked you and used your body for my…"

He cleared his throat. "Fuck, I sound like a total creeper."

She rested her arm on his chest and propped her head up on her hand. "You don't. I liked it too. I wasn't sure about it at first but then I…I was really turned on by it. I'd want to do it again."

"Give me like half an hour," he said.

She poked him in the chest. "Not tonight. It's getting late."

"It isn't," he said. "It's not even seven thirty yet."

She didn't reply. Instead she rested her head on his chest again and closed her eyes. She needed to get dressed and leave. Spending the night with Mark was a very bad idea but God, she was tired. She hadn't slept well last night and getting dressed and going out into the cold and the dark wasn't exactly appealing.

Mark's phone dinged, and she lifted her head again. "Are you going to answer that?"

"It's Luke's ring. I'll text him back later. Do you want to finish dinner?"

She shrugged. What she wanted to do was snuggle with Mark all night and forget that he didn't love her, that he would never agree to anything more than this. His phone dinged again.

"He's texting again," she said.

Mark sighed and reached for his phone, studying the screen. "I'm sure it isn't – shit."

"What's wrong?"

"Your brother is on his way up -"

She sat up at the knock on the door, clutching the sheets to her chest and giving Mark a look of panic. Mark slid out of the bed and yanked his jeans on before grabbing a clean t-shirt. "Stay here, don't make a sound. I'll get him to leave."

She curled up on her side as Mark slipped out of the bedroom and shut the sliding door. She heard him open the front door.

"Hey, Luke. This isn't a good time. I -"

"We need to talk."

Her brother sounded both angry and panicked. She put her hand over her mouth and froze like a mouse when she heard the heavy footsteps walk by the bedroom door.

Shit. Her brother was in the apartment.

Chapter Thirteen

Mark followed Luke into the living room. "Luke, this isn't a great time. Can I -"

"Julien and Pierre are going to be here on Friday. They want to meet." Luke paced back and forth in front of the couch.

"What? Why?"

"Did you even read the texts I sent you?"

"I was busy." His gaze wandered to the bedroom door.

"They say they're going to be here on other business. They say they want to meet us to get an update on the digital storefront."

"Okay, well, we have Chloe working on the marketing, right? Maria says she has interviews lined up next week for the IT part of it. Chloe can be part of the meeting."

"I don't think that's the only reason they're here," Luke said.

"What do you mean?"

"Amy!" Luke almost shouted his sister's name. Mark's gaze was drawn back to his bedroom.

He returned it to Luke in a hurry as Luke scrubbed a hand through his hair. "They want to meet with Amy again as well. They're interested in investing in a casual line wear with her."

"That's a good thing, isn't it?" Mark said. "Amy wants to do a casual line."

"You and I both know they're interested in more than just business with her."

Mark's stomach clenched, and Luke paused in his pacing. "What's wrong? You look like you're gonna puke."

"Nothing," Mark said. "Amy turned them down before."

Luke shrugged. "Doesn't mean she'll turn them down this time. She didn't mind their flirting."

"She won't mix business with pleasure," Mark said. His traitorous gaze wandered to the bedroom door again.

"She was the one who encouraged me to go out with Jane. She has no problem with dating in the workplace," Luke said. "Those two guys are bad news and if Amy sleeps with – Mark! Are you listening to me?"

"Yes." Mark whipped his head around to stare at Luke again. "Amy is a grown woman. She can sleep with whomever she wants."

Nice work, asshole. You almost sound like you believe that.

"You're telling me you'd be fine letting both of those guys have a go at our sister?" Luke gave him an indignant look. "They share their women. Did you know that? You really want our baby sister in the middle of a Julien and Pierre sandwich?"

"She's not my sister."

"She's close enough," Luke said with an irritable look. "Jesus, why are you not more upset about this?"

He was upset. He wanted to kick Luke out, join Amy in his bedroom and make her promise him she wouldn't go anywhere near the two French douchebags. Hell, a big part of him wanted to cuff her to his bed again and keep her there until Julien and Pierre were gone.

Now you're contemplating kidnapping? Jesus, get it together, you asshole!

"Why are you this upset?" He asked. "I get that you're protective of Amy but even this is extreme for you."

Luke stalked to the window and looked out into the darkness. Mark moved closer, then froze. Amy's purse was sitting in the kitchen, tucked under the island but if Luke happened to glance at the floor, he'd see it. He was just contemplating going over and kicking it further under the island when Luke turned around.

"Keep this between you and me, but I'm worried that Julien and Pierre aren't interested in doing a casual line with Amy. I think they just want to get her into their bed and are willing to tell her whatever she wants to hear."

"Amy's an amazing designer." The hair on the back of Mark's neck prickled. "You think she isn't?"

"I didn't say that," Luke replied. "What I said is that Julien and Pierre have it bad for her – Jane said they text and email Amy all the time – and I wonder if they're willing to tempt her with a casual line to get her into their bed."

"You really think they'd invest in a brand-new line of clothing just to sleep with her?"

He hated how that sounded - fuck, he'd hike across the goddamn desert without water just for a chance to sleep with Amy - but Julien and Pierre weren't in love with her.

"I'm more worried that they'll sleep with her and then won't invest in a new line," Luke said. He paced back and forth again before pulling his phone from his pocket. "I'm gonna text Amy, give her the heads up that they're going to be here on Friday."

Mark's eyes widened as he glanced at Amy's purse. Fuck, if her cell phone wasn't on silent...

"Don't text her!" He blurted out.

"What? Why?" Luke's fingers hovered over the keyboard on his phone.

"I saw her just before the end of the day. She said she had a bad headache and was going straight to bed."

"Oh." Luke tucked his phone back into his pocket. "I'll talk to her in the morning at the office."

"She'll be pissed with you if you tell her what you're worried about." He had no idea why he said that. No doubt she had heard every word Luke said.

"Don't I know it," Luke said. "Which is why I'm not going to tell her. I don't want to hurt her feelings and I swear, if it was anyone else but those two assholes, I wouldn't even worry about this. But I can't shake the feeling that they're just using this casual line thing as a way to get to Amy and her goddamn bed."

He ran his hand through his hair again. "I'm just going to remind her that it's a really bad fucking idea to sleep with our investors."

"Sure, okay. Listen, I don't mean to be rude but –"

"Hey, you want to go have a beer? Jane is out with some of her friends from the strip club. I don't have to pick her up until ten."

"Uh, thanks, but I –"

"We could get a bite to eat or..." Luke trailed off as he glanced at the kitchen.

Mark's stomach made an unpleasant flip flop. Luke studied the island, his gaze lingering on the two plates and the wine glass with the faint imprint of lipstick. "You had company?"

"Uh..."

"Holy shit." Luke's face lit up in a grin and he lowered his voice before glancing at Mark's bedroom. "You got a woman in your bedroom."

Mark didn't reply. Luke moved closer and held out his fist. "Nice."

He bumped Luke's fist. Luke glanced at the bedroom again before lowering his voice even more. "Is it Chloe?"

"What? No. I told you, we're just friends."

"Just checking. Who is it?"

"No one you know."

"One-time lay or something more?" Luke asked.

"Luke? Buddy? Do you think you can fucking leave now?"

"Sure. You should introduce her to me and

Jane, we can do a double date or something."

"I'll think about it." He grabbed Luke's arm and pushed him toward the door. "Get out."

Luke shoved his feet into his boots as Mark opened the door. "You can give me details tomorrow."

"Out."

Luke laughed and stepped out into the hallway. "Have fun."

"Thanks." He shut the door and leaned against it, listening as Luke's footsteps faded. He headed back to the bedroom. Amy had her tights and her skirt on and was just slipping into her bra.

"What are you doing?"

She smiled at him. "Getting dressed so I can go home."

"You don't have to leave. It's fine, he didn't know it was you."

"I know. He thought it was Chloe."

He winced. "There's nothing going on -"

"I know that." She pulled her shirt over her head and smoothed her blonde hair. "Thanks for tonight, Mark. I had fun."

"Ames, just wait. Talk to me for a minute, okay?" He took her hand and squeezed it.

"Talk about what?"

"I know you heard what Luke said. Let's talk about it."

"What's there to talk about? My brother thinks that Julien and Pierre are only interested in fucking me."

"Amy, sit. Please." He tried very hard not to use his Dom voice on her and mostly succeeded.

She sighed and sat down on the side of his bed. He sat next to her but when he tried to put his arm around her, she shifted away. She studied the photo of the woman sitting at the man's feet.

"Have Julien and Pierre been in contact with you?" He wondered if she could hear the jealousy in his voice.

"Yep. At least two or three times a week since they went back to Paris."

Jealousy bit a hole in the lining of his stomach and burned like acid. She glanced at his face before looking back at the picture. "I'm not going to fuck them, Mark."

He knew the relief showed on his face. "Luke is just overprotective."

"Yeah, I know."

"Tell me what is actually upsetting you."

She sucked in a big breath and held it for a few seconds before releasing it. "I think Luke is right. I think Julien and Pierre are using the casual line investment as a really fucked up seduction tool. They're not interested in my work, just how quickly they can get me in their bed between them."

His hands clenched into fists and his entire body stiffened. "You're not to go anywhere near their bed, little slave."

She gave him a dry look and he flushed, cursing his inability to keep control around her. "Sorry."

"Anyway, I'll meet with them on Friday, they'll invite me to dinner and we'll talk about the casual line. Then they'll invite me back to their hotel room. When I decline, they'll be gracious but their offer to invest in a casual line will disappear. Just like Luke thinks."

"You don't know that," he said. "You're an amazing designer."

"I'm good at designing business wear," she said. "Luke keeps talking about how we might try a casual wear line next year, but he won't even look at my designs for them. And if Julien and Pierre aren't interested in investing in it, then I'm not sure I'll even be able to convince Luke to try other investors."

"We don't need investors to start a casual line," Mark said.

"It doesn't matter. Luke wants to keep going with the business line, and I understand that. It's successful. If it ain't broke, don't fix it, right?"

"What do you want?" Mark asked.

"Does it matter?" Amy said.

"Yes."

She smiled at him before patting his knee. "Thanks, but I'm not sure that it does. The company employs a lot of people and it would be selfish of me to try something brand new without the financial backing. If it failed, it could bring down the company and a lot of good people would be out of a job."

He wanted to pull her closer but her entire body was tense, and she was leaning away from him. Instead he said, "I don't think that would happen. People would love your casual line, I know it."

"Maybe." She glanced at his alarm clock before standing. "I need to get going."

"Stay the night," he said. "We'll finish dinner and then…"

She smiled again. "I'd better not."

He stood and followed her out of the bedroom. She grabbed her purse and pulled her boots on. He helped her into her jacket and she made a startled noise when she reached for the door handle and he grabbed her wrist.

"Wait." He stepped closer. Every part of him wanted to kiss her, wanted to pick her up and carry her back to his bed, but instead he reached for the collar still around her neck. A shamefully large part of him had been tempted to not say anything. To just let her leave wearing it.

He unbuckled the collar and slid it out from around her neck. Her mouth pursed into an adorable 'o', as she stared at it in his hand. "Oh shit. I completely forgot I was wearing it."

He held it in his hand as she cleared her throat. "Uh, thanks again. I really enjoyed myself."

"You're welcome." He wondered just how pathetic she'd find him if he begged her again to stay the night.

She leaned in and brushed her lips across his cheek. "Good night, Mark."

"Good night, Amy."

∂° ∽

"These are good, Chloe." Amy flipped the page on the sketch pad. "Really good."

Chloe flushed with pleasure. "Thank you, Ms. Dawson."

"I told you to call me Amy," she said as she studied the sketch. "You have talent. It's a bit raw, but it's there. I particularly like this skirt and jacket

253

combo."

She handed the sketch book to Chloe who took it and pressed it against her chest like a schoolgirl. "You have no idea how much it means to me to have you look at my sketches. Thank you again."

"You're welcome. And I wasn't blowing smoke up your ass. You're good."

"Thank you so much."

"Amy?" Jane knocked on her doorway. "You ready? Oh sorry, I didn't mean to interrupt."

"We were just finishing," Amy said. "Come on in. Have you met Chloe yet?"

"I don't think so." Jane shook Chloe's hand. "I'm Jane Smith. I work in finance."

"Hi, Jane. Chloe Matthews, I was just hired in marketing for the new digital storefront."

"Welcome to the team," Jane said.

"Thanks," Chloe replied. "I'll leave you two to your meeting. Thank you again, Amy."

"Chloe, wait. Jane and I are going to the café for lunch. Do you want to join us?"

"I don't want to intrude," Chloe said hesitantly.

"You aren't," Jane said. "The more the merrier."

"Well, if you're sure…"

"We are," Amy said. "Grab your coat and your purse and meet us in the lobby."

જ ✧

"So, did you grow up here?" Amy asked as Chloe sat down beside her at the café table.

"I did," Chloe replied. "My parents moved to Iowa when I was nineteen, but my sister and I decided to stay here. We moved in with my grandmother."

She opened her water and took a drink before twisting in her seat to study the counter at the front of the cafe. "Oh shoot, I forgot to get a package of salad dressing. Maybe I can get Jane to – holy shit."

Amy followed her gaze and suppressed a grin. Luke had obviously stopped in at the café to grab some lunch. Jane was standing at the counter waiting for her salad and Luke was standing next to her. He had given her ass a quick squeeze just as Chloe looked at Jane.

"Uh, did Mr. Dawson just grab Jane's butt?"

Amy laughed. Luke squeezed Jane's ass again and she batted his hand away before checking their table. Her face flushed bright red when she realized Chloe was watching them. She murmured something to Luke who glanced at their table before shrugging. He leaned down, kissed Jane firmly on the mouth and grabbed the wrap from the counter before heading toward the door. He waved at Amy and Chloe. Amy waved back and Luke left the cafe.

"Luke and Jane are dating," Amy said.

"Ah, okay." Chloe twisted back around in her seat. "So, there's no policy against workplace dating?"

"Nope."

Jane slid into the seat next to Amy and gave Chloe an apologetic look. "Sorry."

"For what?"

She cleared her throat. "Um, I don't usually

advertise around the office that Luke and I are dating."

"I won't say anything," Chloe said.

"It's not like a secret or anything," Jane said. "I just don't, uh, want people thinking I'm getting special treatment or anything like that."

"I don't."

Amy broke the awkward silence. "So, Chloe is a budding designer herself."

"Really? That's awesome."

"Mm, I do it more for fun," Chloe said. "I don't have any formal training or anything, but Amy was nice enough to look at my designs."

"She's really good," Amy said.

"Cool," Jane said. "Hey, Luke mentioned that Julien and Pierre are going to be here on Friday."

"They are," Amy said.

"They're the Paris guys who are investing in the international line, right?" Chloe said.

Amy nodded, and Chloe poked at her salad. "Mr. Dawson sent me an email this morning. I'm meeting with them on Friday afternoon."

"Oh God," Jane said. "We need to prepare her, Amy."

Amy laughed as Chloe gave them a curious look. "What?"

"Julien and Pierre are going to be all over you," Jane said. "They're very… fond of the ladies."

"That's a mild way of putting it," Amy said with another laugh. "They're going to try and convince you to bang them, Chloe. Just like they'll try and convince me to bang them when I have dinner with them Friday night."

"Hell, they'll probably try and convince the two of you to have a foursome," Jane said.

Chloe's mouth dropped open. "You're kidding me."

"We're not," Amy said. "They're really nice guys – if you don't mind listening to them talk about themselves – but they're also crazy horndogs."

Jane snickered. "Horndogs... that's an apt description."

"They'll only sleep with a woman if she agrees to sleep with both of them at the same time."

Chloe's mouth, which had just closed, dropped open again. "How do you know that?"

"Oh, they're not shy," Amy said. "They'll tell you themselves if you're with them for longer than ten minutes."

Chloe ate a bite of salad. "Okay, well I appreciate the warning but I'm not sleeping with an investor in the company and I'm certainly not sleeping with two men at once. I'm kind of, uh, straight-laced in the bedroom. I like sex as much as the next girl, but only with one penis at a time."

Both Amy and Jane burst into laughter and Chloe blushed before shrugging. "It's true. Relationships are complicated and messy enough. Could you imagine trying to have a relationship with two men?"

"It's not for the faint of heart," Jane said. "So, I take it you're single right now?"

"I am," Chloe replied. "Actually, I was engaged to a man named John, but he broke it off six months ago."

"I'm sorry," Jane said.

"It was for the best. I have a sister who has some issues with alcohol and a good deal of my time and energy goes toward trying to help her. He didn't like it. He wanted me to accept that she was never going to change and to concentrate more on him."

"John sounds like a dick," Amy said.

Chloe shrugged. "I don't think so. He had a point. I did kind of put my sister before my relationship with him and that's not fair. But it's hard to give up on someone you love and have been trying to help for nearly your entire life, you know? Even if, in the end, it didn't work."

"What do you mean?" Jane asked.

"Almost three months ago, I finally got Lori to agree to go to rehab. She was doing well, but then she left two weeks ago. She's drinking again. John was right – she can't or won't change."

She stared at her salad for a moment, trying not to let the wounds from her past swallow her up. Jane patted her hand a bit timidly. "I'm very sorry, Chloe."

"Thanks. Anyway, enough about my depressing love life. How long have you and Mr. Dawson been dating, Jane?"

౿ ఄ

This is called breaking and entering, you know.

Mark ignored his inner voice. He had a key to Amy's place so technically it wasn't breaking and entering. He stepped inside and closed the door before locking it. He was about to enter the alarm code when he realized she hadn't set the alarm. He scowled at the glowing keypad before taking off his jacket and boots. He crept down the hallway to the stairs.

This is a bad idea, asshole.

Yeah, it probably was. But half an hour ago, it hadn't seemed like a bad idea. To his exhausted mind and body, it had seemed like the best idea in the world. He had slept terribly since Sunday night.

Terribly was an understatement. He didn't think he'd gotten more than a few hours sleep over the last seventy-two hours. He was running on caffeine and sheer willpower alone at this point.

The package he'd ordered Tuesday night after Amy left his place, had arrived at the office this afternoon. He'd had to pay extra for one-day shipping, but he'd wanted it before Friday. He was tempted to take it directly to Amy but resisted. It wasn't something he could just spring on her at the office. She would most likely be resistant to wearing it, but the thought of her meeting with Julien and Pierre was an acid bath eating away at his stomach. He needed something on her that would remind her she belonged to him. His mind had immediately suggested that alternatively, he could just trust that Amy meant what she said about not sleeping with them. He'd found that suggestion disgustingly easy to ignore.

After the Al-Anon meeting, he had driven Chloe home. His place was only a few miles from hers but knowing he would just pace restlessly, he had driven to the club instead. Selene was surprised to see him, but he'd mumbled something about getting caught up on paperwork and locked himself in the small office they shared.

An hour later he was redoing the same goddamn spreadsheet for the third time when Selene walked into the office.

"You look like shit, Mark."

"Thanks, Selene."

"Did you and Amy break up?"

"We'd have to be dating to break up. This isn't dating, remember?" He'd had coffee with Selene on Sunday morning and told her everything.

"I remember. So, why do you look like you haven't slept in three days."

"Because I haven't."

"Why not?"

He pulled at his earlobe before leaning back in his chair. "I don't know."

"I do," Selene said. "This master/slave training thing you have going on with Amy isn't enough for you."

"Yeah, well, it's all I can do," he replied as he stared blearily at the spreadsheet.

"Mark -"

"I don't want to talk about it, okay? Please, Selene, I'm exhausted and not in the mood."

Her face softened and she reached out and took his hand. "Go home, honey. Get some sleep."

"I can't," he said. "I can't sleep without her now."

He cringed at how pathetic he sounded, but Selene just leaned forward and kissed his forehead. "You have to try. Do you need me to cover your shifts this weekend?"

"No," he said. "You already do too much. I'm not pulling my weight around here as it is."

She squeezed his hand. "When you're not as tired, we'll talk about that. Okay?"

"You want to buy me out, Selene? Get a partner who can actually help?"

"Of course not," she said. "But I have something I want to discuss with you."

"We can talk now."

"No. You need sleep. Go home and heat up some milk or something."

He laughed. "I don't think that works."

"At least try it," she said with a small grin. "Go home, Mark."

"Yeah, okay."

He left the club and meant to drive home but half an hour later, he was parked on the street outside of Amy's home. It was only 9:30 but the house was completely dark. It wasn't like Amy to go to bed so early – she was a night owl just like him - but he doubted she was out somewhere. She hated the cold and tended to stay close to home during the winter months. Maybe she had a headache. Maybe she wasn't sleeping well either.

He'd told himself to leave, but the idea of sliding into Amy's bed and curling up against her warm body was a temptation he couldn't resist. He needed sleep and the only way he would get it was in Amy's bed.

So, here he was. Creeping up Amy's stairs like a weird stalker. He told himself to turn around and leave, but then opened her bedroom door. The bedroom blinds were open and cold moonlight spilled into the room, giving him more than enough light to see her curled up in her bed.

He stripped quickly and climbed into the bed behind her. Amy was a sound sleeper and she didn't stir when he pressed up against her warm body. He slid his arm around her and cupped her naked breast before resting his head on the pillow behind hers.

She made a soft snoring sound and stretched a little. Without opening her eyes, she said, "What time is it, Mark?"

"Just before ten," he whispered. He was absurdly pleased that she knew it was him.

"Oh." She yawned and snuggled back against him. She was wearing just a pair of panties and he stroked her smooth thigh before cupping her breast again.

"Is it Thursday?" She asked before yawning a second time.

"No."

"Why are you here?"

"The roads were bad, and your house was closer," he lied. "Do you mind if I sleep here tonight?"

"No, I don't mind."

God, she was adorable when she was all warm and sleepy. He kissed the back of her shoulder. "Thank you, baby."

"You're welcome." Her voice was slowing and becoming lower as she drifted back to sleep. She made a sleepy sound of contentment and then muttered, "Love you, Mark."

His hand squeezed her breast compulsively. He

wondered if his heart pounding against her back would wake her. She didn't move. Already her breathing was deep and even.

He kissed the back of her shoulder again and whispered, "I love you too, Ames."

Chapter Fourteen

She was much warmer than she should be. She kept her house cool, even in the winter, but it was like she had a damn furnace in the bed with her. She tried to wiggle away from the furnace and froze when it squeezed her breast and made a low sound of masculine disapproval.

She opened her eyes and stared at the alarm clock. It was just before five. Normally she never woke up before her alarm went off at six, but she'd gone to bed early last night. Apparently, she really did only need eight hours. She was a little surprised by that considering she'd slept terribly the last few nights and exhaustion was setting in.

Hey, Ames? There's a strange man in your bed.

Not a strange man. Mark. Mark was in her bed. He had climbed into her bed last night even though it wasn't one of their agreed upon nights. But why?

She closed her eyes and strained to remember. Bad roads. Right. The roads were bad, so Mark had stopped. Not that surprising. He had slept over at her place in the past for all sorts of various reasons. Of course, he usually crashed in her guest bedroom. She'd never woken to find Mark's hand on her breast and his morning wood pressing against her ass.

She decided she enjoyed this new sleepover arrangement far more than the previous. She could get way too used to having Mark in her bed. In fact, she had her suspicions that she'd slept so well last night *because* he was in the bed with her.

She rubbed her ass against his erection as need woke in her belly. His low groan lit up her nerve endings and she gasped when he squeezed her breast again and then plucked on her nipple. It hardened, and he kissed between her shoulder blades before pushing his dick against her ass again.

"Good morning, little slave."

All the muscles in her stomach tightened at his low rasp. "Good morning, Sir."

He slid his hand down her stomach and cupped her pussy through her panties. He rubbed her clit through the rapidly dampening fabric and she moaned her need.

"You're not to wear panties to bed anymore," he said. "I want easy access to my slave's pussy when I'm in her bed."

"Yes, Sir," she panted as he continued to rub her.

"Take them off."

She yanked her panties down, squirming and wiggling to get them off her legs and feet as he cupped her breast again and toyed with her nipple.

When she was finally free of them, he pushed his dick between her ass cheeks and rubbed up and down. His groan of pleasure made her pussy wet.

"Have you been fucked in the ass before, little slave?" His hand pulled her thigh back and over his muscled thigh, as his dick slipped between her legs. He moved his hand to her clit and stroked it with a rough touch.

"No," she moaned, arching her hips against him. "That - that's an exit only."

He laughed and nipped at her neck. "Your body belongs to me and I want every part of it."

"You are not fucking me in the ass, Mark Stanford."

She received a hard spank to her pussy for her impertinence. She squealed, but he was already soothing the sting away with light caresses to her clit. Fuck, having her pussy slapped should not make her so wet. But it was kind of hard to deny that it did when Mark lifted his hand and showed her how wet his fingers were.

"Is it a hard limit?" He asked as he lowered his hand to her pussy again.

"I – dammit, it's really hard to think when you're doing that…"

"Doing what?" He pushed her forward on the bed a little before sliding his dick into her pussy.

"Oh!" She curled her hands into the sheets and pushed back against him. "That! Doing that!"

He rubbed her clit as he fucked her with slow, sure strokes. "Has my little slave missed her Master's cock?"

"Yes," she moaned. She reached back and clutched at his hard hip as he pumped in and out of her. "So much."

"But you don't want it in your ass?"

"Um, I – oh fuck!" He pinched her clit and she shuddered all over. "I don't think I'll like it."

"How do you know if you've never tried?" He rocked his hips in a hard motion and she tried not to scream with pleasure when he hit her g-spot.

"I could maybe try it, Sir," she panted as she thrust back against him. "Do you have, um, any lube?"

He made a sound that was half-groan and half-laugh. "Not this morning, little slave. You're not ready for that yet."

"God, make up your mind."

This time her insolence got her a hard slap to the ass. She cried out and squeezed around his cock. He groaned and spanked her again before pushing her onto her stomach. Before she could move, he was kneeling between her thighs and using her hips to pull her onto her knees. He thrust hard into her and she made a muffled squeal into the pillow.

His hand wound in her hair and he pulled her up until she was bracing herself on her hands. He kept a tight grip on her hair and she stared glassy-eyed at the headboard as he pounded into her. The head of his cock brushed against her g-spot with every stroke and she made inarticulate sounds of need and want.

He spanked her ass repeatedly, hard forceful swats that rocked her forward only to be stopped by the grip he had in her hair. The pain in her ass and her scalp pushed her pleasure higher, made her curl her toes and plead for her climax.

When her ass was hot and red, when she was

sure she would lose her mind from need, his hand slipped under her and rubbed her clit. She came immediately, screaming and shaking and squeezing around him. He plunged in and out of her. If not for his hand in her hair, she would have been pushed face-first into the headboard with the power of his thrusts.

He shouted her name and dug his hand into her hip as he stiffened and came inside of her. Warmth flooded her pussy and her inner muscles squeezed and released him as he pulsated inside of her. When he released her hair, she collapsed face-first into the mattress.

With a low groan, he pulled out of her and rolled to the side. Her body trembling, she curled on her side and made a contented sound when he spooned her. He kissed her upper back before resting his head on the pillow behind her.

After a few minutes, she said, "Did it storm last night?"

"What?"

"Did it storm? Is that why the roads were bad?"

There was no reply and she peered over her shoulder at him. His guilt was plastered all over his face.

He cleared his throat. "The roads were fine. I was just near your house and, uh, really tired. I hadn't slept well for a few nights."

"Me neither," she said. "Did you sleep better last night?"

"Yes. Did you?"

"Yes."

"Good."

He kissed her upper back again before touching her ass. "Do you have any of the lotion left that I gave you?"

"Yes. I'll put it on after I shower." She glanced at the alarm clock. It was almost six and, wishing she could spend the entire day in bed with Mark, she pushed back the covers. "I need to shower and get ready for work."

"I should go. I need to go home before I hit the office."

Despite what he said, he stayed in her bed as she walked naked to the master bathroom.

"Hey, Ames?"

"Yeah?"

"Thanks for letting me crash here last night."

"You're welcome, Sir." She gave him a small grin and closed the bathroom door.

❧ ❧

She expected him to be gone when she came downstairs. Instead he was in her kitchen and pouring her a cup of freshly-brewed coffee.

"Thank you."

He looked hot as hell in his rumpled t-shirt and jeans. She wanted to drag him back to the bed and fuck his brains out. Instead, the bracelets on her arms jingling, she sipped some coffee and checked her cell phone.

"Do you mind if I make myself some toast?" Mark asked.

She shook her head before sitting down at the island. "No, help yourself. I've got some of Mom's jam in the fridge if you..."

"What's wrong?"

"What is that?" She pointed to the small rectangular box wrapped with a red ribbon that was sitting in the middle of the island.

"It's a gift for you."

She stared at him before grinning. "Yeah?"

"Yes. Open it."

She pulled the box toward her and untied the ribbon. She pushed the lid off and stared at the necklace resting on soft velvet.

"It's beautiful," she said.

The necklace had bright silver and purple rings in a chainmail weave. A silver and purple heart shaped pendant dangled from the chain. She touched the heart before picking up the necklace.

"Mark, this is so beautiful. Thank you so…"

She picked up the small key that was in the velvet under the necklace. "Why is there a key?"

She glanced again at the heart. It had flipped over in her hand and she studied the padlock closure on the back of it before staring at Mark. "The heart is a padlock."

He nodded and she frowned a little. "Do I attach the key to the necklace or just, like, put it in my pocket?"

"The key stays with me," he said.

"The key stays with you," she repeated before studying the necklace again. She was missing something, something important but she didn't…

"It's a collar," she said as the light came on. "A slave collar."

"Yes."

"You want me to wear this instead of the leather

collar?"

"You'll continue to wear the leather collar in bed. This is," Mark paused, "a day collar."

"Let me get this straight. You said the master/slave thing was only in the bedroom but now you want me to wear a collar in public."

"It looks like a necklace."

"But it's a collar," she said. "One I can't remove unless you remove it for me."

She studied his face for a moment. "Why are you asking me to wear this?"

He didn't reply. She cocked her head at him. "Is it because I'm having dinner with Julien and Pierre tomorrow night?"

"The necklace around your neck -"

"Collar."

"The collar around your neck will serve as a reminder that you belong to me, little slave." Mark's voice was unapologetic.

Somehow that lack of apology, the way he simply acted as if it was his every right to ask her to wear a day collar, was making her ruin a perfectly good pair of panties.

She took a deep breath, a little unnerved at how turned on she was, and said, "I told you I wasn't going to sleep with Julien and Pierre. You don't trust me."

"I trust you," he said.

He didn't say anything else. The silence stretched out between them like warm taffy. She could hear the quiet tick of the clock on the wall.

"What if you lose the key?"

"There's a second key. I'll put it in the

nightstand in my bedroom."

She chewed on her bottom lip and stared at the necklace before holding it and the key out to him.

He took them from her and dropped the key into his pocket after unlocking the padlock. He stood in front of her. "Hold your hair up."

She lifted her hair and shivered all over when he draped the collar around her neck. It was a snug fit around her neck, she supposed it was meant to be, and the click of the small padlock sounded very loud to her.

Mark touched the heart padlock before smiling at her. "It fits you well, little slave."

"Thank you, Sir," she whispered. Her heart was pounding, her nipples were hard peaks and her pussy was pulsing with need.

He studied her flushed face then reached under her skirt. She widened her legs automatically. She was wearing stockings and he touched the wide band at the top of them before brushing his fingers against the soaked crotch of her panties.

Her flush deepened when he smiled. "My little slave likes her Master's gift. Isn't that right?"

"Yes, Sir," she whispered. It was pointless to argue. His fingers were inside her panties now and there was no hiding that she was soaking wet.

"That's my good girl." He brushed a kiss against her mouth. "Would you like your Master to fuck you before you go to work?"

"Yes, please, Sir."

"Turn around."

She turned and he bent her over the island before pushing her skirt up to her waist. As he pulled her panties down her legs, she touched the collar around her throat. She belonged to Mark, and she would wear his collar for as long as he asked her to wear it.

∂ ∾

"Hey, Amy." Jane was walking by her office and she waved.

"Hey, come in for a minute."

Jane stepped into her office and Amy held her arms out. "What do you think of this suit jacket?"

"It's gorgeous," Jane said as she studied the forest green material.

"Thanks. It's a part of the new line and we've been struggling with the shoulders, but I think we've got it now. Help me out of it, would you? The sleeves are only pinned on and I've already poked myself like seventeen times."

Jane laughed and waited for Amy to unbutton the jacket before she helped her slide it down her arms.

"How come you're on this floor?" Amy asked as she took the jacket and draped it over the mannequin.

"Kyla asked me to drop off a file to Mark," Jane said. "Hey, are we still on for shopping on Saturday?"

"Yep. One o'clock at the mall on Barker Street, right?"

"Yes. I was thinking I would invite Chloe. What do you think?" Jane said.

"I think it's a good idea."

"Great. I'll send her an email. I really like her,

Amy."

"Yeah, she's sweet," Amy said.

"She is. That's a gorgeous necklace," Jane said.

Amy touched the heart pendant dangling from the chain. She'd had a meeting with her design team this morning and all of them had complimented her on it. She had blushed then just like she was blushing now. "Thank you."

"Why are you red?" Jane asked.

Amy glanced at her open door. "Mark gave it to me."

"Wow. That's very generous of him. It looks like it cost a fortune."

"It's a slave collar," Amy blurted in a low voice.

Jane stepped closer and studied the necklace. "A slave collar?"

Amy flipped the heart over so Jane could see the padlock closure on the back of it. "It locks with a key and Mark has the key. I can't remove it unless he removes it for me."

"Okay. That's weird and a little sexy at the same time," Jane said. "When did he give it to you?"

"This morning."

"At the office?" Jane said. "That seems…risky."

"No, at my house. He, uh, he came by last night and stayed over."

"I thought you had agreed on Tuesdays and Thursdays."

"We did. I went to bed early because I was exhausted. Mark let himself into the house and crawled into my bed just before ten. He was tired too and we just slept."

"Oh," Jane said.

Amy touched the collar again. "We had sex in the morning though. Twice."

She rubbed her sweaty palm over her skirt. "God. Sorry. I'm oversharing, I know."

Jane laughed. "It's fine. I'm just wondering why he gave you the collar to wear when the master/slave thing is only supposed to be in the bedroom."

"He wants me to be reminded that I belong to him."

"Again, that's weirdly hot."

"You don't think it's over the top?" Amy asked. Her cell phone buzzed on her desk and she walked over and grabbed it.

"It totally is," Jane said. "But that doesn't make it any less hot. I wonder if... what's wrong?"

Amy looked up from her phone screen. "Mark just texted me. He can't come by tonight. Selene needs him to cover for her at the club."

"I'm sorry," Jane said.

Amy shrugged and tried to look like she didn't care. "No big deal. I'll see him on Tuesday night."

"See who Tuesday night?" Luke strolled into her office and slipped his arm around Jane's waist. He kissed her and said, "What are you doing up here?"

"Bringing Mark a file," she said.

"So, you stopped in to see my sister but not me?"

Jane laughed and leaned her head against him. "I was going to stop and see if you wanted to have lunch."

"Sure," Luke said. He glanced at Amy. "Cute necklace, Ames."

"Thanks."

Luke glanced at his watch. "It's eleven thirty, can you take an early lunch?"

"Let me just check with Kyla, but it should be fine," Jane said.

"I'll walk you downstairs and wait while you ask."

"Kyla won't say no with you standing there."

"That's the idea," he said with a grin. "C'mon, gorgeous."

"I'll talk to you later, Amy," Jane said as Luke led her toward the door.

"You bet."

She waited until Jane and Luke were gone before slumping into her chair. She stared out the window at the falling snow. Despite having sex with Mark twice this morning, she'd been looking forward to tonight. She shook off her depression and turned around to open her sketch book. Mark had two jobs and was busy. He enjoyed being with her, but she wouldn't be his number one priority and that was okay. It's not like they were in a relationship, for God's sake.

అం ఴ

"I'm sorry, Mark."

Mark looked away from the wall of screens in front of him. Selene was hurrying into the control room and she sat in the chair next to him.

"It's fine," he said. "How's your dad?"

"Better," she said. "Has it been busy?"

"Steady. Wallace just finished up a show." He glanced at his watch before standing.

"Do you have a minute to talk?" She asked.

"Can it wait?" He snuck another peek at his watch. It was just after eleven. If he hurried, Amy might still be awake when he got to her house.

Selene nodded. There were dark circles under her eyes and she looked tired and unwell. Mark sat down again and took her hands. "Hey? Do you need to go home and get some sleep? I can cover the rest of the shift."

She shook her head. "No. The club doesn't close until three and you have to work at the office tomorrow."

"I don't care about that. You look tired. I know it's difficult when a family member is sick."

"I'm good. Yeah, I'm tired but it helps to be here. Keeps my mind off the fact that my father is dying."

He squeezed her hands. "I'm sorry."

"Me too," she said. "You go home and get some rest. You still look beat. Did you even try the warm milk last night?"

"No, but I got a solid seven hours of sleep. I'm just not caught up yet."

"How did you fall asleep?" Selene asked.

"He masturbates just like the rest of us single bastards." Trent strolled into the control room balancing a muffin and a cup of coffee in one hand. "Daisy brought in muffins if you want one. They're in the staff room."

He sat down in the chair next to Selene and took

a bite of his muffin before pushing a few buttons on the keyboard in front of him. He peered at one of the screens on the wall. "Fuck, the Blue Room bed is soaked in cum. What the hell did Peter do to that chick? It's like she fucking exploded."

"Go home, Mark," Selene repeated. "Get some sleep."

"Yeah, okay." He leaned forward and kissed her cheek. Guilt was brewing in his belly. He wasn't going home. He was going to grab a few items from the toy room and then he was driving straight to Amy's. Watching the club screens all night had him horny as hell.

Is that the only reason you're going to Amy's? What if she's sleeping? You gonna wake her up or just crawl into bed with her like her goddamn boyfriend?

He ignored his inner voice as he left the control room. Staying at Amy's last night had been a mistake. One that he wouldn't make tonight. If his little slave was sleeping, he would wake her, fuck her, and leave. Simple.

Chapter Fifteen

She was brushing her hair when she heard the tell-tale squeal of the front door opening. Her heart knocked against her ribcage and a flush rose in her cheeks. It was Mark. She knew without a doubt that it was. She studied herself in the vanity mirror. She was wearing a baby-doll style nightgown. The light green material hugged her tits and fell to mid-thigh. She watched in the mirror as her nipples tightened into hard buds against the thin material.

Had some part of her known that Mark would

show up? She normally wore nothing to bed but a pair of panties. Yet, here she was wearing a sexy little nightgown with nothing underneath.

The door to her bedroom opened and her hand tightened around the handle of her hair brush. She took a deep breath and ran the brush through her long hair, trying to look nonchalant as Mark stood behind her.

He took the brush from her and set it on the vanity before sweeping her hair aside. He touched the silver and purple collar and then cupped her neck with his big hand. It was a loose grip, but it still sent shivers of need down her spine as he studied her in the mirror.

"Hello, little slave."

"Hello, Sir."

His hand traced her collarbone before brushing the neckline of her nightgown. "This is pretty."

"Thank you, Sir."

He slipped his hand inside her nightgown and cupped her breast, pulling on her erect nipple as she watched in the mirror. His other hand threaded into her hair. He pulled her head back before bending and molding his mouth over hers. She opened immediately for him and he pushed his tongue between her lips. She sucked on it, enjoying his low groan, and he pinched her nipple before pulling away.

"Stay where you are," he instructed as he turned and walked away.

She watched in the mirror as he set a leather bag on the bed and opened it. He produced two floggers, a smaller leather one and a bigger suede one, and something low in her belly tightened. Already her pussy was dampening, preparing her for her Master's cock and she squirmed a little on the chair.

Behind her, Mark pulled out a weird looking contraption. He carried it to the door and attached it to the top of it. When he was finished, two cuffs hung down on short leather straps. He shut the door and tugged on the cuffs before adjusting the straps. When he was satisfied, he took off his suit jacket and draped it across the top of her dresser. He removed his tie and unbuttoned the top two buttons before unfastening his cuff links.

As he rolled up his sleeves, revealing his muscular forearms with their light dusting of dark hair, more pleasure speared into her belly.

"Come, little slave."

She stood. Her legs were trembling, and she walked unsteadily toward him. He pulled her into his embrace and pressed a kiss against her throat as she glanced at the floggers on the bed.

"Are you nervous, little slave?"

"A little."

"Just nervous?"

She shook her head, blushing when he slipped his hand under her nightgown and cupped her bare pussy. "You're soaking wet, slave. Were you touching yourself without my permission?"

Oh God. This was embarrassing. "No."

A grin crossed his face. She bent her head, so he couldn't see the red in her cheeks, but he immediately tipped her head up to face him. "Being wet for your Master is nothing to be ashamed of."

She licked her lips and glanced at the flogger again. "Please fuck me, Master."

"Soon," he said. "Arms up."

She held up her arms and he pulled the nightgown over her head and tossed it on the bed. He eyed her breasts with appreciation before bending and sucking on her right nipple. She moaned and arched her back, weaving her hands into his hair. He sucked on both nipples until they throbbed with need.

When he lifted his head, she made a harsh cry and tried to push his head back to her tits. He slapped her on the ass and she released his hair.

"I'm sorry, Sir."

He didn't reply. She could see his cock tenting the front of his pants and she wanted to touch him but knew better. Instead, she followed contritely when he led her to the door.

"Face the door, little slave."

She did as he asked, staring at the wood as he lifted her left arm and wrapped the cuff around her wrist. He fastened it tight and moved to the right arm, lifting it and cuffing her wrist in the same manner. He stepped back, and she pulled experimentally on the cuffs. She couldn't slip free and her arms were too far apart for her hands to reach the opposite cuff.

She was his prisoner.

A spasm of pleasure went through her belly and she pressed her hot cheek against the cool wood of the door. Mark ran his hand down her back and over her ass before disappearing. When he returned a few seconds later, he was holding a hair clip from her vanity. He pulled her hair into a ponytail and twisted it before clipping it into place.

He kissed the side of her neck and rested one heavy hand on her hip. "What is your safe word?"

"Magnolia."

"Good." He kissed her neck again before moving away. She stared over her shoulder as he picked up the smaller flogger and returned to her.

"Face the door, slave."

Her body trembling, she turned and faced the door. Her hands clenched into fists and she made a startled cry at the first touch of the flogger. Mark moved the flogger continuously against her back in small circles and larger figure eight motions. He avoided her spine and lower back and concentrated on her upper back. Surprisingly, it didn't hurt nearly as much as she thought. It stung, and she could feel her skin growing hot, but she could handle the flogging. In fact, the little stinging bites of pain made her pussy throb pleasantly.

She waited for him to flog her ass, but he continued to concentrate on her upper back. Every ten seconds or so, he stopped flogging and rubbed her lower back.

"How does it feel?" He finally asked.

"Good," she said. "I mean, not *good good*, but not bad."

His low chuckle and the way he slipped his hand between her thighs to rub her clit, made her squirm and pull against her restraints. "Your sweet cream is dripping down your thighs, little slave."

She moaned when he pushed one finger into her tight entrance. She was soaking wet and her nipples were rock hard. She pressed her upper body against the door, spread her thighs and thrust her ass out. Mark's finger probed deeper and she moaned and rocked against his hand.

"So eager," he said with another low laugh.

She cried out in disappointment when he moved his hand away but the strikes from the flogger quickly distracted her. She pressed against the door, closing her eyes and concentrating on the stinging pain.

When he stopped and moved away, she glanced behind her. He had picked up the bigger flogger and she chewed on her bottom lip as he approached her. He held it loosely in his right hand and rubbed her upper back with the other.

"Your skin looks so pretty right now," he said.

"Sir, I…"

She eyed the bigger flogger in his hand and he rubbed his thumb across her bottom lip. "Do you trust me, little slave?"

"Yes, Sir."

"Good. Face the door."

She faced the door, her hands clenching into fists. Mark began the same motion with the bigger flogger, moving his wrist in small circles and figure eights against her upper back. This time the pain was less stingy and more thud-like. She decided she preferred the thudding type of pain more.

She began to relax a little, letting her body sway to the rhythm of the flogger's cyclic strikes. This wasn't so bad. In fact, she could probably –

"Fuck!" Her cry of pain was very loud in the quiet bedroom.

Mark had changed movements, snapping the flogger forward with a hard, overhand strike that sent a brand of fire across her upper back. She arched and cried out again when he repeated the motion twice more.

"Oh fuck!"

He switched to the circle motion and she rested her forehead against the door, panting heavily. That was better. That was –

"Shit! Fuck!"

He had switched techniques again and mother of Mary that burned. She flattened herself against the door, heart pounding, pussy throbbing, and screwed her eyes shut as the flogger landed repeatedly on her back. The thudding pain blocked everything else out and she concentrated on breathing through each strike. It hurt like motherfucking hell, but it was still tinged with just the slightest hint of pleasure.

Each strike that sent pain to her back made her pussy pulse. Even through the pain, she was aware of the moisture that was still sliding down her inner thighs. She moaned and pleaded as tears slipped down her face.

She drew in a hitching breath of relief when Mark switched to the lighter circular strikes. He slowed the pace of the flogging. When he stopped completely, she sagged against the door, breathing in harsh gasps of oxygen. Her arms hurt from being restrained above her and she moaned in complaint when Mark's hands gripped her hips.

He was suddenly as naked as she was, she could feel his hard cock pressing against her ass. He pulled on her hips until she was bent as much as she could be with her arms tied above her. Her head hung down and she stared at the floor of her bedroom as Mark ran his hand over her ass. Her arms complained but he refused to let her go when she tried to wiggle forward and relieve some of the tension on her arms.

"Master, please," she whispered.

He ignored her and spread her thighs apart roughly. She cried out when he pushed his cock deep into her pussy. She was so wet there was no resistance at all. With one hand on her hip and the other on her shoulder to prevent her from headbutting the door, Mark fucked her with hard, short strokes. She moaned and pleaded hoarsely, pulling at the cuffs around her wrists despite the pain in her arms. He fucked her harder, pounding into her as his hand slipped under her. He rubbed her clit and she screamed as her climax rolled over her as relentless as the tide meeting the shore.

Pleasure coursed through every part of her body, making her shake and moan and clench tightly around his thrusting dick. She pulled him in tight, clamping around him and refusing to let him go. He bellowed a curse, his hands digging into her shoulder and her hip before his back arched and he came with a shout that made her ears ring. He rocked back and forth, keeping his cock embedded deep inside of her until he softened.

He pulled out and wrapped one arm around her waist, pulling her into an upright position. She leaned against him as he uncuffed her hands. She was shaking uncontrollably, and tears were streaming down her face. Her back throbbed dully but she couldn't stop the spasms of pleasure that still shook her lower body.

Mark kissed her neck and rubbed her belly and hip. "Such a good girl, sweet slave. You were such a good girl for your Master. I'm so proud of you, baby. You're my good slave."

She kept her eyes shut as Mark lifted her and carried her to the bed. He sat her on the side of it and stopped her from flopping onto her back. "Drink, baby."

She drank from the bottle of water he held to her mouth. It soothed her parched throat and she protested when he pulled it away.

"Open your mouth, Ames."

She opened her mouth and he placed a square of sweet chocolate on her tongue. She sucked on it as he helped her slide under the covers. She was still shaking, and she was grateful when Mark pulled her into his warm embrace.

He rubbed her lower back and pressed kisses across her face. "You were such a good little slave, baby. You did very well for your first flogging."

"Thank you, Sir."

He wiped away the tears on her face and kissed her mouth before reaching over her and grabbing the bottle of water. He sat her up and gave her another few drinks before tucking her under the covers and in his arms again.

"Why am I cold?" She asked as she snuggled closer.

"It's normal," he said. "Do you want more chocolate?"

She shook her head and rested her head on his chest. "I liked it."

He stroked her back. "I liked it too, Ames."

"Will you stay the night?"

"Yes."

She kissed his chest and pressed her ear against his heart. The solid thump soothed her, and she closed her eyes and slept.

ॐ ॐ

Chloe took a deep breath before knocking on Mr. Dawson's office doors. She was meeting with him and the two French investors, and her nerves were trying to get the best of her. The door opened, and she stared in surprise at the blonde woman.

"Amy, hi. I didn't know you would be at the meeting."

"Technically, I'm not," she said as she motioned for Chloe to come in. "Well, I'm going to meet with them later but it's just you and Luke at this meeting."

"Okay," Chloe said. "Hi, Mr. Dawson."

"Call me Luke," he said. "Chloe, I need to talk to you about Mr. Durand and Mr. Morel, and I thought it best to have Amy here while I did."

"Sure." She glanced at Amy. She had a small grin on her face as her brother crossed around his desk and stood next to her.

"Julien and Pierre are," Luke hesitated. He looked distinctly uncomfortable and he glanced at Amy who made a 'go on' gesture.

"The thing is," he said, "they're very charming but sometimes say inappropriate things. They're probably going to, well…"

Feeling sorry for how uncomfortable he looked, Chloe said. "I know. Amy told me how they act around women."

Luke glared at Amy. "You already told her? Why the hell didn't you tell me that?"

"I like watching you squirm, Lukie," Amy said.

He glared at her before giving her a friendly slap on her back. "That's cold, Ames, really … what's wrong?"

Amy had flinched, and Chloe could see the shine of tears in her eyes.

"Nothing," she gasped.

"Something's wrong," Luke said. He reached to touch her back and she twisted away.

"Don't!"

"What the hell?"

"I hurt my back yesterday. It's no big deal, just a pulled muscle," Amy said.

"Shit. Sorry."

"It's fine." Amy touched the purple and silver heart that dangled from her necklace before giving Chloe an apologetic look. "Sorry. Go on, Luke."

Luke shoved his hands into his pockets. "I just wanted to say that if at any point Pierre or Julien say anything that makes you uncomfortable, don't hesitate to let me know. We won't condone harassment of our employees in this office, even from our investors. Okay?"

"Okay," Chloe said. "I'm sure it'll be fine."

"I doubt it," Luke muttered under his breath. "Excuse me for a moment. I need to talk to Mark before the meeting starts."

He left his office and Amy smiled at Chloe. "Pierre and Julien will probably just be very flirty and charming. They don't normally cross the line. But Luke means what he said. If you're offended or uncomfortable, just tell him."

"Like I'm going to destroy a relationship with our investors just because they flirt with me," Chloe said. "I can handle a little flirting."

"Okay, well, just remember what we said."

"I will. Don't worry about it. They're probably not even into redheads with no hips and ghost skin."

Amy laughed. "You're gorgeous and they're going to be flirting up a storm with you."

Luke returned and gave Amy a strained smile. "Ames, are you sure you don't want Jane and me to go to dinner with you tonight?"

"Positive," Amy replied. "Relax, Lukie, I can handle Pierre and Julien perfectly fine on my own."

A scowl crossed his face before he turned to Chloe. "Let's go to the boardroom. You can get your presentation set up before the two Casanovas get here."

Chloe laughed and followed Luke and Amy out the door. "Sounds good."

❧ ❦

"Fuck, am I glad that's over." Luke sank into the office chair across from Mark's desk.

"How did it go?"

"Fine, if you think letting investors flirt with our employees isn't a problem," Luke said. "They were all over Chloe in the meeting, complimenting her in French and trying to get her to go for drinks with them this weekend. I don't even know if they heard a fucking word she said during her marketing presentation. They just nodded and smiled and stared at her tits and her ass, the entire time."

He sat forward and scrubbed his hand through his hair. "I'm starting to second guess our decision to work with them. They're sexually harassing our goddamn employees. I guess Amy warned Chloe ahead of time what they were like. I told her if they made her uncomfortable, not to hesitate in telling me, but what if she doesn't? What if she just files a complaint with the labour board or something?"

"She won't," Mark said. "Chloe isn't like that and she's a lot tougher than she looks. She'll talk to you if it bothered her."

Luke sat back in his chair again. "If they keep this up, I'm talking to them about their behaviour, Mark. I don't care if they pull out of the company."

"Fair enough." Mark glanced at his watch as Luke pulled at his tie. "Did Amy go for dinner with them?"

Luke's lip curled. "Yes. She came in as the meeting ended. You should have seen the way they were all over her. They just jump from woman to woman, it's gross. They left for dinner about ten minutes ago."

"What was Amy wearing?"

Luke frowned at him. "What? Why do you care?"

"I just wondered."

"I don't know what she was wearing. Her work clothes I think." Luke jumped up and paced the room. "I should have gone with them."

"Amy can take care of herself," Mark said. He wished he believed what he was saying. Every part of him was screaming to go to the restaurant and physically carry Amy away from the two French men.

"Yeah, I know. Anyway, did mom text you? Her and dad are going away for the weekend. There's no Sunday dinner."

"Yeah, she sent me a text this morning."

"Okay." Luke headed toward the door. "We still meeting at the gym on Saturday?"

"Ten o'clock. I'll be there."

"See you." Luke left, and Mark sat back in his chair.

His stomach was in knots and he couldn't stop picturing Amy with the two investors.

She isn't going to sleep with them, idiot. She's wearing your collar and she told you she wouldn't fuck them. Don't you trust her?

He did trust her. It was Pierre and Julien he didn't trust.

❧ ❦

"These are incredible, mon ange," Pierre studied the sketches on the screen of her laptop before he took another sip of wine. "Your casual line will be as popular as the business line."

Amy smiled at Pierre before shifting away from Julien. He'd been moving closer to her and his leg was brushing against hers. "Thank you, Pierre. I appreciate yours and Julien's enthusiasm for my work."

"More wine, ma chérie?" Julien went to pour

more into her glass and she covered the top of it with her hand.

"No thank you, I'm driving."

"We would be happy to have our driver return you to your home. Or wherever you may end up this evening," Julien said with a flirty smile. His light green eyes darkened when they dipped to her cleavage. "Drink with us in celebration."

"Celebration of what?" Amy said.

"Why, our investment in your international business line and your new casual line," Pierre said.

She stared at him. "You want to invest in a casual line?"

"Of course we do," Pierre said. "Why would we not?"

"I – thank you," Amy said. "I'm flattered and thrilled."

"Bien," Julien said. "We are happy to do business with such a talented and beautiful woman. Now, ma chérie, what do you think about joining Pierre and me at our hotel room for a nightcap?"

Amy took a deep breath and touched Mark's collar around her neck. Her dreams of creating a casual line were about to be destroyed, but she had no interest in sleeping with either of the French men. Even if she wasn't in love with Mark, she would never sleep with Julien and Pierre.

"That's kind of you to offer but it's late and I'm going to head home."

"Are you certain, mon ange?" Pierre said. "It is not that late." He traced one finger down her arm.

"Let's be straight with each other," Amy said. "I am never going to fuck either of you, together or apart. Ever."

The two French men stared silently at her. She sighed and picked up her purse and her laptop. "Thank you for dinner. I appreciate that you were interested in working with me on a casual line, even if it was only briefly."

She stood up and both men stood as well before Julien grabbed her arm. "Amy, what do you mean, only briefly?"

"I know you're only going to invest in my casual line if I sleep with you," she said.

"Merde, that is far from the truth," Pierre said. "Our investing in your casual line is not dependant on you sleeping with us."

"Of course it isn't," she said. "Look, we all know you'll say whatever tonight, but by tomorrow, you'll be backing out of the agreement to invest in the casual line."

"We will not," Julien said. "I promise you this, Amy."

He glanced at Pierre. "Do we wish to have you in our bed? Very much so. But we are not dogs. We will invest in your casual line because you are a talented designer who will make all of us a lot of money."

She stared at him and Julien nodded. "It is true, mon ange. I promise."

Warmth flooded her belly and she couldn't stop her the grin from spreading across her face. "Thank you."

"You are welcome." Pierre took her hand and lifted it to his mouth, pressing a kiss against her knuckles. "Enjoy your weekend, ma chérie. We will have a contract drawn up and sent to your office, oui?"

"Yes, thank you." Amy shook Julien's hand, her smile widening when he kissed her knuckles as well and gave her a wink.

"A pleasure as always, mon ange."

"Good night."

Amy walked out of the restaurant and hurried to her car. She climbed behind the wheel and then made a loud shriek of excitement before yanking her phone out of her purse. She needed to call Mark and tell him the good news. She scrolled for his name in her contacts before stopping. What was she doing? She couldn't call Mark. One, he was at the club and two, they weren't dating. She couldn't just call him to share the news.

Yes, you can. You're still friends. Call him. Better yet, stop by the club and tell him the good news in person.

Should she? She was aching to see him again and this would be the perfect excuse. She didn't have to stay or anything, but she wanted to see his face when she told him. He'd be thrilled for her and she wanted to see his sweet smile.

She tossed her phone on the seat beside her, started her car, and drove toward the club.

Chapter Sixteen

"Why are you still here, Selene? Go home and enjoy your weekend." Mark didn't look up from the laptop sitting in front of him. He'd brought it into the control room, in hopes of finishing up some reports while he kept an eye on the main floor.

"I will. But let's talk first."

Selene sat down next to him and eyed the report he had open. "How are numbers this month?"

"Good. One of our highest. New memberships are up fifteen percent this month."

Selene smiled in satisfaction. "I was thinking we start doing two shows on Friday night and Saturday night. What do you think?"

"I think it's a good idea. Not sure if Richard will want to do two shows though."

"It doesn't have to be Richard. Wallace or Peter could do the second show. Or you."

"No." Mark stared at the screens on the wall. The thought of doing a show, hell, of even touching someone other than Amy, made him feel sick to his stomach. "I can't."

"Can't or won't?" Selene asked.

"Both."

Selene studied the ends of her long dark hair. "Wallace wants to buy into the club."

He turned to face her. "Seriously?"

"Yes, and I think we should consider it. You've been burning the candle at both ends for two years. You can't keep this up. Not to mention that you're in a relationship now. Do you want to spend every weekend at the club instead of with Amy?"

"We're not in a relationship."

"Keep telling yourself that, sweetheart."

He scowled at Selene, but she just smiled. "If we make Wallace a partner, he can cover the weekend shifts and some of the shifts during the week. You can concentrate solely on the financial side of the business. It takes some of the pressure off you and your weekends are yours again."

"I don't need free weekends. I'm not in a relationship with Amy and - "

"It's not just that," Selene said. "It'll take some of the pressure off me as well. I need a more engaged partner in the club, Mark. You know I love you and I don't want you thinking that I'm trying to edge you out, but we need someone else. Someone who can be here during the week as well."

He leaned back in his chair and tugged at his earlobe. "Shit. I'm sorry."

"Don't be," Selene said. "I knew when we decided to buy the club, what it would be. But in the last two years, the club has grown significantly in membership. We need another, and I think Wallace is perfect for the job."

"Yeah, okay."

"Yeah?" Selene gave him a look of gratitude. "You sure? You can think about it for a few days."

"I don't need to. It makes sense, and I'm not pulling my weight around here."

"That's not what this is about," Selene said. "The growth of the club has put us in this situation and that's not a bad thing."

"I guess you're right."

"I am." She stood and smoothed down her skin-tight dress. "I'm going to have a quick chat with Wallace before I leave. Can you do dinner Sunday night with Wallace and me? Around seven? We can discuss the partnership arrangement."

"Sure. I'll print financials for Wallace to look over."

"Perfect." She leaned forward and kissed him on the forehead. "Thank you, Mark."

"Thanks for not kicking me out completely."

She pinched his cheek. "I'd never do that to you, muffin. You know that."

He gave her an affectionate slap on the ass. "Go home, Selene. Enjoy your weekend."

"Bye, sweetie." She kissed his forehead again and left.

He stared at the laptop in front of him. Everything Selene said made sense and truthfully, he felt relief more than anything. The hectic pace of working two jobs was starting to get to him and the idea of having free time again was intoxicating. If he wasn't working the weekends, he could spend more time with Amy. He could –

You're not in a relationship, moron.

He slumped back in the chair before grabbing the beer on the desk and taking a long drink. It was just after eight. Maybe he should text Amy, just to see if she got home okay.

Home from her date?

He scowled and took another drink of beer. It wasn't a goddamn date.

You're right. Besides, she probably isn't home. She's probably still at the restaurant with those two French bastards. Maybe one of them has his hand on her leg right now. Maybe he's touching what belongs to you and -

"Hey, Mark?" The door to the control room opened.

"What is it, Trent?" He struck at the keys on his laptop with hard short taps.

"Got someone here to see you."

"What?" He spun around in his chair. Amy was standing inside the control room with Trent and he couldn't stop the grin on his face. "Ames? What are you doing here?"

As Trent closed the door and left them alone, she gave him a tentative smile. "Hi. Sorry, I didn't mean to bother you at work. I asked upstairs at the front desk if they would check and see if you had a minute. But then this guy showed up - "

"Trent."

"Trent showed up and told me to follow him. I'm sorry."

"I don't mind," he said. "It's, uh, good to see you."

Christ, he sounded like a smitten schoolboy.

She smiled and joined him at the table. "I won't

take up much of your time, I just… holy shit."

She had glanced at the wall of screens in front of them. He grinned when her mouth dropped open and she leaned over the table to get a better look. She was staring at one of the screens on the bottom row. In the Red Room, Peter and Richard had a woman between them. Her arms were restrained with leather cuffs and she was straddling Peter. His dick was in her pussy and Richard's dick was in her ass. Despite the bright red ball gag in her mouth, there was no denying the look of pure bliss on her face as the two men fucked her roughly.

He watched Amy as she watched them. Her mouth was still open, and her hands were clenched in tight fists against her midsection. Her shirt was stretched tight against her breasts and he could see the way her nipples had hardened. His cock was already straining against his pants and he was tempted to give her open mouth something to suck on.

"Little slave, you are very close to having a cock in your mouth."

She stepped back and closed her mouth with a snap as bright red colour infused her cheeks. "Mark, I – sorry. It's rude of me to watch."

He grinned and stepped behind her. He pressed his dick against her delightful ass and cupped her breast before kissing the side of her neck. "Most people here don't mind being watched."

She moaned and arched her back, pushing more of her breast into his hand. "Yeah, I guess."

He tasted the skin on her throat again just above her new collar. "How was your dinner?"

She turned in his arms and gave him a look of pure delight. "That's why I'm here. Julien and Pierre want to invest in a casual line."

"Ames, that's great!"

"I know, right? At first I didn't think they would because they invited me back to their hotel room and - "

His hand reached down and squeezed her ass, pulling her up against his erection as his nostrils flared. "They what?"

She laughed. "Don't look so surprised. You knew as well as I did that they'd try and lure me back to their hotel room."

He squeezed her ass again as she put her arms around his shoulders. "Anyway, I turned them down and told them point blank that I would never fuck them – together or apart. I was sure Luke would be right and they wouldn't want to invest in the casual line if I didn't sleep with them, but he wasn't right. I wasn't right! They said they still wanted to invest and they're having a contract drawn up for us to look at. Isn't that amazing?"

"I never doubted for a second that they would want to work with you, baby," he said. "I'm so proud of you."

She grinned and pressed a quick kiss against his mouth. "I'm sorry to bother you at work. I really wanted to tell you in person, and I couldn't wait until Monday."

"I'm glad you stopped by," he said.

"Yeah?"

He nodded and cupped her face before bending his head and kissing her. She made a sweet little moan and returned his kiss enthusiastically. He lifted her and set her on the table behind them, pushing between her thighs and rubbing his dick against her.

They kissed repeatedly as he slid his hand under her shirt. He grazed the warm soft skin of her stomach before cupping her breast through her bra and squeezing. She moaned into his mouth before pulling back.

Before he could stop her, she had pushed him back, slid off the table and dropped to her knees in front of him. As her hands unbuttoned his pants, he said, "Ames, baby, what are you doing?"

"Celebrating my good news," she said with an impish grin.

"Not that I don't appreciate your enthusiasm, but I think I should be the one with my face in your – oh fuck…"

Amy had pulled his cock free of his underwear and engulfed him with her warm, wet mouth. His brain went numb as every ounce of his blood went to his dick. He threaded his fingers in her hair and guided her mouth back and forth over his cock.

"Fuck, baby, that's so good. I love your hot mouth on my dick. You're so - "

"Hey, Mark? Shit… sorry."

Amy made a muffled shriek around his cock before pulling back. His heart pounding, he hauled her to her feet. He stuffed his dick back into his pants and hurriedly buttoned them as he looked over his shoulder. Wallace, a small grin on his face, was standing in the doorway of the control room.

"Uh, hey, Wallace."

"Hi. I can come back if…"

"No!" Mark said. "No, that's fine. Uh, Amy just popped by to, uh, tell me something."

Amy groaned and hid her face in her hands as Wallace's grin widened.

"Why don't you take a break so you and Miss Amy can…talk. I'll watch the floor for you."

"That's okay. Amy was just…"

"I was just leaving," Amy said. "Bye, Mark. I'll, uh, see you on Monday."

Keeping her head down, she walked toward the door. Wallace stepped aside. "It was lovely to see you again, Miss Amy."

Christ, he could see Amy's cheeks glowing from across the goddamn room.

She cleared her throat. "You as well, uh, Wallace. Good night."

When she was gone, Wallace said, "Take a break, Mark. Seriously."

"I can't."

"You can. Go play with your slave for an hour or so while I watch the floor."

When Mark opened his mouth to protest, Wallace said, "It'll be good practice for me. Right? Give me a chance to show you what I can do while you're still in the building in case I need assistance."

Mark hesitated, his gaze slipping to the open door. His cock was still hard and throbbing and the temptation to go after Amy was very strong.

"Go," Wallace said. "I'll call you if there are any issues."

Mark grabbed his phone and stuffed it into his

302

pocket. "Thanks, man."

"Don't mention it. Have fun."

❧ ❧

Holy shit. Had she ever been more embarrassed? She had just been caught sucking Mark's dick at his goddamn job. Sure, dick sucking happened to be a common occurrence at this particular workplace, but still…

Amy hurried across the foyer on the top floor of the club. She was absolutely humiliated, but there was a very large part of her that was wishing Wallace hadn't walked through the door. Blowing Mark at work was apparently a huge fucking turn on for her.

So, blow him in his office on Monday.

Yeah, that was never going to happen. The person likely to walk in on them there would be Luke. Just the thought of that made her throw up a little in her mouth.

Lock the door, idiot.

Her footsteps slowed. They could lock the door to his office. The idea wasn't a terrible one. Mark had a couch in his office. Maybe she could suck his dick and then he could fuck her on the couch. Technically they were only supposed to be together Tuesdays and Thursdays, but he broke that rule on Wednesday night. She could break the rule on Monday morning, right?

She nodded to the woman sitting at the front desk before walking toward the front door. God, the thought of not seeing Mark until Monday was killing her. She would be busy on Saturday but after that, she'd spend the rest of the weekend thinking about Mark and wishing –

"Ames!"

She whirled around. Mark was jogging toward her and she didn't protest when he took her hand and tugged her back toward the front desk.

"Good evening, Mr. Stanford."

"Hi, Angie. I need a room."

"Of course." She typed quickly before producing a card key. "Room 212, Mr. Stanford."

"Thank you."

Still holding her hand, Mark took the card key and hurried her toward the sweeping staircase. She tugged at his hand. "What are you doing?"

He stopped at the foot of the stairs and pulled her up against him. He bent his head and kissed her temple before breathing into her ear, "Taking my slave upstairs so I can fuck her."

She shuddered with pleasure, her hand gripping his as he nipped her earlobe. They walked up the stairs and down the hall to their room. The moment they were in the room with the door locked, Mark pushed her up against the wall and kissed her hard.

"Mark, wait," she moaned. "You – you're working."

"I'm on a coffee break."

She giggled as he unbuttoned her shirt. "So, we have fifteen minutes?"

"A little more time than that." He stripped off her shirt and unhooked her bra. He cupped her breasts in his hands. "God, I love your tits. They're incredible."

"Thank you," she said primly.

He grinned at her and turned her around to unzip her skirt. He touched her back with the tips of his fingers. "How's your back?"

"Fine," she said. "It was sore yesterday and only tender today. By tomorrow it won't hurt at all."

"Good." He kissed between her shoulder blades then pushed her skirt down her legs as she kicked off her boots. He peeled off her tights and panties before turning her to face him again and cupping her pussy.

"Why are we here and not downstairs?" She asked.

"Cameras." He tugged on her curls before rubbing the wet lips of her pussy.

"I would think you'd be used to it," she said. Her thighs parted, and she moaned when he rubbed her clit.

"I don't want others watching my little slave being fucked." He gave her a hard slap to her ass, making her cry out and jerk against him, before he stepped back. "No one sees you naked except me. Is that clear, slave?"

"Yes, Sir."

"Good." He unknotted his tie and pulled it free. "Turn around."

She turned immediately and missed his satisfied smile. "Put your arms behind your back."

She did what he asked, pushing her wrists together in the small of her back. He looped his tie around her upper arms and pulled tight until her back was arched. He knotted the tie and tugged on it.

"How's that, little slave?"

"Tight," she said. "I can't move my arms at all, Sir."

"That's the idea."

He turned her around and studied her naked body before glancing up at her face. "You're so beautiful, Amy."

She blinked at him in surprise before giving him a shy smile. "Thank you, Mark."

They stared at each other for a moment before he turned away and stripped off his jacket. He draped it on the small loveseat in the room before unbuttoning his shirt and removing it. She made an appreciative sound in the back of her throat when he took off his pants and briefs.

"Does my slave want to suck her Master's cock?"

"Yes, Sir." She tried to drop to her knees. Fuck, it was difficult to do without the use of her arms. Before she could even really give it an effort, he took her arm and kept her on her feet.

"Please?" She eyed his dick and licked her lips.

Mark made a low groan. "Little slave, you have no idea how much I want your lips wrapped around my cock, but this is your celebration. I'm going to eat your sweet little pussy instead."

"Why not do both?" She said.

For a moment it looked like he was going to push her to her knees, but he backed up a step and took her arm. "As much as I'd love that, I'm technically working and we're on a time limit."

She laughed. "Oh, well in that case – pussy eating it is. Get to it, buster."

Her squeal when he slapped her ass made him grin. She pouted at him and he kissed it away before leading her to the bed.

He pushed her back with a gentle touch until she was lying on her back. She squirmed a little as she tried to get comfortable with her arms tied behind her back. Her back still arched and he studied her breasts before opening her thighs and kneeling between them. He leaned over her and pulled on her nipples. She squeaked and arched her back even more as he bent his head and soothed the sting with his tongue.

"If we had time," he licked between her breasts and up to her collarbone, "I would bring Wallace in and have him work his magic with the rope. You would look so beautiful, little slave."

She moaned. "I – I thought you didn't want anyone else seeing me naked, Sir."

"I could make an exception for Wallace."

Oh fuck. She was way more turned on than she should have been.

Mark touched the tip of one rock-hard nipple. "Of course, he would want something in return."

He rubbed his cock against the soft swell of her stomach as she stared up at him. "What do you mean?"

He reached between her legs and cupped her pussy, rubbing gently at her clit. "Perhaps, once Wallace was finished, when you were bound and helpless, I would allow him to taste my slave's sweet pussy as a thank you."

A gush of wetness covered his fingers even as her cheeks turned a deeper shade of pink. "I – I don't think, I mean, I don't even know him."

His quiet laugh made her blush even more. She closed her eyes as lust and embarrassment fought for dominance. It was a mistake. Immediately, the image of Richard and Peter fucking the bound woman played like a damn porno in her head.

The image flickered, wavered and suddenly she was the bound woman and the two men were not Richard and Peter, but Mark and Wallace. She was straddling Mark, her pussy stuffed full of his cock and his hands on her hips, while Wallace cupped her tits and pushed his cock deep into her ass.

Mark was still rubbing her clit and she moaned as the first flickers of her climax ignited in her belly. Her pussy clenched around nothing and she made another helpless moan of need. Mark moved his hand away and her eyes popped open.

"No! Please, Master! Please fuck me!"

"My slave doesn't want her pussy eaten?"

"I need you to fuck me," she begged. "Please." She couldn't get that damn image out of her head, the idea of being impaled with two thick cocks, of being helpless to stop them from taking what they wanted from her.

She was going to lose her goddamn mind if her Master didn't fuck her soon.

"Please," she begged again.

"What were you thinking about, little slave?" Mark trailed one finger lazily around her nipple.

"Fuck me!"

"Tell me what you were thinking about and I will." He rubbed his cock against her stomach before pressing the head against the entrance of her pussy. His hard hands pushed on her hips, keeping her from arching up to sheath him inside of her. "Tell me, slave."

"You and Wallace," she gasped as her pussy clenched uselessly. "Fucking me together."

Mark's nostrils flared, and she couldn't stop her cry of relief when he shoved his dick into her. He lifted her legs over his shoulders and angled deep, fucking her with hard strokes that made her bounce on the bed. It put added pressure on her shoulders and restrained arms, but the pain only made the pleasure sweeter.

She was so close, her pussy squeezing Mark's dick with every downward stroke. When he rubbed her clit with his thumb, she screamed and climaxed immediately. He held her legs tightly as she shook through her orgasm, and fucked her even harder.

He changed the angle of his thrusts and she screamed again when his cock brushed against her g-spot. He made a hard grin and fucked her until she was screaming and writhing on the bed as her second orgasm engulfed her entire body.

She had no idea when or even if Mark came. Waves of pleasure were still rolling through her, and bright lights were flashing behind her eyelids, and her heart was beating so fast, she thought it might explode. She couldn't seem to catch her breath and her entire body was twitching and jerking.

Vaguely she was aware of being turned on her side, of the pressure on her arms being relieved as he undid the tie, of Mark's warm body pressed against her back. "Breathe, Amy. Take deep breaths, baby."

She gasped in a lungful of air, pushed it out, and gasped in another.

"Good, baby. Do it again."

She did it again.

Again.

Again.

Her heartbeat slowed, and she leaned back against Mark, shivering despite the warmth of his body. He rubbed her hip and kissed her shoulder.

"You okay?"

"Never better," she croaked.

He laughed and sat up. He crossed to the mini-fridge, grabbed a bottle of water, and brought it back. "Drink."

When they'd emptied the bottle, he relaxed next to her on the bed again, stroking the soft skin between her breasts. Without opening her eyes, she said, "Did you come?"

He laughed. "Yes."

"I didn't even notice," she said. "I was too busy screaming and possibly having an orgasm-induced heart attack."

He laughed again, and she opened her eyes and smiled at him. "Thank you. That was about a billion on the orgasm scale."

"My pleasure, Ames."

"Do you have to go back to work now?"

"Not just yet." He kissed the top of her shoulder again.

"Would you really let Wallace…"

"Tie you up?"

She nodded, and he gave her a thoughtful look.

"Yes, probably. If that was something you wanted to try. I have no talent for Shibari and Wallace is very good at it."

"What about – I mean, would you let him taste me?"

"No," he said bluntly. "I wouldn't let him taste you or fuck you."

"Threesomes are hard limits for you?" She wondered if he could see the surprise on her face.

"No. Sharing you is a hard limit for me."

"Oh."

"Do you want to have a threesome with Wallace?"

She considered his question before shaking her head. "No. The fantasy of having sex with both of you did turn me on, but that's all it is. A fantasy. Actually fucking someone other than you, even if you're there? I'm not into it. You're the only one I'll ever want."

He stiffened next to her and gave her a guarded look. "Amy, you know that this is only…"

"Slave training. Yeah, I remember." She hated the bitterness in her voice.

"I'm sorry, I - "

"Don't," she said before sitting up. She slid off the bed before he could stop her and hurried to where her clothes were. "You were perfectly clear what this was, and I agreed to it. You have nothing to apologize for. I should get going though. You're supposed to be working, and the roads aren't great tonight. I want to get home before they get worse."

They dressed in silence. When they were finished, she forced herself to smile at Mark.

"Thanks for taking a coffee break with me."

He tugged on his earlobe. "Congratulations on the casual line. I am really proud of you."

"Thanks."

She wanted to kiss him. She wanted to hug him and tell him that she loved him. Instead, she opened the door, stopping and staring at the empty hallway when Mark called her name.

"Yeah?"

"Are we good?" He asked.

She blinked back the hot tears, pasted a smile on her face and looked over her shoulder. "Yeah, we're good. See you later."

Chapter Seventeen

"Amy, are you sure you're okay?" Jane asked.

Chloe had wandered ahead of them in the mall and was staring at a book on display in the window of the Barnes and Noble.

"Yeah, I'm fine," Amy said.

"You've been quiet all afternoon. Even Chloe has noticed."

"Just a little tired, I think," Amy said. "We should go to the food court and grab a coffee."

"Sure." Jane was giving her a worried look and Amy smiled at her.

"I swear, I'm good. Hey, Chloe?"

Chloe joined them. "What's up?"

"Want to hit the food court? I'm hitting the three o'clock slump and could use a coffee."

"Sure."

The three of them took the escalator to the food court. Once they had their coffees, Jane led them to a table.

"I wore the wrong shoes," Chloe said. "My feet are frackin' killing me."

"Well, I really only want to go to one more store and then I'm done," Jane said. "What about you, Amy?"

"I'm finished with my stuff." Amy sipped at her coffee.

"Oh, I didn't mean that we had to stop," Chloe said. "I'm fine to keep going."

"I told Luke I'd be home by four anyway," Jane said. "He has a new recipe he's trying and -"

"Amy?"

The low raspy voice was oddly familiar. The smell of stale smoke and sweat washed over her as she turned to look behind her.

"Amy? You lookin' good, girl."

She studied the man standing behind her and weaving slightly. His thin face was covered in scabs and his eyes were sunk in their sockets. He was wearing a dirty jacket and a mud-caked scarf was wrapped around his neck. He scratched at one of the sores on his face with long and dirty nails.

"Michael?"

"Yeah, it's me!" He smiled at her revealing rotting bottom teeth and oozing gums where his top teeth used to me. "How you been?"

He shuffled forward and dropped onto the seat beside her. She had to fight the urge to cover her nose.

"I'm good," she said. "How are you?"

"Can't complain," Michael said. "You gonna introduce me to your friends?"

"Jane and Chloe, this is Michael Stanford. Mark's brother."

"Nice to meetcha." Michael smiled at Jane and

then squinted at Chloe. "You look familiar."

"We've met before, Michael," Chloe said. "At Mark's office the other day."

"Right. You're fuckin' him."

Amy winced, and Chloe shook her head. "No, we're just friends."

"Oh, right." He turned back to Amy. "It's been a long time, Amy. You married yet? Got any kids?"

"No," she said. "Where are you living right now, Michael?"

He shrugged. "I got a few different places I crash at. Listen, Amy, can I ask you a favour?" He leaned closer and she held her breath and tried not to flinch. "You think I can borrow a few bucks?"

He scratched nervously at the biggest scab on his cheek. "I hate to ask but I lost my job last week and I need some groceries. You know how it is."

"Uh, sure, Michael." She reached for her purse.

"Amy." Chloe shook her head slightly and Amy hesitated.

"Mind your damn business, Red," Michael said. "This ain't any of your fucking business."

"Michael, watch your language," Amy said.

"Sorry. Listen, I just need something to get some groceries. What do you say, Amy? Can you help your old friend Michael out?"

Feeling sick to her stomach, she took out her wallet and gave him all the cash she had. It was only about two hundred bucks, but Michael's face lit up. He grabbed for it and stuffed it into his pocket.

"Thanks, Amy. I appreciate your generosity."

He stood and scratched again at the sores on his face. "You still working with Mark?"

"Yes."

"Good, that's good. Maybe I'll come by the office someday to see you."

"No," Amy said. "You can't come by the office, Michael. Do you understand? I don't have any more money to give you. This is it."

"Yeah, sure, okay. I'll see you around, Amy."

Michael wandered away. When he disappeared down the escalator, Amy released her breath in a shaky sigh. She felt sick to her stomach and she smiled faintly at Jane when the woman pressed a tissue into her hand. She wiped away the tears that were collecting in her lashes.

"You okay?" Jane said.

"Yeah."

"Amy," Chloe leaned forward, her face even paler than normal, "you shouldn't have -"

"Given him the money, I know. He'll just use it to buy drugs."

"Why did you?"

"Because it's Michael! Because I remember how he was before the drugs really took hold. Because he's Mark's brother and I…"

"You love Mark," Chloe said.

Jane nearly spit out her mouthful of coffee.

"Shit. I'm sorry," Chloe said. "Jesus, I'm a goddamn idiot. I didn't mean to -"

"Jane already knows," Amy said.

"Thank God," Chloe said. "But I'm still sorry. I don't usually go around blurting out secrets, I swear."

"It's fine" Amy said. "Just maybe don't do it around my brother, okay?"

"I won't. Sorry." Chloe's face was bright red, and she looked close to tears.

Jane cleared her throat. "Are you going to tell Mark you saw Michael?"

"No. It'll only upset him."

"From someone with experience with addicts, you should probably tell him," Chloe said. "Michael said he would come by the office to see you and he's pretty wacked out on drugs. Sometimes, that can affect them in ways that you -"

"Michael isn't dangerous and he's not going to hurt me," Amy said. "I know the drugs have done a lot of damage, but when we were kids...he was as sweet as Mark, if not sweeter. He's not a bad man. He's just broken."

"I know but sometimes - "

"We should hit that last store so that Jane can be home by four." Amy stood and grabbed her bags and her coffee. "Ready?"

Jane and Chloe glanced at each other before Jane nodded. "Yeah, we're ready."

๛ ๙

He was losing his damn mind. He couldn't keep sneaking into Amy's house in the middle of the goddamn night like some sex-crazed lunatic. So, why was he creeping into her bedroom at three in the morning?

He'd left the club fully intending to go home to his empty apartment. Only, somehow, someway, he'd ended up at Amy's house again.

Her laptop was on the bed beside her. He smiled and moved it to the nightstand. No doubt she'd been watching movies in bed. He missed watching movies with her.

He stripped off his clothes and climbed into her bed. She didn't stir until he spooned her and kissed her shoulder. She was naked, warm, and so soft. God, did she smell good.

"Hey, Mark?" She stretched and yawned.

"Yeah, baby?"

"What time is it?"

"Late. Go back to sleep."

"Hmm," she said.

He put his arm around her and she reached down and took his hand, linking their fingers together. "How was your day?"

"Fine," he said. "I met your brother at the gym at ten, went back to the apartment, had lunch, and did some work before I went to the club."

"Was it busy?" She yawned again.

He nuzzled his collar around her neck. "Yes. How was your day, baby?"

"Good." She turned in his arms, sliding her arm around his waist and throwing her leg over his hip. He pressed a kiss against her mouth. "I went shopping with Jane and Chloe at the mall."

"Did you have fun?"

"Yes. Jane invited me to have dinner with her and Luke, so I did. Then I," she yawned a third time, "I came home, had a hot bath and watched a movie in bed."

"That sounds really nice."

"It was." She was drifting back to sleep. Her

breathing was deepening, and her body was relaxing against his. "I'm really glad you're here, honey."

"Me too, baby."

"Love you." Her eyes slipped shut and he stroked her hair back from her face.

"I love you too."

৵ ৵

When she woke it was almost eleven. She stretched and grabbed her cell phone. She scrolled through her Facebook and ignored her urge to pee. The bed was warm, the air was cold, and she was half-tempted to fall back asleep. She'd had a really great dream about Mark. For once, it wasn't even a sex dream. He'd just crawled into bed with her and cuddled her. He'd asked about her day and told her about his. She'd felt so safe and warm in his arms and it was like they were a real couple. God, she loved him so much.

She stretched again and ran her hand over the empty side of the bed. What would it be like to wake up to Mark every morning? To feel his hard body next to hers?

Pipe dream, girl. Now get your ass out of bed and go pee before you wet the bed.

She wandered into the master bathroom. Before she was even done, she had decided a return to bed was the right move. She climbed back into bed, her gaze landing on the nightstand as she pulled the covers to her chin.

She stared at the cell phone sitting on it before stretching across the bed and grabbing it. It was Mark's phone and she looked over the side of the

319

bed. Mark's clothes were in an untidy heap on the floor. She set his phone back on the nightstand and leaned against the headboard as her pulse thumped and thudded. It hadn't been a dream. Mark was here.

"Hey, Ames? Wake up, baby. It's almost eleven. I've made you coffee but when I went to make toast, the bread was disgustingly moldy. I mean, we're talking science experiment in your cupboard." Mark strolled into her bedroom, holding two cups of coffee and wearing her silk robe. She stared at him in frozen shock before bursting into giggles.

"What?" He grinned at her and handed over a cup of coffee.

"Nice robe."

"Thank you. I've been told that I look really good in pink."

He moved to his side of the bed and dropped the robe with a remarkable lack of self-consciousness before climbing naked into bed beside her. His phone buzzed as he took a sip of coffee. "I have to answer this email. Sorry."

"It's fine." She sipped at her coffee and picked up her phone, scrolling through Facebook again. She tried to ignore how right it felt to be drinking coffee in bed with Mark. Tried to ignore how it felt like they were in a real relationship.

She finished her coffee and set the empty cup on her nightstand. Mark was still typing away on his phone and she scooted down in the bed, curled on her side and checked her own email before returning to Facebook.

"You're Facebook friends with that giant bouncer from the strip club?" Mark curled up behind her and rested his chin in the crook of her neck.

"His name is Tony and yes. He sent me a friend request after I met him at the hospital when Jane's foster mom was sick."

Mark laughed before kissing her cheek. "You're just full of surprises, Ms. Dawson."

"Tony's really funny," Amy said. "He does stand-up comedy once a month at this bar downtown."

"You're kidding me."

"Nope. Jane, Luke, and I went to his last one. He had the crowd in hysterics."

"Huh," Mark said. He watched as she scrolled through her feed. "Jesus, Mandy Tapkin's kid is ugly."

"Hush." She slapped him lightly on the forearm. "She's not ugly."

"She? I thought that kid was a boy."

She burst into giggles. "She's a girl. Her name is Destiny."

"Of course her name is Destiny," Mark said with a snort. He rubbed her belly with his big, warm hand. "Hey, Ames?"

"Yeah?" She was starting to feel too warm.

"I have a surprise for you."

God, she hoped it involved his tongue and her pussy.

"Oh yeah?"

"Yes. Roll onto your back and close your eyes."

She did what he asked. She spread her legs a little, her hands clutching at the covers as she waited for Mark to move between her legs.

He was doing something on the bed beside her. What was that tapping noise? Was he putting together some sort of restraining device? Maybe he was going to tie her to the bed before he ate her pussy. Maybe he was –

"Okay, open your eyes."

She opened them. Mark had her laptop open and she stared at the Netflix home page before glancing up at him. "Netflix?"

"Yeah!" He gave her an adorable boyish grin. "It's snowing and gloomy and the perfect weather for ordering pizza and having a movie marathon. What do you say, Ames? Wanna watch a movie with me?"

She touched his face. Ran her fingers over the dark stubble on his jaw. Smiled.

"I would love to watch a movie with you, Mark."

&ipsp; &ipsp;

She was a bundle of nerves. Her palms were sweating, and her heart was racing and holy hell, what if Mark wasn't in to her fantasy? What if he found it…weird? Or gross? What if the same look crossed his face that had crossed Tom's when she'd finally worked up the nerve to –

Amy, stop! Relax and take some deep breaths before you pass out.

Her inner voice had a point. She braced her hand against the desk and inhaled and exhaled slowly until the beat of her heart had gone from scared squirrel to panicked possum.

She snorted laughter. Panicked possum? What the fuck was wrong with her?

"Get it together, you idiot!"

The sound of her voice in the silence made her twitch in her too-high-nearly-impossible-to-walk-in heels. She weaved, grabbed the edge of the desk to catch her balance and took another deep breath.

It was Sunday night. She and Mark had spent the afternoon in bed, binge-watching movies, eating pizza and, at one point during a particularly slow part of *Lord of the Rings*, napping. He'd been affectionate and sweet, spooning her in the bed as they watched TV, giving her little kisses throughout the day, but they hadn't had sex.

She had loved every damn minute of it. This was what Boyfriend Mark looked like and she'd never dreamed she'd see it. She had no idea why he was acting this way and she didn't really care. She knew in her heart that this side of him wouldn't last, and so she had soaked up the attention and the love with every fibre of her being. When he came back to his senses and put up that wall again, she would have the memory of this day to cherish.

Mark left just before seven for a business dinner with Selene and Wallace. He asked almost shyly if she wanted him to come back after his dinner. Her immediate yes made him smile and he'd pressed a warm kiss against her mouth before leaving.

Now, she smoothed down her skirt and checked the clock on the wall. Mark said he would be back by nine-thirty and it was twenty after. She smoothed her skirt again. It was a black and white checkered pleated skirt and so damn short, it barely covered her ass. She'd bought it yesterday while shopping and she hadn't even come out of the change room to show Jane. It wasn't like she was going to wear it in public anyway. No, this was purely for her own little fantasy.

What if Mark thinks it's sick? What if he thinks you're sick?

She reached down and adjusted her white thigh-highs. She'd had to buy those as well. The white shirt she already owned. It had shrunk in the wash and was way too tight across the tits. She'd meant to donate it and never got around to it. She studied the buttons before unbuttoning one more. She was wearing a push up bra and her tits were practically falling out of the damn shirt. She supposed that was the idea.

She touched the silver and purple collar around her throat before touching her hair a little self-consciously. She had put it in two pigtails to complete the school girl look. When she'd stared at herself in the mirror in her bedroom, she'd been both amused and a little turned on by her costume.

She studied the desk in her office. Before getting dressed in her outfit, she had cleared everything off the desk. Well, almost everything. Her gaze dropped to the wooden ruler lying in the middle of the desk and her nipples hardened as an almost painful cramp of pleasure flooded her lower belly.

The front door slammed, and her pulse ratcheted back up to scared squirrel levels.

"Ames! I'm back!"

"In the office," she called.

She hurried to the whiteboard she had set up in her office. She eyed the sucker she'd grabbed from the kitchen cupboard before unwrapping it and popping it into her mouth. If she was going to try and live out this fantasy, she might as well go full throttle, right?

She picked up the whiteboard marker and began to write under the lines that were already there. She could hear Mark's footsteps in the hallway and she tried to control her breathing as her hand trembled. Her usual neat handwriting was a barely-legible chicken scratch at this point.

"Hey, Ames. Did you eat? Do you want…"

She turned, put her hand on her hip and pulled the sucker from her mouth before pouting at him. "Mr. Stanford, you gave me too many lines. It's not fair. My hand hurts."

There was a moment of perfect silence as Mark looked her up and down. She tried not to fidget and popped the sucker back into her mouth as Mark's gaze dropped to the desk. He stared at the ruler before lifting his gaze to hers.

Every muscle in her stomach and pelvis tightened and then loosened at the look of pure lust in his eyes. The crotch of her white panties dampened, and she almost abandoned her little fantasy right there and begged Mark to fuck her.

Instead, she sucked on her sucker as Mark leaned against the doorjamb and studied her mouth.

"It isn't fair, Sir," she said again.

He didn't reply, and she could feel sweat

breaking out on her forehead.

Please, Mark, oh please, be into this. Please, please, please.

Mark shoved his hands into his pockets and walked into the office. "You misbehaved, Ms. Dawson. Misbehaving means punishment."

"But writing a hundred lines is stupid. It's gonna take me forever and I'm supposed to meet Jenny at the mall in, like, an hour," she said as he leaned against the desk and folded his arms across his broad chest.

She sucked enthusiastically on her sucker before stepping toward him. His gaze dropped to her tits and she ran one finger across his broad chest just above his crossed arms.

"Maybe we could think of a different punishment, Mr. Stanford?" She gave him a coy smile as he raised one eyebrow.

"What did you have in mind, Ms. Dawson?" He pulled the sucker from her mouth with a low pop and dropped it into the trash can.

"Well," she licked her lips and traced her fingers over his crossed arms and down his flat abdomen. "Maybe I could, you know, do *something* for you."

She stared at the way his pants tented at the crotch. Before she could touch his dick, he caught her wrist and squeezed hard.

She gasped and pouted at him. "Ouch, Sir."

"What are you trying to say, Ms. Dawson?"

She crinkled her nose at him. "I could, you know…"

"No, I don't know. Clear communication is

important. Wouldn't you agree, Ms. Dawson?"

"Yes, Sir," she said.

"Then be clear."

"I could," a nervous giggle escaped from her lips, "I could, like, suck your cock for you."

His nostrils flared, and his hand tightened around her wrist. "Excuse me?"

"I could suck your cock," she repeated in a low voice.

"I'm your teacher, Ms. Dawson."

"Yes. But I, like, turned eighteen two weeks ago, Sir. So, you know, you wouldn't, like, get in trouble or anything."

A cold grin crossed his face and she shivered and tried to tug her wrist free of his grip. He refused to let her go, instead pulling her closer until the tips of her breasts brushed against his hard chest.

"Do you really think I would accept an offer of cock sucking from one of my students, Ms. Dawson?"

"I – I don't know," she whispered.

"How many cocks have you sucked?"

She flushed bright red at his question and looked at the floor. "I don't, I mean…"

His hard hand gripped her chin and forced it up. "Answer me. How many cocks have you sucked?"

"One," she said. "I sucked Evan Thorne's cock after the football game."

He laughed derisively, and new shame flooded through her.

"Let me guess. You sucked Evan's cock and he followed you around like a little puppy dog for weeks after that, doing whatever you asked him to do. So now you think getting on your knees and wrapping those soft little lips around a dick is the perfect way to get the boys to do what you want. Is that right?"

She tried to pull her head free, but he refused to let her go. "Answer me, Ms. Dawson."

"Yes!" She said. "Yes, I do, Sir."

He cupped the back of her head and she moaned helplessly when he put his mouth to her ear and his warm breath washed over it.

"There's only one problem with your plan, Ms. Dawson. I'm not a boy. Offering to suck my cock isn't going to make me forget that you've misbehaved, or let you leave this room without punishment."

"Please, Sir," she moaned and tried to touch him. He grabbed both of her wrists in a hard grip and pushed her back.

"You will finish your punishment, Ms. Dawson."

He released her wrists and pointed at the white board. She glared at him and reached for the marker. Before she could resume writing lines, he said, "Of course, I do understand the importance of honouring your commitments."

She swung around and gave him a suspicious look. "What do you mean, Sir?"

"You're meeting your friend in an hour."

"I'm supposed to be," she said sulkily. "But I'll never finish this in time."

"True, you won't," he said. "But I'm willing to offer a different punishment. One that will be much quicker and allow you to meet your friend like you promised."

"What type of punishment?"

He picked up the ruler and her insides cramped with pleasure. He tapped it thoughtfully on one hard thigh. "Have you been spanked before, Ms. Dawson?"

She backed up a step, her hands automatically reaching down to cover her bottom. "No. I – my parents don't believe in it."

Another smile of derision. "Of course they don't. Their perfect little princess would never do anything to deserve a spanking. Would she?"

She crossed her arms nervously over her torso as he stood. There was an armless, straight-backed chair in the corner of the room and he picked it up and brought it over. He sat down and smiled at her. "You can continue to write lines and miss your chance to hang out with your friends, or you can be spanked and join your friends."

She chewed at her bottom lip before staring at the lines on the whiteboard.

"Make your choice, Ms. Dawson. I don't have all day."

She worried her bottom lip again. Owen Kipten was going to be at the mall and she'd had a crush on him for months. So did Jenny. If she didn't show up, Jenny would be all over Owen and she was a total slut. She'd probably fuck him in a change room at the mall or something, and Amy would lose her chance with him.

"Okay," she said in a low voice.

"Okay what, Ms. Dawson?"

"I – I'll do the spanking."

She approached him cautiously and he patted his lap. She blinked at him. "You want me to bend over your lap, Sir?"

"Yes," he said.

"Uh, okay." She started to lean over him, and he shook his head.

"Your panties, Ms. Dawson."

"Uh, what about them?"

"Pull them down."

She backed up a step and gave him a horrified look. "What? No, I can't do that!"

"You offered to suck my cock, Ms. Dawson, but balk at me seeing your bare bottom?"

She flushed. Her nipples were hard pearls in her bra and she was feeling hot and uncomfortable and turned on all at the same time.

"Do I have to, Sir?" She whispered.

"Yes."

She bit her lip and reached under her skirt. His eyes flared with dark lust when she pulled her plain white cotton panties down. They were only mid-thigh when he held his hand up. "That's good. Come here."

She shuffled forward and took a deep breath before bending over his lap. She tried not to touch him, but he pushed on her lower back with his hard hand and she fell against his thighs with a small 'oof'.

His erection dug into her stomach and she took in another deep lungful of air as his hands lifted the back of her skirt and the cool air hit her naked ass. She eeped in surprise when his hand wrapped around one pigtail and tugged. She turned her head. He released her pigtail and held out the ruler to her.

"Hold this, Ms. Dawson."

She took it with a trembling hand and turned her gaze back to the floor. Her entire body jerked when he slapped her right ass cheek and he steadied her with one hand on her lower back.

Without speaking, he spanked each cheek repeatedly. She cringed and moaned, trying not to wiggle, and failing miserably. He spanked the back of her thighs, just below her ass and she cried out and tried to push his hand away with her free hand.

He caught it and twisted it behind her back. "Try to stop me again and you'll get extra spankings. Understand, Ms. Dawson?"

"Yes," she said.

He spanked her hard. "Try again."

"Yes, Sir!" She cried out. "I understand, Sir."

"Good." He released her hand. She let it drop down and gripped the leg of the chair. She squeezed it and the ruler in her left hand as he spanked her until her skin was bright red and her ass and upper thighs were throbbing.

When he pushed his hand between her thighs and touched her pussy, she squealed in alarm and tried to climb off his lap. He kept her pinned to his thighs and parted her pussy lips to push two fingers deep inside of her.

"Mr. Stanford! You shouldn't touch me there," she cried desperately.

"You're very wet, Ms. Dawson. You seem to be enjoying your punishment."

"I'm not!" She cried. "I'm not!"

He rubbed her clit and she shrieked and writhed against his fingers. Already she was so close, and she made a pleading noise when he pulled his hand away.

"The ruler, Ms. Dawson."

She stared at it in her hand. Her ass was already burning and suddenly the idea of being spanked with the ruler was not nearly as appealing.

She turned her head, tears dripping down her cheek and into her ear. "I'll be a good girl, Sir. Please don't spank me with the ruler."

His smile was somehow both cold and reassuring. His hand rubbed her burning ass. "The ruler, Ms. Dawson. Don't make me ask again."

Her hand shaking, she handed him the ruler. He patted her bottom as she faced the floor and closed her eyes. The first spank with the ruler made her squeal. She clutched the chair legs with both hands and squeezed her eyes shut as tears streamed down her face. He spanked her repeatedly, each slap of the ruler leaving a burning strip of pain across her flesh.

When he spanked her upper thighs with the ruler, she buried her mouth in the crook of her arm and screamed. He spanked her upper thighs four more times before stopping and rubbing her ass and thighs. When her heartbeat had slowed he spanked her ass again, the sound of the wooden ruler hitting her flesh very loud.

He stopped again and pushed his hand between her thighs. His fingers rubbed and pinched her clit and she screamed again. This time it was a scream of pure pleasure. He grunted in surprise when she climaxed all over his leg, her entire body shuddering and bucking against his lap.

She collapsed against his lap, her head hanging down and gasping for air as spasms shook her pussy and her legs twitched. She could barely stand when he helped her up off his lap and she swayed on her heels. He cupped the back of her neck and kissed her hard, forcing his tongue past her lips and tasting every part of her mouth. His other hand yanked at her blouse. Buttons popped off and rolled across the office floor as he shoved her shirt down her arms and reached for her bra clasp. He unhooked it and yanked it off her body before squeezing and kneading her breasts.

Her ass and the back of her thighs were burning but she didn't protest when he turned her around and pushed her roughly over the desk. She rested her hot cheek against the smooth wood, listening to his harsh pants and the sound of his zipper. He crowded up against her, pushing her legs apart with his hard thighs as he shoved her skirt up around her waist. She cried out as the pressure of his hair-rough skin rubbed against her sensitive skin.

He lifted her hips, spread her legs even farther until she could feel her underwear digging into her thighs and plunged his cock into her tight warmth. She cried out again, her pussy clenching around him. Each stroke was pleasure and pain as his pelvis smacked into her painful ass and legs. It didn't stop her from meeting each of his thrusts with a hot eagerness. The desk scraped across the floor as she pounded into her and she screamed his name and came again when he reached under her and rubbed at her clit.

His cock swelled, thickened, stretched her with every single stroke and he gasped her name before coming deep inside of her. He thrust back and forth as her pussy squeezed him tight.

When he collapsed against her back, his breath hot on her flesh and his heart pounding against her spine, she made a weak laugh. "You okay back there?"

"Jesus," he rasped, "that was the best fucking fantasy ever, Ames."

She laughed again. "I'm glad you enjoyed it. Can you get off me though? You're kind of heavy."

"Fuck, sorry." He eased out of her and steadied her when she straightened and immediately wobbled on her heels.

He pulled his pants up as she kicked off her heels and shoved her panties the rest of the way down her legs. She stepped out of them. He cupped her head and pulled her into his arms.

"Thank you," he said. "That was unfuckingbelievable."

She kissed his throat. "It was really good."

He laughed hoarsely. "Yeah, good doesn't even begin to describe it. Turn around, baby."

She turned, and he lifted her skirt to look at her butt. "Let's get an ice pack and the aloe vera gel."

She gave him a nervous look. "Ice pack for my butt? How bad is it back there?"

"Not that bad, but you are going to bruise this time," he said. "The ice will help with any swelling and maybe minimize some of the bruising. Go to the bedroom, Ames, and I'll grab the ice and bring it to you."

"Are you – I mean, are you staying the night?'
She asked.

He cleared his throat. "I stopped at home after
my meeting and picked up some fresh clothes and
toiletries. But, uh, I don't have to stay if you don't -
"

"I do," she said. "I want you to spend the night
with me."

"Okay." He kissed her. "Bed now, I'll be right
there to do aftercare."

"Yes, Sir," she said.

Chapter Eighteen

Monday afternoon, Amy eased her ass into her office chair and winced. Fuck, but did her ass hurt. Actually, she decided, it was more her upper thighs that hurt. They had started to bruise already, stripes of dark purple in the perfect width of the ruler. She had studied them in the mirror this morning, feeling pride and a weird kind of fulfillment.

She wasn't the only one. Mark had joined her and stared at the marks on her ass and backs of her thighs. He hadn't even tried to hide the look of satisfaction on his face as he touched the marks with his fingertips. He had smoothed more lotion into them for her after she showered, and she had hissed her way through the pain. He offered no apology for the bruises and once more, she was oddly content that he didn't.

Of course, that had been this morning before a two-hour sit-down meeting with her design team. Now, she was in desperate need of some Advil and maybe a bag of frozen peas to sit on.

She climbed to her feet with a light groan and

left her office. She'd grab a coffee from the kitchen and see if there was any Advil in the cupboard. As she walked down the hall toward reception, she heard Brenda's voice rise in alarm.

"Sir! Sir, I told you he isn't here. If you don't leave, I'm going to call security."

Amy hurried forward. She groaned when she saw Michael, even dirtier and smellier than he was on Saturday, standing by the desk in reception.

"I don't care! I know he's here and I'm not leaving until I see him."

"Michael?"

He turned and stared at her. His pupils were blown out and he was ticking nervously. "Amy! Hey! How the fuck are you?"

"Michael, hush," Amy said.

"I'm glad to see you. Hey, thanks for your help on Saturday."

"You're welcome. You should go though."

He scowled at her. "I need to see Mark."

"He's not here," Brenda said. "I told you that." She glanced at Amy. "Mark and Luke are at a meeting."

"Okay," Amy said. "Why don't you -"

"You need to leave!" Brenda said shrilly when Michael leaned against her desk.

"I ain't fucking leaving," Michael said. "You're gonna have to drag me out of here before -"

"Michael, stop!" Amy said. "Come to my office, okay?"

"Amy -"

"It's fine, Brenda."

"Yeah, Brenda, it's fine," Michael said. "We're

friends."

"Can you call Mark on his cell phone and ask him to come back to the office right now, please, Brenda?" Amy said as she led Michael toward her office. She needed to get him out of sight before he made a bigger scene. Already people were poking their heads out of their office, drawn by the sound of his shouting, and she cringed at the thought of Mark being humiliated by the actions of his brother.

"Hurry, Michael," she said.

"I'm comin'," he puffed behind her.

He followed her into her office and she shut the door. "Michael, I -"

"Oh, hey, pretty lady!"

Jane was sitting in one of the beanbag chairs and she jumped to her feet. "Um, hi. Amy, I'm sorry, I stopped in because I had a file for you. I didn't mean to interrupt."

"You haven't," Amy said. "Michael is just here to see Mark."

"He's not in the office. He and Luke are at a meeting." Jane eyed Michael when he wandered over to the mannequin and touched the fabric draped across it with one grimy finger.

"I know. Brenda's calling him right now," Amy said. "You should go, Jane."

She gave her a bright false smile and Jane shook her head. "No, I don't think I should."

"It's fine. Mark will be here any moment."

"I'll wait," Jane said.

"This is a real nice office you got here." Michael stared out the window before grinning at her. "You always did real well, didn't you, Amy?"

"Why don't you sit down, Michael? Jane and I will go to the kitchen and get you a coffee, okay?" Amy said.

"Nah, I don't need one. Actually, I stopped by because I was hoping to see you again. Wondered if I could borrow a few more bucks."

She shook her head. "No, I'm sorry. I told you on Saturday that I wouldn't give you money again."

A scowl crossed his face and Amy took Jane's hand when he stalked toward them. "That ain't fair, Amy. You got more money than you know what to do with."

"I don't have any to give you," she said. "You took all of it on Saturday."

"Bitch," he snarled at her. "Why you gotta be such a fucking selfish bitch, Amy?"

She swallowed down the fear that was rising in her throat. "You need to leave now, Michael."

"I don't have to do anything you tell me," Michael said. He reached into his pocket and pulled out a switch knife. He clicked the button and the blade popped free, shiny and terrifyingly sharp.

Bitter, cold fear blossomed like a malignant flower in her belly.

"Michael, put that away. What do you think Mark will say if he sees you threatening me with a knife?"

"I don't fucking care what that little bastard says or does no more. He leaves me to starve on the street like a dog. He knows I need my medicine, but he won't give me the money for it." Michael's face twisted and he scratched at the sores before pointing the knife at her. "He's as selfish as you are, bitch."

Jane's hand was cold and clammy in her own. Amy retreated backwards toward the door, tugging the smaller woman with her.

"Stop moving!" Michael shouted.

She stopped, the malignant flower growing into her chest. "Michael, I can't give you money that I don't have. I gave it all to you on Saturday. There's nothing in my wallet. I can go to a bank machine though. Why don't you wait here, and we'll run to the bank machine and bring you - "

"You must think I'm a real fucking idiot," Michael said.

"I don't."

"You do." He eyed the bracelets around her wrists. "Give me your jewelry."

"Michael - "

"Give it to me!" He waved the knife at her and she held up her hands.

"Okay." She slipped the bracelets off her arms and placed them in his shaking palm. He stuffed them in the pocket of his jacket. He studied Jane and said, "Give me your ring and that necklace."

Her fingers trembling, Jane handed them over. He added them to his pocket and stared at Amy again. "I want your necklace too."

"I can't give it to you."

"Yes, you fucking can!"

"No," she said. "It's locked and I don't have the key. See?"

She tried to turn the heart pendant over to show him the closure and cringed back when he raised his knife.

"Give me the fucking necklace, Amy, or I'll cut your pretty little fingers off. You think you can draw all your pictures without your fingers? Huh?"

"I don't have the key," she repeated. "I swear. It's locked, and I can't open it."

"Fuck that!" Michael said. "Stop lying to me, you stupid bitch!"

"She's not lying, Michael."

Mark's low, calm voice spoke behind her, and relief poured through her in a big swooping rush that stole her breath.

"Hey, little brother." Michael's grin was cold and humourless.

When Jane was tugged away from her, Amy turned to see her brother pushing Jane behind him. His face pale, he reached for her next.

"Don't you fucking touch her, Luke," Michael said.

He held his hands up. "Michael, put the knife down."

"Fuck you, Luke. You know I always hated you. You smug fucking bastard. You took my brother from me!"

"Calm down, Michael." Mark moved beside her but when he tried to plant his big body between hers and his brother's, Michael shook his head again.

"Don't do that, asshole."

"I have money for you." Mark reached for his wallet. "I'll give you what I have and then you can - "

"I want that fucking necklace!" Michael said shrilly.

"It needs a key to open it," Mark said. "The key is in my pocket."

"Then fucking get it!" Michael waved the knife at him.

Mark reached into his pocket and produced the small silver key. Amy turned toward Mark and lifted her chin.

He smiled at her and stroked the soft skin of her throat. "It'll be okay, Ames."

His hands remarkably steady, he unlocked the necklace from around her throat and pulled it free. He faced his brother, taking a few steps forward as Michael backed up.

"Give it to me!"

Mark held the necklace out. Michael stared at him mistrustfully and reached for the necklace. Before he could grab it, Mark dropped it. It hit the floor with a soft clunk and Michael made a scream of rage.

"I fucking hate you, you spoiled little brat!"

He rushed forward and raised the knife, bringing it down in a deadly short arc. Mark blocked his brother's arm with his forearm before punching him hard in the stomach.

Michael dropped the knife and bent over, gagging and coughing. Without speaking, Mark pulled him into a standing position and punched him in the face. Blood flew from his mouth, landing on the beanbag chair with a wet splat as Michael stumbled back. His eyes rolled up in his head and he fell to the floor in a crumpled heap.

Luke cupped Jane's face. "Call 9-1-1 and go to my office and lock the door. Now."

"Amy, go with her," Mark said.

"Mark - "

"Go, Amy."

She turned and took Jane's hand as Mark crouched beside his brother. Jane pulled her out of the office. She got one last glimpse of Mark's pale face as he placed his hand on his brother's shoulder.

&c ∞

She was pacing in the kitchen when she heard the key in the lock. Luke had almost begged her to stay with him and Jane, but she had refused, knowing Mark would come to her.

He appeared in her kitchen, looking so exhausted and miserable that her heart broke for him. She wanted to rush to him and hug her, but the wall was up. She could see it in his eyes.

"How is he?" She asked.

"He's fine. In jail. He'll be there for – he has a lot of outstanding warrants. The officer said that I shouldn't expect him to get out of prison any time soon in the next five years."

He barked harsh laughter before yanking on his earlobe.

"I'm sorry, honey," she said.

"I'm not." His tone was cold. "He tried to hurt you. He can rot in prison for all I care."

"Mark - "

"Why are you wearing that again?" He pointed to the purple and silver collar around her neck. "You shouldn't wear it. It almost got you killed."

"It's not your fault, honey."

"It is!" He took a deep breath and shoved his

hand into his pocket, withdrawing the key. "Here, take this."

"No," she said.

"Take it!" He almost begged.

"I won't."

He gave her a look of frustration and dropped the key on the table. "I need to go. I just wanted to make sure you were okay."

"Don't leave me," she said.

"I have to."

"No, you don't."

He stared at her before his face crumpled and he turned away. She ran forward and forced him back around before throwing her arms around him. He stood rigid and unyielding against her.

"Honey," she whispered, "don't push me away. Not tonight."

He threw his arms around her waist and buried his face in her throat. "I'm sorry, baby. I'm so sorry."

"Shh, it's not your fault." She tugged his head back and pressed a kiss against his mouth. "I'm fine. It's not your fault."

"When I saw him with the knife and standing in front of you. When I thought…"

His voice broke and he kissed her hard on the mouth. "I need you, Ames.

She took his hand and led him upstairs to her bedroom. They undressed each other. He laid her down in the middle of her bed before stretching out between her thighs. He kissed her curls, her inner thighs and each of her hipbones before burying his mouth in her pussy. She moaned and clutched at his head, ignoring the throb of pain in her ass and back of her thighs as he used his lips and tongue and fingers to bring her to a pulse-pounding climax. When she was weak and shuddering, he slid up her body. She wrapped her thighs around his lean hips and reached between them to grasp his cock.

"Please, Sir."

He shook his head and kissed her on the mouth. "Not tonight, baby. It's just Mark."

She stared at him and he kissed her again, teasing her mouth open with gentle licks. He sucked on her bottom lip and then her tongue.

When he released her, she smoothed her fingers across his jaw. "Please, Mark."

He reached down and guided his cock into her pussy. She moaned and squeezed his waist with her legs as he dropped to his forearms. His hard chest pressed against her breasts and he rested his forehead against hers for a moment before lifting his head.

"I love you, Amy."

She touched his face and blinked back tears. "I love you too."

He moved with long slow strokes. She met each of them with a gentle rise of her hips. They kissed repeatedly and when his strokes turned harder and more urgent, she gripped his waist and urged him on with soft cries.

Their hips slapped together in a quickening rhythm, his pelvic bone grinding against her clit with every stroke. She moaned, pleaded, cried his name.

"I love you," he gasped out as his back arched.

They climaxed together, holding onto each other as the pleasure consumed them both. When he slipped out of her, she clung to him and kissed his warm mouth. "I love you."

"I love you too." He lay on his back and she curled on her side, easing some of the pressure on her butt and thighs. She rested her head on his chest as he stroked her back with his warm hands.

"So," she finally said, "you have to admit that vanilla sex isn't all that bad."

He laughed and kissed her forehead. "Vanilla sex with you is incredible."

"I know," she said. "I'm, like, so good at sex."

His laughter rumbled out of his chest and she planted a kiss on his collarbone. "God, I love you so much."

"I love you too."

"So, when do we tell my parents and my brother?"

She tensed, waiting for him to tell her nothing had changed. To tell her that he loved her but that he couldn't be with her.

"How about Sunday during family dinner?"

Her muscles relaxed, and she kissed his chest again. "Yeah. That should liven it up, right?"

"I'll make sure to sit near the door so when your father and brother try to beat the hell out of me, I can make a quick exit."

"God, you're so manly. It's really hot thinking about you running down the street with my father and brother chasing after you."

He laughed and hugged her. "Don't joke about it, it'll probably happen."

She lifted her head and studied his face. "It won't, honey. They'll be happy for us. I know they will."

He lifted her hand to his mouth and kissed her knuckles.

"Why have you changed your mind about telling them?" She asked.

"Because I love you and I will always love you. I won't lose your family because I'll never lose you. You're stuck with me for life, Amy Dawson."

"Most romantic marriage proposal ever," she said.

He grinned. "You want to marry me?"

"Of course I do," she said. "Maybe not tomorrow, but I'm free next Thursday."

"I'll clear my calendar."

She kissed him before resting her chin on his chest. "We may not have until Sunday to tell my brother. He's going to ask about the necklace. Probably tomorrow."

"Probably."

"I won't tell him about the master/slave thing, but I – I won't lie about loving you."

"I don't want you to," he said. "If he asks you about it tomorrow, just call me. I'll come to your office and we'll tell him together."

"Okay," she said. "I love you, Mark."

"I love you too, Ames. You wanna try another round of vanilla sex?"

She laughed and nuzzled his collarbone. "You read my mind, Mr. Stanford."

వా ⚶

"Amy, this skirt is just not working." Rachel, a bright orange swatch of fabric draped over her arm, walked into her office. "I've pinned the hell out of it and it still doesn't fit right. I need a human mannequin and Jenna's gone for lunch. Drop your pants, lady."

Amy laughed and kicked off her shoes before unbuttoning her pants. "Sure. Shut the door, would you?"

Rachel shut the door to her office and returned as Amy pushed her pants down her legs. Rachel crouched and said, "Turn around for me. The skirt's got a million pins in the back and I'm going to try and not poke you but no promises...oh my God, Amy, your thighs!"

Amy's eyes widened. She was wearing boy shorts and they hid the bruising on her ass but the stripes of bruises on the back of her thighs were exposed. Rachel touched the back of one thigh. "These bruises look like they were made on purpose. Like they're - "

"Hey, Ames?" Luke opened her door without knocking and strolled into the room. "You want to have lunch and – what the hell? Are those bruises?"

He stared at her legs and Amy whirled around and snatched the fabric from Rachel, holding it in front of her body. "Luke! Out!"

"Are those bruises?" He repeated. "What the fuck, Amy? Where did you - "

"Luke, get out!"

He turned and strode jerkily to the door. "Come and see me in my office, Amy. Immediately."

He slammed the door behind him and Rachel

gave Amy a wide-look of anxiety. "Amy? Are you okay?"

"I'm fine," she said. "Go take a lunch break, I'll come and see you later. Okay?"

"Yeah, okay."

She took the fabric from Amy and left. Amy yanked her pants on and took a few deep breaths before walking to Luke's office. She passed Mark's office and hesitated. It was empty, and she bit her lip in thought. She wasn't going in there to tell Luke about her and Mark. She wouldn't text him and tell him to meet her in Luke's office. If Luke even suspected that Mark had left those bruises...

She shuddered and gripped her elbows before continuing to Luke's office. She knocked on the doors, opened them and stepped inside. Luke was pacing behind his desk like an angry bull and he glared at her. "What the fuck are those bruises from, Amy?"

"Calm down, Luke."

"Don't tell me to calm down. My baby sister has bruises all over her legs and don't you dare tell me that you fell down. They're *stripes* of bruising, Ames. They're actual goddamn stripes like someone took a – a cane to you or... who are you dating? Who's the goddamn asshole who is abusing you?"

Shit. He was way too perceptive for his own good.

She pressed her lips together and tried to think of how to word it. "It's not abuse, Luke. Okay? I – I wanted it to happen and I -"

"Fucking hell, it's those goddamn French

dickheads, isn't it?" Luke's hands clenched into fists. "I will fucking kill those bastards. Jesus Christ, Amy!"

"It wasn't them," Amy said. "Luke, it wasn't Pierre and Julien."

"Bullshit, it wasn't! You had dinner with them Friday night. Did you let them hurt you just so you could get a goddamn casual line?"

"What? You asshole!" Amy shouted. "No, I didn't fucking let them hurt me just to get a casual line. You arrogant dickhead. They're investing in my casual line because they see my potential."

"Amy," Luke gave her a sick look before running both hands through his hair, "this is abuse, Ames. Okay? I am fucking shredding the contract. We don't need them to invest in an international line, and you don't have to let them do this to you just to get -"

"I didn't. Goddammit, Luke, I didn't whore myself out to them. Julien and Pierre didn't do this to me."

"Then who?" He shouted. He came around the desk and took her by the arms. "Who the fuck hurt you, Amy? Tell me who did this before I -"

"It was me."

She whirled around and stared at Mark. His cheeks were red from the cold and he was wearing his coat. He shut the doors to Luke's office before standing next to her and taking her hand. "I made those marks on your sister, Luke."

"What?" Luke staggered back. "You – no, what?"

"I love her," Mark said. "I love her and I -"

"You hurt her?" Luke said.

"I love her," Mark said. "There's something you need to know about me. I'm a Dom and I own a club called Secrets. I've been a dominant for -"

"You son of a bitch!"

Amy screamed when Luke grabbed Mark and tore him away from her. He punched him in the face and shoved him back against the wall before punching him in the stomach. "You fucking son of a bitch! She's your fucking sister, you sick motherfucker!"

He punched Mark in the face again. Mark made no effort to fight back or defend himself, and Amy ran forward and grabbed Luke's arm when he tried to punch Mark again.

"Stop it!" She shouted. "Stop it, Luke! I love him, and I asked him to do it."

He blinked at her before stumbling away from her. "Amy?" He whispered. "He-he's your brother."

"No," she said. "He isn't. You're my brother, Luke. Mark is your best friend and I'm in love with him. I have been since I was nineteen years old."

"You can't possibly be okay with what he's doing to you," Luke said.

"I am. I want him to do it."

Luke's face paled. She didn't try and stop him when he stalked to the doors of his office and yanked them open. He left, slamming the doors behind him. She turned and hurried back to Mark.

"Oh, honey," she said. A bruise was already rising on one cheekbone, and blood was trickling from his left nostril. "We need to get you to the hospital."

"No," he said. "I'm okay."

"Your nose might be broken."

"It's not."

"I'm so sorry."

"It isn't your fault," he said. "It's mine. I knew this would happen. We can't be together, Amy. Not after this. Not after -"

"Don't." She pressed a tissue against his nose and cupped his face with her other hand. "This is not going to tear us apart. Do you hear me, Mark Stanford? I love you. You love me. In it for life, remember?"

"For life," he said in a low voice.

"That's right. Luke will come around, I promise you."

"He won't," Mark said. "He thinks I'm sick and when he tells your parents -"

"He's not going to tell my parents. If he does, I'll kick his ass. We'll give him a day or two to cool down and then we'll talk to him again. We'll make him understand."

She pressed a kiss against his mouth. "You're not sick, honey."

"You're not either," he said. "You know that right?"

"Yes. I know, and I have you to thank for it," she said. "It'll be okay, Mark. I promise you."

"I love you, Ames."

"I love you too."

Chapter Nineteen

Luke snuck into the house. It was dark and quiet, he suspected that Jane had been sleeping for hours, and he crept down the hallway to the kitchen. He flicked the light on and screamed when he saw Jane sitting at the island.

"What the hell?" He said. "Why are you sitting in the dark?"

"Because I was waiting for you to get home and listening to you scream like a girl is never not funny to me," Jane said with a grin.

He scowled at her and stalked across the room to the fridge. He grabbed a bottle of water and twisted the cap off, wincing when it sent pain shooting through his swollen knuckles.

Jane slipped off the stool and opened the freezer, grabbing a bag of peas as he sat down at the island and drank half the bottle of water in two large gulps.

She tugged his hand to the island and rested the bag of peas on it. "Amy told me what happened. Where have you been?"

He sighed. "I drove around the city about seventeen times. Then I went to a bar to get drunk. I had two drinks and then went to the gym and worked out for three hours."

"Do you feel better?"

"What do you think?" He drank more water. "Did you know, Jane? Did you know about Amy and Mark?"

"Yes. Amy told me a while ago."

"You kept it from me." He gave her a hurt look of accusation and she squeezed his forearm.

"Amy asked me not to tell anyone and I said I wouldn't."

"But I'm your -"

"You're my man and I love you," she said, "but that doesn't mean I have to tell you everything. Especially when someone asks me to keep it to myself."

"He beats her," Luke said. "Did you know that? He beats her until she's bruised. Did she tell you that part?"

"She told me that they both enjoy the impact play of the BDSM lifestyle," Jane said.

"Impact play? Is that what they call beating a woman now?" Luke said. "I never thought my best friend would abuse my sister and everyone would be okay with it. Least of all the woman I love."

"Stop it, Luke!" Jane said. She slid off the stool and crowded up to him, cupping his face and staring intently at him. "You're a good man, the best man I know, and I love you. But, honey, you're being a first-class dickhead right now."

He stared at her before slumping and closing his

eyes. "She's my baby sister, Jane."

"I know, honey." She put her arms around him and he hugged her as she rubbed his back. "She's also a grown woman who has certain tastes in the bedroom that, while they may not be your thing, does not make her sick or the victim of abuse. You need to stop thinking that way. Do you hear me?"

She leaned back and studied his face. "Mark and Amy love each other. Very much. You can see it, can't you?"

"I -I don't know," he said. "I thought he looked at her like she was his sister, like he -"

"He doesn't, and it's not fair of you to think he should. He may have grown up with you guys, but he is not related to you. He's not your brother. He's not Amy's brother. He loves her, and she loves him. You need to be happy for them."

"What if I try and I can't?" He said.

She cupped his face and rubbed her thumb across his cheekbone. "Then you're going to lose them both."

❧ ❦

Amy opened her front door and stared at her brother.

"Hey, Amy."

"Hello, Luke."

"Can I come in?"

She stepped back, and he joined her in the hallway. He took off his boots and jacket and followed her to the kitchen. She sat down and stared silently at him as he slid onto the stool across from her. "You, uh, alone?"

"Mark is at his Al-Anon meeting," she said. "He'll be back soon."

"Right," he said. "I'm sorry, Amy."

"What are you sorry for, Luke? Are you sorry that you accused me of whoring myself out to get Pierre and Julien to invest in my casual line? Are you sorry for trying to beat up the man I love and calling him a sick son of a bitch? Or maybe you're sorry for the way you believe that you have the right to tell me how to live my life?"

He winced. "Amy, I -"

"Or, perhaps you're sorry that you're one judgemental asshole who made his best friend feel like garbage the day after he was forced to call the police on his own damn brother."

"I'm sorry for all of it," he said.

"You should be. Mark told me you'd react this way and I defended you, Lukie. I said you wouldn't be upset. Mark is terrified of losing you, of losing our parents. We're his only family, and you hurt him."

"I didn't mean to. I was surprised and shocked and, you're my baby sister, Amy. The thought of someone hurting you…"

"I know." She took his hand and squeezed tightly. "I love you, Lukie, I do. But I love Mark too. I want to be with him. I will be with him. I want you to be a part of our lives but if you can't accept that -"

"I can," he said. "I can accept that you and Mark are in love and that you want to be together, Ames. The other stuff – the being a dominant at some club - that might take me a little longer. But I promise you I'll try."

"Good," she said.

"I'm sorry for what I said about Julien and Pierre. I don't think they would only give you a casual line because you slept with him."

"I was at Mark's apartment when you came over to talk to him. I was the woman in his bedroom."

"Gross," Luke said before he flinched. "Sorry, I didn't mean it like that."

She couldn't help but laugh. "I know."

"I believe in you and your casual line. I really do. I was just worried about them because they're…"

"Horndogs?"

"Yeah. We don't need them to invest in a casual line, Amy. We can do it ourselves."

"I know. But I'm fine with working with them. They know I'm not going to sleep with them."

"Okay."

There was silence and Luke drummed his fingers on the island. "So, are you going to tell Mom and Dad about you and Mark?"

"Yes. On Sunday night."

"That's good. They'll be happy for you, Ames."

"I think so too."

"What's with the necklace?" He asked. "Why is it locked and why does Mark have the key?"

She shrugged. "It's a thing with us. You don't want to know the details, okay?"

"Yeah, okay," he said.

కొ ∾

Balancing the ice cream and beer in one hand, Mark opened the door to Amy's house. "Amy? I'm home, baby. I picked up a six pack of beer and a tub of Rocky Road. Just to be clear, the beer is for you and the ice cream is for me. Sometimes I like to eat my feelings."

He kicked off his boots and wandered into the kitchen, holding the tub of ice cream and the beer. Luke was sitting at the island with Amy and his stomach tightened. "Hey, Luke."

"Hi, Mark."

Amy took the ice cream and the beer from him and pressed a kiss against his mouth. "Hi, honey."

She took out the tub of ice cream and set it on the island before placing two spoons next to it. She opened a beer and took a swig then kissed Mark again. "You two talk and eat your ice cream. I've got some work to do."

She left the kitchen with her beer and Mark sat down in her spot. There was an awkward silence and he cleared his throat before opening the ice cream and grabbing a spoonful. He passed it to Luke who took his own spoonful.

"It's good," he said as he swallowed the ice cream.

"Yeah," Mark said. "My favourite."

"I know."

They both ate a few more spoonfuls of ice cream before Luke sighed and set his spoon on the island. "I'm sorry." He stared at the bruise on Mark's cheek. "I'm sorry for punching you. I'm sorry for what I said. It was wrong of me and I didn't mean it."

"Didn't you?" Mark said.

Luke considered it before shaking his head. "No, I didn't. I was really shocked, but I've done a lot of thinking over the past day, and I talked with Jane about it. I don't think you're sick or that you beat women. I just... I had no idea, Mark. We've been best friends since we were kids and I suddenly feel like I don't even know you."

"You know me, "Mark said. "You know me better than anyone, except maybe Amy. I didn't want to keep this from you, but I – I knew you would be disgusted by it, and I didn't want to lose you or your family. I didn't want to lose Amy. I told her I fell in love with her when she was a teenager, but the truth is, I've loved her since we were kids, Luke. She is the only woman for me. I will spend the rest of my life loving her, with or without your approval."

He ate another spoonful of ice cream as Luke stared at the top of the island. "How long have you been together?"

"We spent a couple nights together a while ago, and then I-I told her I couldn't be with her because I was afraid of losing you and your parents."

Luke groaned and scooped himself out another mouthful of ice cream. "That's why you guys got so weird and angry with each other. Fuck, it's my fault you were fighting."

"No, it isn't. I was the one who pushed her away because I was afraid. I tried to stay away from her, but I couldn't. Once I'd been with her, I couldn't..."

He sighed and shoved another bite of ice cream

into her mouth. "I can't live without her, Luke. As for the Dom thing at the club - that's a part of who I am, and I won't apologize for it. I'm part owner at Secrets and it's important to me. Amy understands that it's important and she supports me."

"That's good," Luke said.

"I'm not asking you to understand it and I won't force you to talk about it with me, but I don't want to keep it a secret from you anymore either. It's been eight years and I'm tired of keeping secrets."

"Yeah, I get it," Luke said. "I'm happy for you and Amy, I really am, man. I'm sorry for how I acted. I promise not to be such a dickhead in the future."

"Thanks, Luke. I love you," Mark said.

"Yeah, I love you too, my little snuggle bunny. Now stop hogging the damn Rocky Road."

જે ન્

"Love, the pork roast was divine," Gary said as he pushed his empty plate away. "Kids, wasn't it amazing?"

"It is," Luke said. "Best pork I've ever eaten, Mom."

Clara laughed and poked Luke in the arm. "I can tell when you're mocking me, Lukie. Jane, dearest, pass me the pickles, would you?"

Jane passed her the pickles and Clara took a couple before passing them to Gary. "Have a pickle, sweetheart."

"Mom? Dad?" Amy cleared her throat as Gary and Clara looked down the table at her.

"What is it, Ames?" Clara said.

"Mark and I have something to tell you." She gave Mark a nervous look. He picked up her hand and kissed her knuckles before giving her an encouraging smile. "Mark and I are dating. We, um, we're in love. We're going to move in together."

"Gross," Luke said.

"Shut up, Luke," Amy said.

"You shut up."

"No, you shut up."

"No, you shut up."

"Both of you shut up," Jane said.

Luke gaped at her and she giggled before kissing his cheek. "Sorry, honey. I couldn't resist."

"Mom?" Amy was studying her mother's face anxiously. "Say something."

Clara sat back in her chair before turning to her husband and grinning at him. "Pay up."

"Dammit," Gary said. He pulled his wallet from his pocket and began counting out twenties.

"What's going on?" Amy said.

"Your father is paying me the money he owes me."

"Money for what?"

"The bet he lost."

"What bet?" Luke said.

"Oh, we started a little bet back in…when was it, dear?"

Gary made a snorting noise. "When Amy was twenty-two."

"Ah, that's right. We made a bet about when you and Mark would finally admit you loved each other and start dating. Your father said it wouldn't happen until you were in your thirties. I said your twenties. I won."

"Don't look so smug, sweetie," Gary said. "Amy turns thirty in like two months. You almost lost."

"But I didn't, did I?" Clara said with a cheeky grin as she took the money from her husband and tucked it into her bra.

"You bet on us?" Amy said.

"Of course we did," Clara said. "We bet on all sorts of things with you kids. Have ever since you were born. God, it would have been dreadfully boring if we hadn't. Why, I made like two grand off of Luke when he was a teenager."

"Mom!" Luke gave her an indignant look.

"It's true." Clara smiled at Amy and Mark. "Congratulations, you two. Your father and I couldn't be happier for you."

"Let's get back to this betting thing," Luke said. "How exactly did you make two grand off of me?"

"Oh sweetie, it was so long ago, who can remember?" Clara said. "Who wants dessert?"

"Do you have any more bets on us?" Luke asked.

"Maybe," Clara said before winking at her husband. "Gary, do you want pie?"

"Yes please, sweetheart. Want me to grab the ice cream from the freezer downstairs?"

"That would be wonderful. Thank you."

Her father left the dining room and Jane gathered up some of the plates as Clara picked up the bowl of leftover potatoes. She and Jane headed toward the kitchen with Luke trailing after them.

"Seriously, Mom, what are these bets?"

Mark put his arm around Amy and she leaned against his broad chest. He kissed her and tugged the heart padlock on her necklace. "That went surprisingly well."

She laughed. "I guess we weren't hiding our feelings as well as we thought."

"Guess not." He nuzzled her temple. "I love you, Ames."

"I love you too, Mark."

END

Please enjoy a sample chapter of Ramona Gray's novel "Undeniably Theirs", Book Three in the Undeniable Series

UNDENIABLY THEIRS
Copyright ©2018 Ramona Gray

Chloe stared at the amber liquid. She normally avoided liquor of any kind, afraid she had the mutated gene or weakness or whatever the hell it was that ran in their family. Becoming like Lori or her mother was a low-grade fear in the pit of her stomach that never really went away.

But tonight.

Fuck tonight.

Tonight she deserved a goddamn drink. One drink didn't make her a damn drunk. She had stopped at the first bar she came across. That this bar was attached to a hotel made no difference to her.

Her grandmother didn't live right in the Badlands. But she was close enough to its outskirts that a place like this, only ten minutes from her grandma's home, was on the seedier side. No doubt her sister frequented this place on a regular basis.

It was confirmed when a man slid onto the stool next to her and placed his hand on her leg. "Hey, Lori, you looking to make some extra cash tonight? I can get us a room upstairs and -"

She pushed his hand off her leg as he squinted at her. "Sorry, you ain't who I thought you was."

He hopped off the stool and nearly fell on his ass before catching himself on the edge of the bar.

Straightening his ratty coat around him, he gave her an oddly dignified bow, before staggering away.

She returned to her drink. Lifted the cheap glass. Studied the cheap bourbon in the dim light.

Drank.

It burned her throat and made her eyes water. She coughed, wiped her mouth and coughed again before setting the glass down.

There was movement to her right. The bartender – an overweight blonde with mileage on her face and a smoker's cough – appeared almost immediately. She purposely didn't look, purposely ignored the little shiver that went down her back at the surprisingly deep, surprisingly sober sounding voice of the man who sat beside her.

"I'll take a whiskey and another of whatever my friend is having."

"No." Chloe stared at the bartender, "I don't want another drink. You have me mistaken for someone else. I'm not Lori, and I'm not gonna blow you for a goddamn drink."

There was silence beside her. The bartender's overgrown eyebrows were raised in astonishment. She gave Chloe a girl-you-are-a-fucking-idiot look before smiling at the man.

"One whiskey, coming right up, sweetheart. I'll get you the good stuff."

"Thank you."

Another little shiver. God, his voice was insanely deep. She decided it wouldn't hurt to take one quick glance at the man who was probably one of many men in this bar who had fucked Lori for a handful of drinks and a carton of cigarettes.

She turned her head, peeked, and froze.

Holy shit. He was beautiful.

Adonis beautiful.

Dark hair, dark eyes, sexy stubble, beautiful.

She looked him up and down without a speck of shame. When one stumbled upon a god in broad daylight – well, dim bar light – one did not just simply look away. He was dressed in a leather jacket and jeans with dark boots. The jacket stretched across his broad shoulders and the jeans hugged his thick thighs. Her core tightened at the sizeable bulge at his crotch.

His clothing was too expensive for a place like this. He looked out of place. A glitch in the regularly scheduled programming. A pearl in a sea of pebbles.

His smile revealed perfect white teeth. "Hello, not Lori. My name is -"

"I'm not interested in your name."

"Fair enough," he said. "Is there anything about me you are interested in?"

She paused. "No."

His grin really should come attached with a warning sign of impending danger. "Did you... hesitate?"

"No."

"Huh. I could have sworn there was hesitation." His dark eyes studied her, made her feel like a bug trapped under glass.

She fidgeted on the bar stool, smoothed down her red hair, and told herself to just stand up and leave already.

"So, tell me, Red. What's a girl like you doing

in a place like this?"

"Seriously? That's the pick-up line you're going to use?" She said.

"Not a pick-up line. I'm genuinely curious what a girl like you is doing in this bar. You don't exactly fit in with the rest of the clientele."

"Neither do you."

"True."

"Besides, you know nothing about me," she said. "Maybe I'm a drunk. Maybe I go to whatever bar I find."

"Maybe. But drunks don't normally turn down free drinks. Nor do they wear seven hundred dollar Dawson suits."

"Into fashion, are we?" She studied his hands. One rested on the bar and the other was curled around his drink. They were big hands. Rough hands. Hands that were meant for –

Tangling in your hair? Undressing you? Making you come?

Her traitorous skin flamed bright red.

She raised her gaze to his face. The look on it suggested that maybe he knew why she was blushing.

"I'm not particularly into fashion," he said, "but I have recently become more knowledgeable about that particular brand."

"Why?"

"Well, I -"

"Lori? Bitch, where you been?" A heavy hand fell on her shoulder and she cringed. "You wanna give me a handie in the bathroom? I'll buy you a fuckin' drink if you – ow! Jesus, fuck!"

The weight of his hand disappeared. The man sitting beside her was now standing. The stranger who had touched her was on his knees on the dirty floor. Her new friend was bending his thumb at an almost impossible angle.

"The lady isn't Lori," he said. "Apologize, please."

"Let me the fuck go, you fucking – OW! Motherfucker!"

Oh God. Chloe stared at the drunk's thumb as the man bent it back even further. The drunk was starting to cry, snot bubbling out of one nostril, as her new friend made a polite smile.

"Apologize to the lady."

"I'm sorry," the drunk moaned. "I'm sorry, lady. I thought you was someone else."

"That's fine," Chloe said.

The god in leather released the drunk immediately and the man climbed to his feet and staggered away. The bartender approached and leaned her sizeable rack against the bar. She had unbuttoned three of the buttons, and Chloe stared at the spray-tanned flesh bulging out from the top of her bra.

"You need another drink, sweetheart?"

"No, thank you," the man said.

"Okay, well, my name is Gina. You need anything, you just holler. Okay?" She traced one pink-painted talon down his forearm. "Anything."

"Thank you, Gina."

He waited until she left before turning to Chloe. "You okay?"

"Yes, thank you. That was um, very nice and

also terrifying to watch."

"I didn't mean to frighten you."

"No, I didn't mean that you – I should go."

He rested his hand on her forearm. "Stay and tell me why you're here."

She couldn't tell this complete stranger her sob story. The smart thing to do was to leave. Instead of leaving, she said, "Lori is my sister. She's a drunk. I was visiting her tonight and it didn't go well. I stopped in at a bar because – honestly, I don't really know why, I hate drinking. But here I am, at the first bar I found. Apparently, she spends a lot of time here trading sexual favours for alcohol. The worst part is – I'm not even surprised by that. She's ruining my life. I don't know how to stop allowing her to take all the good things from me. I'm not strong enough to kick her out of my life."

She glanced at him, saw pity in his eyes, and slid off the barstool. She rarely spoke about her sister outside of Al-Anon meetings. She didn't want anyone's pity, let alone this sexy stranger's.

"Wait," he said.

"I have to go." She hurried across the bar and pushed open the door to the hotel lobby. The lobby was empty and the clerk standing behind the desk didn't look up from his cell phone. There was a narrow hallway to her right. She walked a few steps into it and leaned against the wall. Her heart pounding and sick to her stomach, she fought back the hot tears. What was wrong with her? Why did she -

"Red?"

Her eyes flew open and she stared at the

stranger from the bar. He stood in front of her and she had to crane her neck to look at him. He was well over six feet and – holy god – how was it possible he looked even better in the fluorescent light of the hallway?

"Are you okay?" He asked.

"I don't want your pity," she said. "I don't – that isn't what I want."

"What do you want?" His big hand smoothed a strand of hair away from her cheek.

"I want to forget about her for one night," she whispered. "I want to do something to get her out of my goddamn head for just one night. Can you help me with that?"

"Yes." He stepped closer and slipped his arm around her waist. His hand cupped her hip and he bent until his mouth was hovering over hers.

She waited.

He didn't move and she realized that she needed to make the first step. He was willing to help her forget, but not until she showed him that it was what she really wanted. They stood in the hallway, his warm breath washing over her mouth.

Chloe, a night of sex with a stranger isn't going to help you forget.

It might.

It won't. Don't be an idiot, Chloe. You know nothing about this guy. He could be a serial killer for all you know.

She pressed her mouth against his. He immediately took control of the kiss, teasing her lips apart with small licks and nips. He sucked on her bottom lip and then ran the tip of his tongue across her upper one. She moaned into his mouth and he deepened the kiss, sliding his tongue into her mouth to taste and tease.

When he released her, the voice in her head was quiet. She bit her bottom lip. "I want to have sex with you."

"I want to have sex with you too," he said. "I don't live around here. Do you?"

"No. I'll get us a room here."

He frowned. "I'll get the room."

She pulled back, and ran a hand over her swollen mouth. It was suddenly important that she pay for the room. She supposed it made her feel less like a whore. "I pay for the room or this doesn't happen."

He studied her and then nodded. "All right."

She took his hand and he followed her out of the narrow hallway and toward the front desk.

About the Author

Ramona Gray is a Canadian romance author. She currently lives in Alberta with her awesome husband and her mutant Chihuahua. She's addicted to home improvement shows, good coffee, and reading and writing about the steamier moments in life.

If you would like more information about Ramona, please visit her at:

www.ramonagray.ca

Books by Ramona Gray

Individual Books

The Escort
Saving Jax
The Assistant
One Night
Sharing Del
Filthy Appeal

Other World Series

The Vampire's Kiss (Book One)
The Vampire's Love (Book Two)
The Shifter's Mate (Book Three)
Rescued By The Wolf (Book Four)
Claiming Quinn (Book Five)
Choosing Rose (Book Six)
Elena Unbound (Book Seven)

Undeniable Series

Undeniably His
Undeniably Hers
Undeniably Theirs

Working Men Series

The Mechanic
The Carpenter
The Bartender
The Welder
The Electrician
The Landscaper